FINE WEATHER, JEEVES

Summer Stories from the World of Wodehouse

ABOUT THE AUTHOR

P. G. Wodehouse (1881–1975) is widely regarded as the greatest comic writer of the twentieth century. Wodehouse wrote more than 70 novels and 200 short stories, creating numerous much-loved characters – the inimitable Jeeves and Wooster, Lord Emsworth and his beloved Empress of Blandings, Mr Mulliner, Ukridge, and Psmith. His humorous articles were published in more than 80 magazines, including *Punch*, over six decades. He was also a highly successful music lyricist, once with over five musicals running on Broadway simultaneously. P. G. Wodehouse was awarded the Mark Twain Prize for 'an outstanding and lasting contribution to the happiness of the world'.

Also by P. G. Wodehouse

Jeeves and Wooster

The Inimitable Jeeves
Carry On, Jeeves
Very Good, Jeeves
Thank You, Jeeves
Right Ho, Jeeves
The Code of the Woosters
Joy in the Morning
The Mating Season
Ring for Jeeves
Jeeves and the Feudal Spirit
Jeeves in the Offing
Stiff Upper Lip, Jeeves
Much Obliged, Jeeves
Aunts Aren't Gentlemen

Blandings Castle

Something Fresh
Leave it to Psmith
Summer Lightning
Full Moon
Pigs Have Wings
A Pelican at Blandings
Sunset at Blandings

Uncle Fred

Uncle Fred in the Springtime
Uncle Dynamite
Cocktail Time
Service with a Smile

Monty Bodkin

The Luck of the Bodkins

Standalone novels

The Pothunters
Piccadilly Jim
A Damsel in Distress
The Adventures of Sally
The Small Bachelor
Money for Nothing
Big Money
Hot Water
Laughing Gas
Summer Moonshine
The Girl in Blue

FINE WEATHER, JEEVES

Summer Stories from the World of Wodehouse

P. G. Wodehouse

PENGUIN BOOKS

PENGUIN BOOKS

UK | USA | Canada | Ireland | Australia
India | New Zealand | South Africa

Penguin Books is part of the Penguin Random House group of companies whose addresses can be found at global.penguinrandomhouse.com

This collection first published by Penguin Books in 2024

www.penguin.co.uk

A CIP catalogue record for this book is available from the British Library

ISBN: 978–1–804–95021–0

Please be aware that the stories in this collection were originally published in the 1910s, 1920s and 1930s and contain language, themes or characterisations which you may find outdated.

Typeset in 12.5/14.75pt Garamond MT Std by Jouve (UK), Milton Keynes
Printed and bound in Great Britain by Clays Ltd, Elcograf S.p.A.

The authorised representative in the EEA is Penguin Random House Ireland, Morrison Chambers, 32 Nassau Street, Dublin D02 YH68

www.greenpenguin.co.uk

Contents

Introduction

As I write this it is late March, and England has been on the receiving end of a nigh-Biblical deluge. Across the country, weather forecasters have left the thunderclouds on their maps for weeks without fear of refutation. Any unpaved ground resembles Agincourt at half-time. Biblical patriarchs have been seen ushering zoo animals into large MDF structures and muttering things like 'I told you so.' If rain, to misquote Madeline Bassett, is fairy tears, then something has gone seriously awry in fairyland.

And yet despite the clouds overhead, my spirits are undimmed, because I have just finished reading the collection of stories you hold in your hand, and have been transported to the Wodiverse, where it is generally summer, and where no matter what trials assail our heroes, the endings of their stories usually offer them at least a ray of sunshine.

This collection, ranging from the going at Goodwood to the turrets of Tudsleigh Court, shows Wodehouse to great advantage, in a field where he spent most of his career – that of shorter fiction, then a key strut of the literary world and the way many writers made their start. Lots of old favourites – Ukridge, Jeeves and Wooster, Bingo Little, Mr Mulliner, Anatole – make welcome appearances in this collection. There are implausible wagers of chefs, there are romances that hinge on the swing of a mashie or the brim of a gentleman's hat. There are two separate kidnaps. All the usual stuff, as Wodehouse himself might airily dismiss it.

But there are also plenty of surprises in store, fictional realms where the casual reader might not think Wodehouse had a toehold. For example, 'The Romance of a Bulb-Squeezer', which presents a hero whose entire miserable job is to photograph beautiful women, and which introduces as its antagonist the indescribably hideous mayor of Tooting East. Or 'First Aid for Dora', which ushers the reader into one of the most dangerous territories in Wodehouse's entire oeuvre – the parlour of a bestselling lady novelist, living just off Wimbledon Common.

He wouldn't like it – he was aware before the joke was first made about the risks of dissecting frogs – but I have a theory about Wodehouse's work, which is that it essentially follows the lines of Shakespearean comedy. There is youth, there is almost always love, the stakes are small but real, and very often the action transplants our heroes from the safe environment of the city to the countryside, where all sorts of weird inversions and chaos can occur. I think this is why so many Jeeves and Wooster stories begin with him being summoned by one aunt or another – because it is outside the safe haven of the Drones Club and the metrop that true Wodehousian mayhem can be unleashed.

As you might expect, the individual jokes throughout this collection are extraordinarily good. A young woman unhappy in love 'flung herself on the sofa and was now chewing the cushion in an ecstasy of grief. She gulped like a bull-pup swallowing a chunk of steak.' When the hopeless golfer Ferdinand Dibble exiles himself to a seaside resort where the standard of play lies even below his own weak standards, he finds that after a week, 'he had gone through the entire menagerie like a bullet through a cream puff . . . . Ferdinand Dibble was faced on the eighth morning of his visit by the startling fact that he had no more worlds to conquer.' Wodehouse can make the seam between a sub-par golfer and Alexander the Great so invisibly small that any right-thinking reader will be startled into a smile.

This breadth of allusion is another feature of the Wodiverse, and yet not an essential one. Wodehouse's work is not a crossword puzzle to be solved. The allusions he makes don't have to be teased out or described at length in laborious endnotes. If you get the reference, all to the good; if not, like an omnibus, there'll be another one along very soon, which you can pick up if you like. I don't doubt I have missed dozens. But the comedy frequently sits in the enormous gaps between the allusion made and what is actually being described. 'Percy continued to stare before him like a man who has drained the wine cup of life to its lees, only to discover a dead mouse at the bottom.' This is a glancing reference to Tennyson's 'Ulysses' which – and this is crucial, particularly given how dated Tennyson's stuff has been looking lately – *in no way affects the quality of the joke.*

'Like Hamlet on a less impressive occasion,' another narrator writes, 'I wanted to slay this man when he was full of bread, with all his crimes, broad-blown, as flush as May, at drinking, swearing, or about some act that had no relish of salvation in it.' Bear in mind that this is about Ukridge, who has borrowed the narrator's dress-clothes without permission, meaning he's had to borrow some from his landlord. The genius lies in even drawing the comparison with the Moody Dane.

Another pet theory of mine – call this one the Code of the Wodehouses – is that so much of the charm of P. G.'s work is to make each separate element of the work look easy. This applies not only to his plots, which he frequently puzzled over for weeks or months until they were watertight, and over which he agonised in letters to his friends, but to every sentence. I don't know if Wodehouse was familiar with the Italian Renaissance idea of *sprezzatura* – to work so terribly hard that you make difficult things seem easy, and never let on just how much effort they've cost you – but even if he did know the word, he wouldn't have been caught dead admitting it. The reader doesn't have to do any work, and in fact the stories are good *because* they don't let on that they cost hundreds of hours of sweat. Any chump can strain for effect and then invite the world to witness them straining. But to slog and then conceal the slog is harder.

As he aged, Wodehouse was dismissed as having remained in a world that would be almost completely alien to anyone without their own Duchy, and was scorned by some critics as a soul marooned in a world that no longer existed. The real genius of his work is that, as Evelyn Waugh once famously observed, *it never did exist.* It's not as if Wodehouse kept writing stories about Blandings Castle long after the place was sold off to the National Trust. The whole thing is a fever dream. The greatest strength of the work is that it transports the reader to an entirely different realm, one where essentially trivial people are grappling, in essentially trivial ways, with the real problems of life and young love.

Far from being a shipwrecked Edwardian, Wodehouse was deeply in tune with the fiction of the time – it is remarkable to read his letters describing lunch with George Orwell just after the war, reading Evelyn Waugh and marvelling at the satire of *Put Out More Flags*, and giving his views of the latest fiction – but any criticism that alleges he should somehow have turned his pen to gritty social realism ignores not only the breadth of what fiction can do but how comic writing works. Readers still pick up these stories precisely because of the delightful inversion of what *matters*. To the heroes in this collection of stories, some parts of modern life matter intensely (a golf handicap, the snug fit of a Bodmin's hat). Other things that get a lot of people worked up don't matter at all (the revolution of the proletariat).

This element of his writing, his steadfast refusal to grapple with the Great Issues of the Twentieth Century, is in fact essential to the comedy. Throughout the great pantheon, from *The Diary of a Nobody* via Adrian Mole to Bridget Jones, the inability to see things in their proper proportion is a vital ingredient of what makes comic characters actually comic. The outlook is essentially an anti-extremist one and, in uncertain times, it is a genuine pleasure to take refuge among a cast of characters who simply cannot imagine anything ghastlier than eating sardines for tea.

The dialect matches this cream-puff *Weltanschauung*. When Bertie Wooster is forced against his will to host a tea party for a group of communists (due to a complicated plot I won't spoil for you now), the following discussion takes place between Bertie and Comrade Rowbotham, who fixes him with a glittering eye and asks:

'Are you of the movement?'
'Well – er—'
'Do you yearn for the Revolution?'
'Well, I don't know that I exactly yearn.'

Time and again, from Rowbotham to Spode, Wodehouse and his cast remain deeply sceptical of anyone who can capitalise letters in everyday dialogue to describe their obsessions. These stories were refuges for millions of readers from the horrors of the twentieth century; they remain delightful oases of good humour and escapes from the dull or frightening realities of life even now, well into the twenty-first. This world has an innocence about it, and it allows us, however briefly, to recapture our own.

That's enough theory, and probably far more than Wodehouse would ever have admitted to, even in the direst extremity. So I will simply conclude by saying that I enjoyed these stories immensely, and I hope you do too. Nothing remains but to pour yourself a glass of something strong (maybe go easy on the Buck-U-Uppo), collapse back onto the nearest cushioned surface, and take comfort in these thirteen delicious slices of Plum Pie.

Andrew Hunter Murray, 2024

FINE WEATHER, JEEVES

Summer Stories from the World of Wodehouse

June

The Amazing Hat Mystery

A bean was in a nursing home with a broken leg as the result of trying to drive his sports-model Poppenheim through the Marble Arch instead of round it, and a kindly Crumpet had looked in to give him the gossip of the town. He found him playing halma with the nurse, and he sat down on the bed and took a grape, and the Bean asked what was going on in the great world.

'Well,' said the Crumpet, taking another grape, 'the finest minds in the Drones are still wrestling with the great Hat mystery.'

'What's that?'

'You don't mean you haven't heard about it?'

'Not a word.'

The Crumpet was astounded. He swallowed two grapes at once in his surprise.

'Why, London's seething with it. The general consensus of opinion is that it has something to do with the Fourth Dimension. You know how things go. I mean to say, something rummy occurs and you consult some big-brained bird and he wags his head and says "Ah! The Fourth Dimension!" Extraordinary nobody's told you about the great Hat mystery.'

'You're the first visitor I've had. What is it, anyway? What hat?'

'Well, there were two hats. Reading from left to right, Percy Wimbolt's and Nelson Cork's.'

The Bean nodded intelligently.

'I see what you mean. Percy had one, and Nelson had the other.'

'Exactly. Two hats in all. Top hats.'

'What was mysterious about them?'

'Why, Elizabeth Bottsworth and Diana Punter said they didn't fit.'

'Well, hats don't sometimes.'

'But these came from Bodmin's.'

The Bean shot up in bed. 'What?'

'You mustn't excite the patient,' said the nurse, who up to this point had taken no part in the conversation.

'But, dash it, nurse,' cried the Bean, 'you can't have caught what he said. If we are to give credence to his story, Percy Wimbolt and Nelson Cork bought a couple of hats at Bodmin's – at *Bodmin's,* I'll trouble you – and they didn't fit. It isn't possible.'

He spoke with strong emotion, and the Crumpet nodded understandingly. People can say what they please about the modern young man believing in nothing nowadays, but there is one thing every right-minded young man believes in, and that is the infallibility of Bodmin's hats. It is one of the eternal verities. Once admit that it is possible for a Bodmin hat not to fit, and you leave the door open for Doubt, Schism, and Chaos generally.

'That's exactly how Percy and Nelson felt, and it was for

that reason that they were compelled to take the strong line they did with E. Bottsworth and D. Punter.'

'They took a strong line, did they?'

'A very strong line.'

'Won't you tell us the whole story from the beginning?' said the nurse.

'Right ho,' said the Crumpet, taking a grape. 'It'll make your head swim.'

'So mysterious?'

'So absolutely dashed uncanny from start to finish.'

You must know, to begin with, my dear old nurse (said the Crumpet), that these two blokes, Percy Wimbolt and Nelson Cork, are fellows who have to exercise the most watchful care about their lids, because they are so situated that in their case there can be none of that business of just charging into any old hattery and grabbing the first thing in sight. Percy is one of those large, stout, outsize chaps with a head like a watermelon, while Nelson is built more on the lines of a minor jockey and has a head like a peanut.

You will readily appreciate, therefore, that it requires an artist hand to fit them properly and that is why they have always gone to Bodmin. I have heard Percy say that his trust in Bodmin is like the unspotted faith of a young curate in his bishop and I have no doubt that Nelson would have said the same, if he had thought of it.

It was at Bodmin's door that they ran into each other on the morning when my story begins.

'Hullo,' said Percy. 'You come to buy a hat?'

'Yes,' said Nelson. 'You come to buy a hat?'

'Yes.' Percy glanced cautiously about him, saw that he was alone (except for Nelson, of course) and unobserved, and drew closer and lowered his voice. 'There's a reason!'

'That's rummy,' said Nelson. He, also, spoke in a hushed tone. 'I have a special reason, too.'

Percy looked warily about, and lowered his voice another notch.

'Nelson,' he said, 'you know Elizabeth Bottsworth?'

'Intimately,' said Nelson.

'Rather a sound young potato, what?'

'Very much so.'

'Pretty.'

'I've often noticed it.'

'Me, too. She is so small, so sweet, so dainty, so lively, so viv— what's-the-word? – that a fellow wouldn't be far out in calling her an angel in human shape.'

'Aren't all angels in human shape?'

'Are they?' said Percy, who was a bit foggy on angels. 'Well, be that as it may,' he went on, his cheeks suffused to a certain extent, 'I love that girl, Nelson, and she's coming with me to the first day of Ascot, and I'm relying on this new hat of mine to do just that extra bit that's needed in the way of making her reciprocate my passion. Having only met her so far at country houses, I've never yet flashed upon her in a topper.'

Nelson Cork was staring.

'Well, if that isn't the most remarkable coincidence I ever came across in my puff!' he exclaimed, amazed. 'I'm buying my new hat for exactly the same reason.'

A convulsive start shook Percy's massive frame. His eyes bulged.

'To fascinate Elizabeth Bottsworth?' he cried, beginning to writhe.

'No, no,' said Nelson, soothingly. 'Of course not. Elizabeth and I have always been great friends, but nothing more. What I meant was that I, like you, am counting on this forthcoming topper of mine to put me across with the girl I love.'

Percy stopped writhing.

'Who is she?' he asked, interested.

'Diana Punter, the niece of my godmother, old Ma Punter. It's an odd thing, I've known her all my life – brought up as kids together and so forth – but it's only recently that passion has burgeoned. I now worship that girl, Percy, from the top of her head to the soles of her divine feet.'

Percy looked dubious.

'That's a pretty longish distance, isn't it? Diana Punter is one of my closest friends, and a charming girl in every respect, but isn't she a bit tall for you, old man?'

'My dear chap, that's just what I admire so much about her, her superb statuesqueness. More like a Greek goddess than anything I've struck for years. Besides, she isn't any taller for me than you are for Elizabeth Bottsworth.'

'True,' admitted Percy.

'And, anyway, I love her, blast it, and I don't propose to argue the point. I love her, I love her, I love her, and we are lunching together the first day of Ascot.'

At Ascot?'

'No. She isn't keen on racing, so I shall have to give Ascot a miss.'

'That's Love,' said Percy, awed.

'The binge will take place at my godmother's house in

Berkeley Square, and it won't be long after that, I feel, before you see an interesting announcement in the *Morning Post.'*

Percy extended his hand. Nelson grasped it warmly.

'These new hats are pretty well bound to do the trick, I should say, wouldn't you?'

'Infallibly. Where girls are concerned, there is nothing that brings home the gravy like a well-fitting topper.'

'Bodmin must extend himself as never before,' said Percy.

'He certainly must,' said Nelson.

They entered the shop. And Bodmin, having measured them with his own hands, promised that two of his very finest efforts should be at their respective addresses in the course of the next few days.

Now, Percy Wimbolt isn't a chap you would suspect of having nerves, but there is no doubt that in the interval which elapsed before Bodmin was scheduled to deliver he got pretty twittery. He kept having awful visions of some great disaster happening to his new hat: and, as things turned out, these visions came jolly near being fulfilled. It has made Percy feel that he is psychic.

What occurred was this. Owing to these jitters of his, he hadn't been sleeping any too well, and on the morning before Ascot he was up as early as ten-thirty, and he went to his sitting room window to see what sort of a day it was, and the sight he beheld from that window absolutely froze the blood in his veins.

For there below him, strutting up and down the pavement, were a uniformed little blighter whom he recognised as Bodmin's errand boy and an equally foul kid in mufti.

And balanced on each child's loathsome head was a top hat. Against the railings were leaning a couple of cardboard hatboxes.

Now, considering that Percy had only just woken from a dream in which he had been standing outside the Guildhall in his new hat, receiving the Freedom of the City from the Lord Mayor, and the Lord Mayor had suddenly taken a terrific swipe at the hat with his mace, knocking it into hash, you might have supposed that he would have been hardened to anything. But he wasn't. His reaction was terrific. There was a moment of sort of paralysis, during which he was telling himself that he had always suspected this beastly little boy of Bodmin's of having a low and frivolous outlook and being temperamentally unfitted for his high office: and then he came alive with a jerk and let out probably the juiciest yell the neighbourhood had heard for years.

It stopped the striplings like a high-powered shell. One moment, they had been swanking up and down in a mincing and affected sort of way: the next, the second kid had legged it like a streak and Bodmin's boy was shoving the hats back in the boxes and trying to do it quickly enough to enable him to be elsewhere when Percy should arrive.

And in this he was successful. By the time Percy had got to the front door and opened it, there was nothing to be seen but a hatbox standing on the steps. He took it up to his flat and removed the contents with a gingerly and reverent hand, holding his breath for fear the nap should have got rubbed the wrong way or a dent of any nature been made in the gleaming surface; but apparently all was well. Bodmin's boy might sink to taking hats out of their boxes and fooling about with them, but at least he hadn't gone to the last awful extreme of dropping them.

The lid was OK absolutely: and on the following morning Percy, having spent the interval polishing it with stout, assembled the boots, the spats, the trousers, the coat, the flowered waistcoat, the collar, the shirt, the quiet grey tie, and the good old gardenia, and set off in a taxi for the house where Elizabeth was staying. And presently he was ringing the bell and being told she would be down in a minute, and eventually down she came, looking perfectly marvellous.

'What ho, what ho!' said Percy.

'Hullo, Percy,' said Elizabeth.

Now, naturally, up to this moment Percy had been standing with bared head. At this point, he put the hat on. He wanted her to get the full effect suddenly in a good light. And very strategic, too. I mean to say, it would have been the act of a juggins to have waited till they were in the taxi, because in a taxi all toppers look much alike.

So Percy popped the hat on his head with a meaning glance and stood waiting for the uncontrollable round of applause.

And instead of clapping her little hands in girlish ecstasy and doing spring dances round him, this young Bottsworth gave a sort of gurgling scream not unlike a coloratura soprano choking on a fish-bone.

Then she blinked and became calmer.

'It's all right,' she said. 'The momentary weakness has passed. Tell me, Percy, when do you open?'

'Open?' said Percy, not having the remotest.

'On the Halls. Aren't you going to sing comic songs on the Music Halls?'

Percy's perplexity deepened.

'Me? No. How? Why? What do you mean?'

'I thought that hat must be part of the make-up and that you were trying it on the dog. I couldn't think of any other reason why you should wear one six sizes too small.'

Percy gasped. 'You aren't suggesting this hat doesn't fit me?'

'It doesn't fit you by a mile.'

'But it's a Bodmin.'

'Call it that if you like. I call it a public outrage.'

Percy was appalled. I mean, naturally. A nice thing for a chap to give his heart to a girl and then find her talking in this hideous, flippant way of sacred subjects.

Then it occurred to him that, living all the time in the country, she might not have learned to appreciate the holy significance of the name Bodmin.

'Listen,' he said gently. 'Let me explain. This hat was made by Bodmin, the world-famous hatter of Vigo Street. He measured me in person and guaranteed a fit.'

'And I nearly had one.'

'And if Bodmin guarantees that a hat shall fit,' proceeded Percy, trying to fight against a sickening sort of feeling that he had been all wrong about this girl, 'it fits. I mean, saying a Bodmin hat doesn't fit is like saying . . . well, I can't think of anything awful enough.'

'That hat's awful enough. It's like something out of a two-reel comedy. Pure Chas Chaplin. I know a joke's a joke, Percy, and I'm as fond of a laugh as anyone, but there is such a thing as cruelty to animals. Imagine the feelings of the horses at Ascot when they see that hat.'

Poets and other literary blokes talk a lot about falling in

love at first sight, but it's equally possible to fall out of love just as quickly. One moment, this girl was the be-all and the end-all, as you might say, of Percy Wimbolt's life. The next, she was just a regrettable young blister with whom he wished to hold no further communication. He could stand a good deal from the sex. Insults directed at himself left him unmoved. But he was not prepared to countenance destructive criticism of a Bodmin hat.

'Possibly,' he said, coldly, 'you would prefer to go to this bally race meeting alone?'

'You bet I'm going alone. You don't suppose I mean to be seen in broad daylight in the paddock at Ascot with a hat like that?'

Percy stepped back and bowed formally.

'Drive on, driver,' he said to the driver, and the driver drove on.

Now, you would say that that was rummy enough. A full-sized mystery in itself, you might call it. But wait. Mark the sequel. You haven't heard anything yet.

We now turn to Nelson Cork. Shortly before one-thirty, Nelson had shoved over to Berkeley Square and had lunch with his godmother and Diana Punter, and Diana's manner and deportment had been absolutely all that could have been desired. In fact, so chummy had she been over the cutlets and fruit salad that it seemed to Nelson that, if she was like this now, imagination boggled at the thought of how utterly all over him she would be when he sprang his new hat on her.

So when the meal was concluded and coffee had been drunk and old Lady Punter had gone up to her boudoir with a digestive tablet and a sex-novel, he thought it would be a sound move to invite her to come for a stroll along Bond Street. There was the chance, of course, that she would fall into his arms right in the middle of the pavement: but if that happened, he told himself, they could always get into a cab. So he mooted the saunter, and she checked up, and presently they started off.

And you will scarcely believe this, but they hadn't gone more than halfway along Bruton Street when she suddenly stopped and looked at him in an odd manner.

'I don't want to be personal, Nelson,' she said, 'but really I do think you ought to take the trouble to get measured for your hats.'

If a gas main had exploded beneath Nelson's feet, he could hardly have been more taken aback.

'M-m-m-m . . .' he gasped. He could scarcely believe that he had heard aright.

'It's the only way with a head like yours. I know it's a temptation for a lazy man to go into a shop and take just whatever is offered him, but the result is so sloppy. That thing you're wearing now looks like an extinguisher.'

Nelson was telling himself that he must be strong.

'Are you endeavouring to intimate that this hat does not fit?'

'Can't you feel that it doesn't fit?'

'But it's a Bodmin.'

'I don't know what you mean. It's just an ordinary silk hat.'

'Not at all. It's a Bodmin.'

'I don't know what you are talking about.'

'The point I am trying to drive home,' said Nelson,

stiffly, 'is that this hat was constructed under the personal auspices of Jno Bodmin of Vigo Street.'

'Well, it's too big.'

'It is not too big.'

'I say it is too big.'

'And I say a Bodmin hat cannot be too big.'

'Well, I've got eyes, and I say it is.'

Nelson controlled himself with an effort.

'I would be the last person,' he said, 'to criticise your eyesight, but on the present occasion you will permit me to say that it has let you down with a considerable bump. Myopia is indicated. Allow me,' said Nelson, hot under the collar, but still dignified, 'to tell you something about Jno Bodmin, as the name appears new to you. Jno is the last of a long line of Bodmins, all of whom have made hats assiduously for the nobility and gentry all their lives. Hats are in Jno Bodmin's blood.'

'I don't . . .'

Nelson held up a restraining hand.

'Over the door of his emporium in Vigo Street the passers-by may read a significant legend. It runs: "Bespoke Hatter to the Royal Family". That means, in simple language adapted to the lay intelligence, that if the King wants a new topper he simply ankles round to Bodmin's and says: "Good morning, Bodmin, we want a topper." He does not ask if it will fit. He takes it for granted that it will fit. He has bespoken Jno Bodmin, and he trusts him blindly. You don't suppose His Gracious Majesty would bespeak a hatter whose hats did not fit. The whole essence of being a hatter is to make hats that fit, and it is to this end that Jno Bodmin has strained every nerve for years. And that is why I say again – simply and without heat – This hat is a Bodmin.'

Diana was beginning to get a bit peeved. The blood of the Punters is hot, and very little is required to steam it up. She tapped Bruton Street with a testy foot.

'You always were an obstinate, pig-headed little fiend, Nelson, even as a child. I tell you once more, for the last time, that that hat is too big. If it were not for the fact that I can see a pair of boots and part of a pair of trousers, I should not know that there was a human being under it. I don't care how much you argue, I still think you ought to be ashamed of yourself for coming out in the thing. Even if you didn't mind for your own sake, you might have considered the feelings of the pedestrians and traffic.'

Nelson quivered.

'You do, do you?'

'Yes, I do.'

'Oh, you do?'

'I said I did. Didn't you hear me? No, I suppose you could hardly be expected to, with an enormous great hat coming down over your ears.'

'You say this hat comes down over my ears?'

'Right over your ears. It's a mystery to me why you think it worth while to deny it.'

I fear that what follows does not show Nelson Cork in the role of a parfait gentil knight, but in extenuation of his behaviour I must remind you that he and Diana Punter had been brought up as children together, and a dispute between a couple who have shared the same nursery is always liable to degenerate into an exchange of personalities and innuendos. What starts as an academic discussion on hats turns only too swiftly into a raking-up of old sores and a grand parade of family skeletons.

It was so in this case. At the word 'mystery', Nelson uttered a nasty laugh.

'A mystery, eh? As much a mystery, I suppose, as why your Uncle George suddenly left England in the year 1920 without stopping to pack up?'

Diana's eyes flashed. Her foot struck the pavement another shrewd wallop.

'Uncle George,' she said haughtily, 'went abroad for his health.'

'You bet he did,' retorted Nelson. 'He knew what was good for him.'

Anyway, he wouldn't have worn a hat like that.'

'Where they would have put him if he hadn't been off like a scalded kitten, he wouldn't have worn a hat at all.'

A small groove was now beginning to appear in the paving stone on which Diana Punter stood.

'Well, Uncle George escaped one thing by going abroad, at any rate,' she said. 'He missed the big scandal about your Aunt Clarissa in 1922.'

Nelson clenched his fists. 'The jury gave Aunt Clarissa the benefit of the doubt,' he said hoarsely.

'Well, we all know what that means. It was accompanied, if you recollect, by some very strong remarks from the Bench.'

There was a pause.

'I may be wrong,' said Nelson, 'but I should have thought it ill beseemed a girl whose brother Cyril was warned off the Turf in 1924 to haul up her slacks about other people's Aunt Clarissas.'

'Passing lightly over my brother Cyril in 1924,' rejoined Diana, 'what price your cousin Fred in 1927?'

They glared at one another in silence for a space, each realising with a pang that the supply of erring relatives had now given out. Diana was still pawing the paving stone, and Nelson was wondering what on earth he could ever have seen in a girl who, in addition to talking subversive drivel about hats, was eight feet tall and ungainly, to boot.

'While as for your brother-in-law's niece's sister-in-law Muriel . . .' began Diana, suddenly brightening.

Nelson checked her with a gesture.

'I prefer not to continue this discussion,' he said, frigidly.

'It is no pleasure to me,' replied Diana, with equal coldness, 'to have to listen to your vapid gibberings. That's the worst of a man who wears his hat over his mouth – he will talk through it.'

'I bid you a very hearty good afternoon, Miss Punter,' said Nelson.

He strode off without a backward glance.

Now, one advantage of having a row with a girl in Bruton Street is that the Drones is only just round the corner, so that you can pop in and restore the old nervous system with the minimum of trouble. Nelson was round there in what practically amounted to a trice, and the first person he saw was Percy, hunched up over a double and splash.

'Hullo,' said Percy.

'Hullo,' said Nelson.

There was a silence, broken only by the sound of Nelson ordering a mixed vermouth. Percy continued to stare before him like a man who has drained the wine cup of life to its lees, only to discover a dead mouse at the bottom.

'Nelson,' he said at length, 'what are your views on the Modern Girl?'

'I think she's a mess.'

'I thoroughly agree with you,' said Percy. 'Of course, Diana Punter is a rare exception, but, apart from Diana, I wouldn't give you twopence for the modern girl. She lacks depth and reverence and has no sense of what is fitting. Hats, for example.'

'Exactly. But what do you mean Diana Punter is an exception? She's one of the ringleaders – the spearhead of the movement, if you like to put it that way. Think,' said Nelson, sipping his vermouth, 'of all the unpleasant qualities of the Modern Girl, add them up, double them, and what have you got? Diana Punter. Let me tell you what took place between me and this Punter only a few minutes ago.'

'No,' said Percy. 'Let me tell you what transpired between me and Elizabeth Bottsworth this morning. Nelson, old man, she said my hat – my Bodmin hat – was too small.'

'You don't mean that?'

'Those were her very words.'

'Well, I'm dashed. Listen. Diana Punter told me my equally Bodmin hat was too large.'

They stared at one another.

'It's the Spirit of something,' said Nelson. 'I don't know what, quite, but of something. You see it on all sides. Something very serious has gone wrong with girls nowadays. There is lawlessness and licence abroad.'

'And here in England, too.'

'Well, naturally, you silly ass,' said Nelson, with some asperity. 'When I said abroad, I didn't mean abroad, I meant abroad.'

He mused for a moment.

'I must say, though,' he continued, 'I am surprised at what you tell me about Elizabeth Bottsworth, and am inclined to think there must have been some mistake. I have always been a warm admirer of Elizabeth.'

'And I have always thought Diana one of the best, and I find it hard to believe that she should have shown up in such a dubious light as you suggest. Probably there was a misunderstanding of some kind.'

'Well, I ticked her off properly, anyway.'

Percy Wimbolt shook his head.

'You shouldn't have done that, Nelson. You may have wounded her feelings. In my case, of course, I had no alternative but to be pretty crisp with Elizabeth.'

Nelson Cork clicked his tongue.

'A pity,' he said. 'Elizabeth is sensitive.'

'So is Diana.'

'Not so sensitive as Elizabeth.'

'I should say, at a venture, about five times as sensitive as Elizabeth. However, we must not quarrel about a point like that, old man. The fact that emerges is that we seem both to have been dashed badly treated. I think I shall toddle home and take an aspirin.'

'Me, too.'

They went off to the cloakroom, where their hats were, and Percy put his on.

'Surely,' he said, 'nobody but a half-witted little pipsqueak who can't see straight would say this was too small?'

'It isn't a bit too small,' said Nelson. 'And take a look at this one. Am I not right in supposing that only a female giantess with straws in her hair and astigmatism in both eyes could say it was too large?'

'It's a lovely fit.'

And the cloakroom waiter, a knowledgeable chap of the name of Robinson, said the same.

'So there you are,' said Nelson.

'Ah, well,' said Percy.

They left the club, and parted at the top of Dover Street.

Now, though he had not said so in so many words, Nelson Cork's heart had bled for Percy Wimbolt. He knew the other's fine sensibilities and he could guess how deeply they must have been gashed by this unfortunate breaking-off of diplomatic relations with the girl he loved. For, whatever might have happened, however sorely he might have been wounded, the way Nelson Cork looked at it was that Percy loved Elizabeth Bottsworth in spite of everything. What was required here, felt Nelson, was a tactful mediator – a kindly, sensible friend of both parties who would hitch up his socks and plunge in and heal the breach.

So the moment he had got rid of Percy outside the club he hared round to the house where Elizabeth was staying and was lucky enough to catch her on the front door steps. For, naturally, Elizabeth hadn't gone off to Ascot by herself. Directly Percy was out of sight, she had told the taxi-man to drive her home, and she had been occupying the interval since the painful scene in thinking of things she wished she had said to him and taking her hostess's dog for a run – a Pekingese called Clarkson.

She seemed very pleased to see Nelson, and started to

prattle of this and that, her whole demeanour that of a girl who, after having been compelled to associate for a while with the Underworld, has at last found a kindred soul. And the more he listened, the more he wanted to go on listening. And the more he looked at her, the more he felt that a lifetime spent in gazing at Elizabeth Bottsworth would be a lifetime dashed well spent.

There was something about the girl's exquisite petiteness and fragility that appealed to Nelson Cork's depths. After having wasted so much time looking at a female Carnera like Diana Punter, it was a genuine treat to him to be privileged to feast the eyes on one so small and dainty. And, what with one thing and another, he found the most extraordinary difficulty in lugging Percy into the conversation.

They strolled along, chatting. And, mark you, Elizabeth Bottsworth was a girl a fellow could chat with without getting a crick in the neck from goggling up at her, the way you had to do when you took the air with Diana Punter. Nelson realised now that talking to Diana Punter had been like trying to exchange thoughts with a flagpole sitter. He was surprised that this had never occurred to him before.

'You know, you're looking perfectly ripping, Elizabeth,' he said.

'How funny!' said the girl. 'I was just going to say the same thing about you.'

'Not really?'

'Yes, I was. After some of the gargoyles I've seen today – Percy Wimbolt is an example that springs to the mind – it's such a relief to be with a man who really knows how to turn himself out.'

Now that the Percy *motif* had been introduced, it should

have been a simple task for Nelson to turn the talk to the subject of his absent friend. But somehow he didn't. Instead, he just simpered a bit and said: 'Oh no, I say, really, do you mean that?'

'I do, indeed,' said Elizabeth earnestly. 'It's your hat, principally, I think. I don't know why it is, but ever since a child I have been intensely sensitive to hats, and it has always been a pleasure to me to remember that at the age of five I dropped a pot of jam out of the nursery window on to my Uncle Alexander when he came to visit us in a deerstalker cap with ear-flaps, as worn by Sherlock Holmes. I consider the hat the final test of a man. Now, yours is perfect. I never saw such a beautiful fit. I can't tell you how much I admire that hat. It gives you quite an ambassadorial look.'

Nelson Cork drew a deep breath. He was tingling from head to foot. It was as if the scales had fallen from his eyes and a new life begun for him.

'I say,' he said, trembling with emotion, 'I wonder if you would mind if I pressed your little hand?'

'Do,' said Elizabeth cordially.

'I will,' said Nelson, and did so. 'And now,' he went on, clinging to the fin like glue and hiccoughing a bit, 'how about buzzing off somewhere for a quiet cup of tea? I have a feeling that we have much to say to one another.'

It is odd how often it happens in this world that when there are two chaps and one chap's heart is bleeding for the other chap you find that all the while the second chap's heart is bleeding just as much for the first chap. Both bleeding, I mean to say, not only one. It was so in the case of Nelson Cork and Percy Wimbolt. The moment he had left Nelson,

Percy charged straight off in search of Diana Punter with the intention of putting everything right with a few well-chosen words.

Because what he felt was that, though at the actual moment of going to press pique might be putting Nelson off Diana, this would pass off and love come into its own again. All that was required, he considered, was a suave go-between, a genial mutual pal who would pour oil on the troubled w.'s and generally fix things up.

He found Diana walking round and round Berkeley Square with her chin up, breathing tensely through the nostrils. He drew up alongside and what-hoed, and as she beheld him the cold, hard gleam in her eyes changed to a light of cordiality. She appeared charmed to see him and at once embarked on an animated conversation. And with every word she spoke his conviction deepened that of all the ways of passing a summer afternoon there was none fruitier than having a friendly hike with Diana Punter.

And it was not only her talk that enchanted him. He was equally fascinated by that wonderful physique of hers. When he considered that he had actually wasted several valuable minutes that day conversing with a young shrimp like Elizabeth Bottsworth, he could have kicked himself.

Here, he reflected, as they walked round the square, was a girl whose ear was more or less on a level with a fellow's mouth, so that such observations as he might make were enabled to get from point to point with the least possible delay. Talking to Elizabeth Bottsworth had always been like bellowing down a well in the hope of attracting the attention of one of the smaller infusoria at the bottom.

It surprised him that he had been so long in coming to this conclusion.

He was awakened from this reverie by hearing his companion utter the name of Nelson Cork.

'I beg your pardon?' he said.

'I was saying,' said Diana, 'that Nelson Cork is a wretched little undersized blob who, if he were not too lazy to work, would long since have signed up with some good troupe of midgets.'

'Oh, would you say that?'

'I would say more than that,' said Diana firmly. 'I tell you, Percy, that what makes life so ghastly for girls, what causes girls to get grey hair and go into convents, is the fact that it is not always possible for them to avoid being seen in public with men like Nelson Cork. I trust I am not uncharitable. I try to view these things in a broad-minded way, saying to myself that if a man looks like something that has come out from under a flat stone it is his misfortune rather than his fault and that he is more to be pitied than censured. But on one thing I do insist, that such a man does not wantonly aggravate the natural unpleasantness of his appearance by prancing about London in a hat that reaches down to his ankles. I cannot and will not endure being escorted along Bruton Street by a sort of human bacillus the brim of whose hat bumps on the pavement with every step he takes. What I have always said and what I shall always say is that the hat is the acid test. A man who cannot buy the right-sized hat is a man one could never like or trust. Your hat, now, Percy, is exactly right. I have seen a good many hats in my time, but I really do not think that I have ever come across a more perfect specimen of all that a hat should be. Not too large, not too small, fitting snugly to the head like the skin on a sausage. And you have just the kind of head that a silk hat shows off. It gives you a sort of look . . . how shall I describe it? . . . it conveys the idea of a master of men. Leonine is the word I want. There is something about the way it rests on the brow and the almost imperceptible tilt towards the south-east . . .'

Percy Wimbolt was quivering like an Oriental muscle-dancer. Soft music seemed to be playing from the direction of Hay Hill, and Berkeley Square had begun to skip round him on one foot.

He drew a deep breath.

'I say,' he said, 'stop me if you've heard this before, but what I feel we ought to do at this juncture is to dash off somewhere where it's quiet and there aren't so many houses dancing the "Blue Danube" and shove some tea into ourselves. And over the pot and muffins I shall have something very important to say to you.'

'So that,' concluded the Crumpet, taking a grape, 'is how the thing stands; and, in a sense, of course, you could say that it is a satisfactory ending.

'The announcement of Elizabeth's engagement to Nelson Cork appeared in the Press on the same day as that of Diana's projected hitching-up with Percy Wimbolt: and it is pleasant that the happy couples should be so well matched as regards size.

'I mean to say, there will be none of that business of a six-foot girl tripping down the aisle with a five-foot-four man, or a six-foot-two man trying to keep step along the sacred edifice with a four-foot-three girl. This is always good for a laugh from the ringside pews, but it does not make for wedded bliss.

'No, as far as the principals are concerned, we may say that all has ended well. But that doesn't seem to me the important point. What seems to me the important point is this extraordinary, baffling mystery of those hats.'

'Absolutely,' said the Bean.

'I mean to say, if Percy's hat really didn't fit, as Elizabeth Bottsworth contended, why should it have registered as a winner with Diana Punter?'

'Absolutely,' said the Bean.

'And, conversely, if Nelson's hat was the total loss which Diana Punter considered it, why, only a brief while later, was it going like a breeze with Elizabeth Bottsworth?'

'Absolutely,' said the Bean.

'The whole thing is utterly inscrutable.'

It was at this point that the nurse gave signs of wishing to catch the Speaker's eye.

'Shall I tell you what I think?'

'Say on, my dear young pillow-smoother.'

'I believe Bodmin's boy must have got those hats mixed. When he was putting them back in the boxes, I mean.'

The Crumpet shook his head, and took a grape.

'And then at the club they got the right ones again.'

The Crumpet smiled indulgently.

'Ingenious,' he said, taking a grape. 'Quite ingenious. But a little far-fetched. No, I prefer to think the whole thing, as I say, has something to do with the Fourth Dimension. I am convinced that that is the true explanation, if our minds could only grasp it.'

'Absolutely,' said the Bean.

First Aid for Dora

Never in the course of a long and intimate acquaintance having been shown any evidence to the contrary, I had always looked on Stanley Featherstonehaugh Ukridge, my boyhood chum, as a man ruggedly indifferent to the appeal of the opposite sex. I had assumed that, like so many financial giants, he had no time for dalliance with women – other and deeper matters, I supposed, keeping that great brain permanently occupied. It was a surprise, therefore, when, passing down Shaftesbury Avenue one Wednesday afternoon in June at the hour when *matinée* audiences were leaving the theatres, I came upon him assisting a girl in a white dress to mount an omnibus.

As far as this simple ceremony could be rendered impressive, Ukridge made it so. His manner was a blend of courtliness and devotion; and if his mackintosh had been a shade less yellow and his hat a trifle less disreputable, he would have looked just like Sir Walter Raleigh.

The bus moved on, Ukridge waved, and I proceeded to make inquiries. I felt that I was an interested party. There had been a distinctly 'object-matrimony' look about the back of his neck, it seemed to me; and the prospect of having to support a Mrs Ukridge and keep a flock of little Ukridges in socks and shirts perturbed me.

'Who was that?' I asked.

'Oh, hallo, laddie!' said Ukridge, turning. 'Where did you

spring from? If you had come a moment earlier, I'd have introduced you to Dora.' The bus was lumbering out of sight into Piccadilly Circus, and the white figure on top turned and gave a final wave. 'That was Dora Mason,' said Ukridge, having flapped a large hand in reply. 'She's my aunt's secretary-companion. I used to see a bit of her from time to time when I was living at Wimbledon. Old Tuppy gave me a couple of seats for that show at the Apollo, so I thought it would be a kindly act to ask her along. I'm sorry for that girl. Sorry for her, old horse.'

'What's the matter with her?'

'Hers is a grey life. She has few pleasures. It's an act of charity to give her a little treat now and then. Think of it! Nothing to do all day but brush the Pekingese and type out my aunt's rotten novels.'

'Does your aunt write novels?'

'The world's worst, laddie, the world's worst. She's been steeped to the gills in literature ever since I can remember. They've just made her president of the Pen and Ink Club. As a matter of fact, it was her novels that did me in when I lived with her. She used to send me to bed with the beastly things and ask me questions about them at breakfast. Absolutely without exaggeration, laddie, at breakfast. It was a dog's life, and I'm glad it's over. Flesh and blood couldn't stand the strain. Well, knowing my aunt, I don't mind telling you that my heart bleeds for poor little Dora. I know what a foul time she has, and I feel a better, finer man for having given her this passing gleam of sunshine. I wish I could have done more for her.'

'Well, you might have stood her tea after the theatre.'

'Not within the sphere of practical politics, laddie. Unless you can sneak out without paying, which is dashed difficult to do with these cashiers watching the door like weasels, tea even at an ABC shop punches the pocket-book pretty hard, and at the moment I'm down to the scrapings. But I'll tell you what, I don't mind joining you in a cup, if you were thinking of it.'

'I wasn't.'

'Come, come! A little more of the good old spirit of hospitality, old horse.'

'Why do you wear that beastly mackintosh in mid-summer?'

'Don't evade the point, laddie. I can see at a glance that you need tea. You're looking pale and fagged.'

'Doctors say that tea is bad for the nerves.'

'Yes, possibly there's something in that. Then I'll tell you what,' said Ukridge, never too proud to yield a point, 'we'll make it a whisky-and-soda instead. Come along over to the Criterion.'

It was a few days after this that the Derby was run, and a horse of the name of Gunga Din finished third. This did not interest the great bulk of the intelligentsia to any marked extent, the animal having started at a hundred to three, but it meant much to me, for I had drawn his name in the sweepstake at my club. After a monotonous series of blanks stretching back to the first year of my membership, this seemed to me the outstanding event of the century, and I celebrated my triumph by an informal dinner to a few friends. It was some small consolation to me later to remember that I had wanted to include Ukridge in the party, but failed to get hold of him. Dark hours were to follow, but at least Ukridge did not go through them bursting with my meat.

There is no form of spiritual exaltation so poignant as that which comes from winning even a third prize in a sweepstake. So tremendous was the moral uplift that, when eleven o'clock arrived, it seemed silly to sit talking in a club and still sillier to go to bed. I suggested spaciously that we should all go off and dress and resume the revels at my expense half an hour later at Mario's, where, it being an extension night, there would be music and dancing till three. We scattered in cabs to our various homes.

How seldom in this life do we receive any premonition of impending disaster. I hummed a gay air as I entered the house in Ebury Street where I lodged, and not even the usually quelling sight of Bowles, my landlord, in the hall as I came in could quench my bonhomie. Generally, a meeting with Bowles had the effect on me which the interior of a cathedral has on the devout, but tonight I was superior to this weakness.

'Ah, Bowles,' I cried, chummily only just stopping myself from adding 'Honest fellow!' 'Hallo, Bowles! I say, Bowles, I drew Gunga Din in the club sweep.'

'Indeed, sir?'

'Yes. He came in third, you know.'

'So I see by the evening paper, sir. I congratulate you.'

'Thank you, Bowles, thank you.'

'Mr Ukridge called earlier in the evening, sir,' said Bowles.

'Did he? Sorry I was out. I was trying to get hold of him. Did he want anything in particular?'

'Your dress-clothes, sir.'

'My dress-clothes, eh?' I laughed genially. 'Extraordinary

fellow! You never know—' A ghastly thought smote me like a blow. A cold wind seemed to blow through the hall. 'He didn't *get* them, did he?' I quavered.

'Why, yes, sir.'

'Got my dress-clothes?' I muttered thickly clutching for support at the hatstand.

'He said it would be all right, sir,' said Bowles, with that sickening tolerance which he always exhibited for all that Ukridge said or did. One of the leading mysteries of my life was my landlord's amazing attitude towards this hell-hound. He fawned on the man. A splendid fellow like myself had to go about in a state of hushed reverence towards Bowles, while a human blot like Ukridge could bellow at him over the banisters without the slightest rebuke. It was one of those things which make one laugh cynically when people talk about the equality of man.

'He got my dress-clothes?' I mumbled.

'Mr Ukridge said that he knew you would be glad to let him have them, as you would not be requiring them tonight.'

'But I do require them, damn it!' I shouted, lost to all proper feeling. Never before had I let fall an oath in Bowles's presence. 'I'm giving half a dozen men supper at Mario's in a quarter of an hour.'

Bowles clicked his tongue sympathetically.

'What am I going to do?'

'Perhaps if you would allow me to lend you mine, sir?'

'Yours?'

'I have a very nice suit. It was given to me by his lordship the late Earl of Oxted, in whose employment I was for many years. I fancy it would do very well on you, sir.

His lordship was about your height, though perhaps a little slenderer. Shall I fetch it, sir? I have it in a trunk downstairs.'

The obligations of hospitality are sacred. In fifteen minutes' time six jovial men would be assembling at Mario's, and what would they do, lacking a host? I nodded feebly.

'It's very kind of you,' I managed to say.

'Not at all, sir. It is a pleasure.'

If he was speaking the truth, I was glad of it. It is nice to think that the affair brought pleasure to someone.

That the late Earl of Oxted had indeed been a somewhat slenderer man than myself became manifest to me from the first pulling on of the trousers. Hitherto I had always admired the slim, small-boned type of aristocrat, but it was not long before I was wishing that Bowles had been in the employment of someone who had gone in a little more heartily for starchy foods. And I regretted, moreover, that the fashion of wearing a velvet collar on an evening coat, if it had to come in at all, had not lasted a few years longer. Dim as the light in my bedroom was, it was strong enough to make me wince as I looked in the mirror.

And I was aware of a curious odour.

'Isn't this room a trifle stuffy, Bowles?'

'No, sir. I think not.'

'Don't you notice an odd smell?'

'No, sir. But I have a somewhat heavy cold. If you are ready, sir, I will call a cab.'

Moth balls! That was the scent I had detected. It swept upon me like a wave in the cab. It accompanied me like a fog all the way to Mario's, and burst out in its full fragrance when I entered the place and removed my overcoat. The cloakroom waiter sniffed in a startled way as he gave me my check, one or two people standing near hastened to remove themselves from my immediate neighbourhood, and my friends, when I joined them, expressed themselves with friend-like candour. With a solid unanimity they told me frankly that it was only the fact that I was paying for the supper that enabled them to tolerate my presence.

The leper-like feeling induced by this uncharitable attitude caused me after the conclusion of the meal to withdraw to the balcony to smoke in solitude. My guests were dancing merrily, but such pleasures were not for me. Besides, my velvet collar had already excited ribald comment, and I am a sensitive man. Crouched in a lonely corner of the balcony, surrounded by the outcasts who were not allowed on the lower floor because they were not dressed, I chewed a cigar and watched the revels with a jaundiced eye. The space reserved for dancing was crowded and couples either revolved warily or ruthlessly bumped a passage for themselves, using their partners as battering rams. Prominent among the ruthless bumpers was a big man who was giving a realistic imitation of a steam-plough. He danced strongly and energetically, and when he struck the line, something had to give.

From the very first something about this man had seemed familiar; but owing to his peculiar crouching manner of dancing, which he seemed to have modelled on the ring style of Mr James J. Jeffries, it was not immediately that I was able to see his face. But presently, as the music stopped and he straightened himself to clap his hands for an encore, his foul features were revealed to me.

It was Ukridge. Ukridge, confound him, with my dress-clothes fitting him so perfectly and with such unwrinkled smoothness that he might have stepped straight out of one of Ouida's novels. Until that moment I had never fully realised the meaning of the expression 'faultless evening dress'. With a passionate cry I leaped from my seat, and, accompanied by a rich smell of camphor, bounded for the stairs. Like Hamlet on a less impressive occasion, I wanted to slay this man when he was full of bread, with all his crimes, broad-blown, as flush as May, at drinking, swearing, or about some act that had no relish of salvation in it.

'But, laddie,' said Ukridge, backed into a corner of the lobby apart from the throng, 'be reasonable.'

I cleansed my bosom of a good deal of that perilous stuff that weighs upon the heart.

'How could I guess that you would want the things? Look at it from my position, old horse. I knew you, laddie, a good true friend who would be delighted to lend a pal his dress-clothes any time when he didn't need them himself, and as you weren't there when I called, I couldn't ask you, so I naturally simply borrowed them. It was all just one of those little misunderstandings which can't be helped. And, as it luckily turns out, you had a spare suit, so everything was all right, after all.'

'You don't think this poisonous fancy dress is mine, do you?'

'Isn't it?' said Ukridge, astonished.

'It belongs to Bowles. He lent it to me.'

'And most extraordinarily well you look in it, laddie,' said Ukridge. 'Upon my Sam, you look like a duke or something.'

'And smell like a second-hand clothes store.'

'Nonsense, my dear old son, nonsense. A mere faint

suggestion of some rather pleasant antiseptic. Nothing more. I like it. It's invigorating. Honestly, old man, it's really remarkable what an air that suit gives you. Distinguished. That's the word I was searching for. You look distinguished. All the girls are saying so. When you came in just now to speak to me, I heard one of them whisper "Who is it?" That shows you.'

'More likely "What is it?"'

'Ha, ha!' bellowed Ukridge, seeking to cajole me with sycophantic mirth. 'Dashed good! Deuced good! Not "Who is it?" but "What is it?" It beats me how you think of these things. Golly, if I had a brain like yours – But now, old son, if you don't mind, I really must be getting back to poor little Dora. She'll be wondering what has become of me.'

The significance of these words had the effect of making me forget my just wrath for a moment.

'Are you here with that girl you took to the theatre the other afternoon?'

'Yes. I happened to win a trifle on the Derby, so I thought it would be the decent thing to ask her out for an evening's pleasure. Hers is a grey life.'

'It must be, seeing you so much.'

'A little personal, old horse,' said Ukridge reprovingly. 'A trifle bitter. But I know you don't mean it. Yours is a heart of gold really. If I've said that once, I've said it a hundred times. Always saying it. Rugged exterior but heart of gold. My very words. Well, goodbye for the present, laddie. I'll look in tomorrow and return these things. I'm sorry there was any misunderstanding about them, but it makes up for everything, doesn't it, to feel that you've helped brighten life for a poor little downtrodden thing who has few pleasures.'

'Just one last word,' I said. 'One final remark.'

'Yes?'

'I'm sitting in that corner of the balcony over there,' I said. 'I mention the fact so that you can look out for yourself. If you come dancing underneath there, I shall drop a plate on you. And if it kills you, so much the better. I'm a poor downtrodden little thing, and I have few pleasures.'

Owing to a mawkish respect for the conventions, for which I reproach myself, I did not actually perform this service to humanity. With the exception of throwing a roll at him – which missed him but most fortunately hit the member of my supper party who had sniffed with the most noticeable offensiveness at my camphorated costume – I took no punitive measures against Ukridge that night. But his demeanour, when he called at my rooms next day, could not have been more crushed if I had dropped a pound of lead on him. He strode into my sitting room with the sombre tread of the man who in a conflict with Fate has received the loser's end. I had been passing in my mind a number of good snappy things to say to him, but his appearance touched me to such an extent that I held them in. To abuse this man would have been like dancing on a tomb.

'For heaven's sake what's the matter?' I asked. 'You look like a toad under the harrow.'

He sat down creakingly, and lit one of my cigars.

'Poor little Dora!'

'What about her?'

'She's got the push!'

'The push? From your aunt's, do you mean?'

'Yes.'

'What for?'

Ukridge sighed heavily.

'Most unfortunate business, old horse, and largely my fault. I thought the whole thing was perfectly safe. You see, my aunt goes to bed at half-past ten every night, so it seemed to me that if Dora slipped out at eleven and left a window open behind her she could sneak back all right when we got home from Mario's. But what happened? Some dashed officious ass,' said Ukridge, with honest wrath, 'went and locked the damned window. I don't know who it was. I suspect the butler. He has a nasty habit of going round the place late at night and shutting things. Upon my Sam, it's a little hard! If only people would leave things alone and not go snooping about—'

'What happened?'

'Why, it was the scullery window which we'd left open, and when we got back at four o'clock this morning the infernal thing was shut as tight as an egg. Things looked pretty rocky, but Dora remembered that her bedroom window was always open, so we bucked up again for a bit. Her room's on the second floor, but I knew where there was a ladder, so I went and got it, and she was just hopping up as merry as dammit when somebody flashed a great beastly lantern on us, and there was a policeman, wanting to know what the game was. The whole trouble with the police force of London, laddie, the thing that makes them a hissing and a byword, is that they're snoopers to a man. Zeal, I suppose they call it. Why they can't attend to their own affairs is more than I can understand. Dozens of murders going on all the time, probably, all over Wimbledon, and all this bloke would do was stand and wiggle his infernal lantern and ask what the game was. Wouldn't be satisfied with a plain statement that it was all right. Insisted on rousing the house to have us identified.'

Ukridge paused, a reminiscent look of pain on his expressive face.

'And then?' I said.

'We were,' said Ukridge, briefly.

'What?'

'Identified. By my aunt. In a dressing gown and a revolver. And the long and the short of it is, old man, that poor little Dora has got the sack.'

I could not find it in my heart to blame his aunt for what he evidently considered a high-handed and tyrannical outrage. If I were a maiden lady of regular views, I should relieve myself of the services of any secretary-companion who returned to roost only a few short hours in advance of the milk. But, as Ukridge plainly desired sympathy rather than an austere pronouncement on the relations of employer and employed, I threw him a couple of tuts, which seemed to soothe him a little. He turned to the practical side of the matter.

'What's to be done?'

'I don't see what you can do.'

'But I must do something. I've lost the poor little thing her job, and I must try to get it back. It's a rotten sort of job, but it's her bread and butter. Do you think George Tupper would biff round and have a chat with my aunt, if I asked him?'

'I suppose he would. He's the best-hearted man in the world. But I doubt if he'll be able to do much.'

'Nonsense, laddie,' said Ukridge, his unconquerable optimism rising bravely from the depths. 'I have the utmost confidence in old Tuppy. A man in a million. And he's such a dashed respectable sort of bloke that he might have her jumping through hoops and shamming dead before she knew what was happening to her. You never know. Yes, I'll try old Tuppy. I'll go and see him now.'

'I should.'

'Just lend me a trifle for a cab, old son, and I shall be able to get to the Foreign Office before one o'clock. I mean to say, even if nothing comes of it, I shall be able to get a lunch out of him. And I need refreshment, laddie, need it sorely. The whole business has shaken me very much.'

It was three days after this that, stirred by a pleasant scent of bacon and coffee, I hurried my dressing and, proceeding to my sitting room, found that Ukridge had dropped in to take breakfast with me, as was often his companionable practice. He seemed thoroughly cheerful again, and was plying knife and fork briskly like the good trencherman he was.

'Morning, old horse,' he said agreeably.

'Good morning.'

'Devilish good bacon, this. As good as I've ever bitten. Bowles is cooking you some more.'

'That's nice. I'll have a cup of coffee, if you don't mind me making myself at home while I'm waiting.' I started to open the letters by my plate, and became aware that my guest was eyeing me with a stare of intense penetration through his pince-nez, which were all crooked as usual. 'What's the matter?'

'Matter?'

'Why,' I said, 'are you looking at me like a fish with lung trouble?'

'Was I?' He took a sip of coffee with an overdone carelessness. 'Matter of fact, old son, I was rather interested. I see you've had a letter from my aunt.'

'What?'

I had picked up the last envelope. It was addressed in a strong female hand, strange to me. I now tore it open. It was even as Ukridge had said. Dated the previous day and headed 'Heath House, Wimbledon Common', the letter ran as follows:

DEAR SIR,

I shall be happy to see you if you will call at this address the day after tomorrow (Friday) at four-thirty.

Yours faithfully,

JULIA UKRIDGE

I could make nothing of this. My morning mail, whether pleasant or the reverse, whether bringing a bill from a tradesman or a cheque from an editor, had had till now the uniform quality of being plain, straightforward, and easy to understand; but this communication baffled me. How Ukridge's aunt had become aware of my existence, and why a call from me should ameliorate her lot, were problems beyond my unravelling, and I brooded over it as an Egyptologist might over some newly-discovered hieroglyphic.

'What does she say?' inquired Ukridge.

'She wants me to call at half-past four tomorrow afternoon.'

'Splendid!' cried Ukridge. 'I knew she would bite.'

'What on earth are you talking about?'

Ukridge reached across the table and patted me affectionately on the shoulder. The movement involved the upsetting of a full cup of coffee, but I suppose he meant well. He sank back again in his chair and adjusted his pince-nez in order to get a better view of me. I seemed to fill him with honest joy, and he suddenly burst into a spirited eulogy, rather like some minstrel of old delivering an extempore boost of his chieftain and employer.

'Laddie,' said Ukridge, 'if there's one thing about you that I've always admired it's your readiness to help a pal. One of the most admirable qualities a bloke can possess, and nobody has it to a greater extent than you. You're practically unique in that way. I've had men come up to me and ask me about you. "What sort of a chap is he?" they say. "One of the very best," I reply. "A fellow you can rely on. A man who would die rather than let you down. A bloke who would go through fire and water to do a pal a good turn. A bird with a heart of gold and a nature as true as steel." '

'Yes, I'm a splendid fellow,' I agreed, slightly perplexed by this panegyric. 'Get on.'

'I am getting on, old horse,' said Ukridge with faint reproach. 'What I'm trying to say is that I knew you would be delighted to tackle this little job for me. It wasn't necessary to ask you. I *knew*.'

A grim foreboding of an awful doom crept over me, as it had done so often before in my association with Ukridge.

'Will you kindly tell me what damned thing you've let me in for now?'

Ukridge deprecated my warmth with a wave of his fork. He spoke soothingly and with a winning persuasiveness. He practically cooed.

'It's nothing, laddie. Practically nothing. Just a simple little act of kindness which you will thank me for putting in your way. It's like this. As I ought to have foreseen from the first, that ass Tuppy proved a broken reed. In that matter of Dora, you know. Got no result whatever. He went to see my aunt the day before yesterday, and asked her to take Dora on again, and she gave him the miss-in-balk. I'm not surprised. I never had any confidence in Tuppy. It was a mistake ever sending him. It's no good trying frontal attack in a delicate business like this. What you need is strategy. You want to think what is the enemy's weak side and then attack from that angle. Now, what is my aunt's weak side, laddie? Her weak side, what is it? Now think. Reflect, old horse.'

'From the sound of her voice, the only time I ever got near her, I should say she hadn't one.'

'That's where you make your error, old son. Butter her up about her beastly novels, and a child could eat out of her hand. When Tuppy let me down I just lit a pipe and had a good think. And then suddenly I got it. I went to a pal of mine, a thorough sportsman – you don't know him. I must introduce you some day – and he wrote my aunt a letter from you, asking if you could come and interview her for *Woman's Sphere.* It's a weekly paper, which I happen to know she takes in regularly. Now, listen, laddie. Don't interrupt for a moment. I want you to get the devilish shrewdness of this. You go and interview her, and she's all over you. Tickled to death. Of course, you'll have to do a good deal of Young Disciple stuff, but you won't mind that. After you've soft-soaped her till she's purring like a dynamo, you get up to go. "Well," you say, "this has been the proudest occasion of my life, meeting one whose work I have so long admired." And she says, "The pleasure is mine, old horse." And you slop over each other a bit more. Then you say sort of casually, as if it had just occurred to you, "Oh, by the way, I believe my cousin" – or sister – No, better make it cousin – "I believe my cousin, Miss Dora Mason, is your secretary, isn't she?" "She isn't any such dam' thing," replies my aunt. "I sacked her three days ago." That's your cue, laddie. Your face falls, you register concern, you're frightfully cut up. You start in to ask her to let Dora come back. And you're such pals by this time that she can refuse you nothing. And there you are! My dear old son, you can take it from me that if you only keep your head and do the Young Disciple stuff properly the thing can't fail. It's an iron-clad scheme. There isn't a flaw in it.'

'There is one.'

'I think you're wrong. I've gone over the thing very carefully. What is it?'

'The flaw is that I'm not going anywhere near your infernal aunt. So you can trot back to your forger chum and tell him he's wasted a good sheet of letter-paper.'

A pair of pince-nez tinkled into a plate. Two pained eyes blinked at me across the table. Stanley Featherstonehaugh Ukridge was wounded to the quick.

'You don't mean to say you're backing out?' he said, in a low, quivering voice.

'I never was in.'

'Laddie,' said Ukridge, weightily, resting an elbow on his

last slice of bacon, 'I want to ask you one question. Just one simple question. Have you ever let me down? Has there been one occasion in our long friendship when I have relied upon you and been deceived? Not one!'

'Everything's got to have a beginning. I'm starting now.'

'But think of her. Dora! Poor little Dora. Think of poor little Dora.'

'If this business teaches her to keep away from you, it will be a blessing in the end.'

'But, laddie—'

I suppose there is some fatal weakness in my character, or else the brand of bacon which Bowles cooked possessed a peculiarly mellowing quality. All I know is that, after being adamant for a good ten minutes, I finished breakfast committed to a task from which my soul revolted. After all, as Ukridge said, it was rough on the girl. Chivalry is chivalry. We must strive to lend a helping hand as we go through this world of ours, and all that sort of thing. Four o'clock on the following afternoon found me entering a cab and giving the driver the address of Heath House, Wimbledon Common.

My emotions on entering Heath House were such as I would have felt had I been keeping a tryst with a dentist who by some strange freak happened also to be a duke. From the moment when a butler of super-Bowles dignity opened the door and, after regarding me with ill-concealed dislike, started to conduct me down a long hall, I was in the grip of both fear and humility. Heath House is one of the stately homes of Wimbledon; how beautiful they stand, as the poet says: and after the humble drabness of Ebury Street it frankly overawed me. Its keynote was an extreme neatness which seemed to sneer at my squashy collar and reproach my baggy trouser-leg. The farther I penetrated over the polished floor, the more vividly was it brought home to me that I was one of the submerged tenth and could have done with a haircut. I had not been aware when I left home that my hair was unusually long, but now I seemed to be festooned by a matted and offensive growth. A patch on my left shoe which had had a rather comfortable look in Ebury Street stood out like a blot on the landscape. No, I was not at my ease; and when I reflected that in a few moments I was to meet Ukridge's aunt, that legendary figure, face to face, a sort of wistful admiration filled me for the beauty of the nature of one who would go through all this to help a girl he had never even met. There was no doubt about it – the facts spoke for themselves – I was one of the finest fellows I had ever known. Nevertheless, there was no getting away from it, my trousers did bag at the knee.

'Mr Corcoran,' announced the butler, opening the drawing room door. He spoke with just that intonation of voice that seemed to disclaim all responsibility. If I had an appointment, he intimated, it was his duty, however repulsive, to show me in; but, that done, he dissociated himself entirely from the whole affair.

There were two women and six Pekingese dogs in the room. The Pekes I had met before, during their brief undergraduate days at Ukridge's dog college, but they did not appear to recognise me. The occasion when they had lunched at my expense seemed to have passed from their minds. One by one they came up, sniffed, and then moved away as if my bouquet had disappointed them. They gave the impression that they saw eye to eye with the butler in his estimate of the young visitor. I was left to face the two women.

Of these – reading from right to left – one was a tall, angular, hawk-faced female with a stony eye. The other, to whom I gave but a passing glance at the moment, was small, and so it seemed to me, pleasant-looking. She had bright hair faintly powdered with grey, and mild eyes of a china blue. She reminded me of the better class of cat. I took her to be some casual caller who had looked in for a cup of tea. It was the hawk on whom I riveted my attention. She was looking at me with a piercing and unpleasant stare, and I thought how exactly she resembled the picture I had formed of her in my mind from Ukridge's conversation.

'Miss Ukridge?' I said, sliding on a rug towards her and feeling like some novice whose manager, against his personal wishes, has fixed up with a match with the heavyweight champion.

'I am Miss Ukridge,' said the other woman. 'Miss Watterson, Mr Corcoran.'

It was a shock, but, the moment of surprise over, I began to feel something approaching mental comfort for the first time since I had entered this house of slippery rugs and supercilious butlers. Somehow I had got the impression from Ukridge that his aunt was a sort of stage aunt, all stiff satin and raised eyebrows. This half-portion with the mild blue eyes I felt I could tackle. It passed my comprehension why Ukridge should ever have found her intimidating.

'I hope you will not mind if we have our little talk before Miss Watterson,' she said with a charming smile. 'She has come to arrange the details of the Pen and Ink Club dance which we are giving shortly. She will keep quite quiet and not interrupt. You don't mind?'

'Not at all, not at all,' I said in my attractive way. It is not exaggerating to say that at this moment I felt debonair. 'Not at all, not at all. Oh, not at all.'

'Won't you sit down?'

'Thank you, thank you.'

The hawk moved over to the window, leaving us to ourselves.

'Now we are quite cosy,' said Ukridge's aunt.

'Yes, yes,' I agreed. Dash it, I liked this woman.

'Tell me, Mr Corcoran,' said Ukridge's aunt, 'are you on the staff of *Woman's Sphere*? It is one of my favourite papers. I read it every week.'

'The outside staff.'

'What do you mean by the outside staff?'

'Well, I don't actually work in the office, but the editor gives me occasional jobs.'

'I see. Who is the editor now?'

I began to feel slightly less debonair. She was just making conversation, of course, to put me at my ease, but I wished she would stop asking me these questions. I searched desperately in my mind for a name – any name – but as usual on these occasions every name in the English language had passed from me.

'Of course. I remember now,' said Ukridge's aunt, to my profound relief. 'It's Mr Jevons, isn't it? I met him one night at dinner.'

'Jevons,' I burbled. 'That's right. Jevons.'

'A tall man with a light moustache.'

'Well, fairly tall,' I said, judicially.

'And he sent you here to interview me?'

'Yes.'

'Well, which of my novels do you wish me to talk about?'

I relaxed with a delightful sense of relief. I felt on solid ground at last. And then it suddenly came to me that Ukridge in his woollen-headed way had omitted to mention the name of a single one of this woman's books.

'Er – oh, all of them,' I said hurriedly.

'I see. My general literary work.'

'Exactly,' I said. My feeling towards her now was one of positive affection.

She leaned back in her chair with her fingertips together, a pretty look of meditation on her face.

'Do you think it would interest the readers of *Woman's Sphere* to know which novel of mine is my own favourite?'

'I am sure it would.'

'Of course,' said Ukridge's aunt, 'it is not easy for an author to answer a question like that. You see, one has moods in which first one book and then another appeals to one.'

'Quite,' I replied. 'Quite.'

'Which of my books do *you* like best, Mr Corcoran?'

There swept over me the trapped feeling one gets in nightmares. From six baskets the six Pekingese stared at me unwinkingly.

'Er – oh, all of them,' I heard a croaking voice reply. My voice, presumably, though I did not recognise it.

'How delightful!' said Ukridge's aunt. 'Now, I really do call that delightful. One or two of the critics have said that my work was uneven. It is so nice to meet someone who doesn't agree with them. Personally, I think my favourite is *The Heart of Adelaide*.'

I nodded my approval of this sound choice. The muscles which had humped themselves stiffly on my back began to crawl back into place again. I found it possible to breathe.

'Yes,' I said, frowning thoughtfully, 'I suppose *The Heart of Adelaide* is the best thing you have written. It has such human appeal,' I added, playing it safe.

'Have you read it, Mr Corcoran?'

'Oh, yes.'

'And you really enjoyed it?'

'Tremendously.'

'You don't think it is a fair criticism to say that it is a little broad in parts?'

'Most unfair.' I began to see my way. I do not know why, but I had been assuming that her novels must be the sort you find in seaside libraries. Evidently they belonged to the other class of female novels, the sort which libraries ban. 'Of course,' I said, 'it is written honestly, fearlessly, and shows life as it is. But broad? No, no!'

'That scene in the conservatory?'

'Best thing in the book,' I said stoutly.

A pleased smile played about her mouth. Ukridge had been right. Praise her work, and a child could eat out of her hand. I found myself wishing that I had really read the thing, so that I could have gone into more detail and made her still happier.

'I'm so glad you like it,' she said. 'Really, it is most encouraging.'

'Oh, no,' I murmured modestly.

'Oh, but it is. Because I have only just started to write it, you see. I finished chapter one this morning.'

She was still smiling so engagingly that for a moment the full horror of these words did not penetrate my consciousness.

'*The Heart of Adelaide* is my next novel. The scene in the conservatory, which you like so much, comes towards the middle of it. I was not expecting to reach it till about the end of next month. How odd that you should know all about it!'

I had got it now all right, and it was like sitting down on the empty space where there should have been a chair. Somehow the fact that she was so pleasant about it all served to deepen my discomfiture. In the course of an active life I have frequently felt a fool, but never such a fool as I felt then. The fearful woman had been playing with me, leading me on, watching me entangle myself like a fly on flypaper. And suddenly I perceived that I had erred in thinking of her eyes as mild. A hard gleam had come into them. They were like a couple of blue gimlets. She looked like a cat that had caught a mouse, and it was revealed to me in one sickening age-long instant why Ukridge went in fear of her. There was that about her which would have intimidated the Sheik.

'It seems so odd, too,' she tinkled on, 'that you should have come to interview me for *Woman's Sphere*. Because they published an interview with me only the week before last. I thought it so strange that I rang up my friend Miss Watterson, who is the editress, and asked her if there had not been some mistake. And she said she had never heard of you. *Have* you ever heard of Mr Corcoran, Muriel?'

'Never,' said the hawk, fixing me with a revolted eye.

'How strange!' said Ukridge's aunt. 'But then the whole thing is so strange. Oh, must you go, Mr Corcoran?'

My mind was in a slightly chaotic condition, but on that one point it was crystal clear. Yes, I must go. Through the door if I could find it – failing that, through the window. And anybody who tried to stop me would do well to have a care.

'You will remember me to Mr Jevons when you see him, won't you?' said Ukridge's aunt.

I was fumbling at the handle.

'And, Mr Corcoran.' She was still smiling amiably, but there had come into her voice a note like that which it had had on a certain memorable occasion when summoning Ukridge to his doom from the unseen interior of his Sheep's Cray Cottage. 'Will you please tell my nephew Stanley that I should be glad if he would send no more of his friends to see me. Good afternoon.'

I suppose that at some point in the proceedings my hostess must have rung a bell, for out in the passage I found my old chum, the butler. With the uncanny telepathy of his species he appeared aware that I was leaving under what might be called a cloud, for his manner had taken on a warder-like grimness. His hand looked as if it was itching to grasp me by the shoulder, and when we reached the front door he eyed the pavement wistfully, as if thinking what a splendid spot it would be for me to hit with a thud.

'Nice day,' I said, with the feverish instinct to babble which comes to strong men in their agony.

He scorned to reply, and as I tottered down the sunlit street I was conscious of his gaze following me.

'A very vicious specimen,' I could fancy him saying. 'And mainly due to my prudence and foresight that he hasn't got away with the spoons.'

It was a warm afternoon, but to such an extent had the recent happenings churned up my emotions that I walked the whole way back to Ebury Street with a rapidity which caused more languid pedestrians to regard me with a pitying contempt. Reaching my sitting room in an advanced state of solubility and fatigue, I found Ukridge stretched upon the sofa.

'Hallo, laddie!' said Ukridge, reaching out a hand for the cooling drink that lay on the floor beside him. 'I was wondering when you would show up. I wanted to tell you that it won't be necessary for you to go and see my aunt after all. It appears that Dora has a hundred quid tucked away in a bank, and she's been offered a partnership by a woman she knows who runs one of these typewriting places. I advised her to close with it. So she's all right.'

He quaffed deeply of the bowl and breathed a contented sigh. There was a silence.

'When did you hear of this?' I asked at length.

'Yesterday afternoon,' said Ukridge. 'I meant to pop round and tell you, but somehow it slipped my mind.'

The Romance of a Bulb-Squeezer

Somebody had left a copy of an illustrated weekly paper in the bar-parlour of the Angler's Rest; and, glancing through it, I came upon the ninth full-page photograph of a celebrated musical comedy actress that I had seen since the preceding Wednesday. This one showed her looking archly over her shoulder with a rose between her teeth, and I flung the periodical from me with a stifled cry.

'Tut, tut!' said Mr Mulliner, reprovingly. 'You must not allow these things to affect you so deeply. Remember, it is not actresses' photographs that matter, but the courage which we bring to them.'

He sipped his hot Scotch.

I wonder if you have ever reflected (he said gravely) what life must be like for the men whose trade it is to make these pictures? Statistics show that the two classes of the community which least often marry are milkmen and fashionable photographers – milkmen because they see women too early in the morning, and fashionable photographers because their days are spent in an atmosphere of feminine loveliness so monotonous that they become surfeited and morose. I know of none of the world's workers whom I pity more sincerely than the fashionable photographer; and yet – by one of those strokes of irony which make the thoughtful man waver between sardonic laughter and sympathetic tears – it is the ambition of every youngster who enters the profession some day to become one.

At the outset of his career, you see, a young photographer is sorely oppressed by human gargoyles: and gradually this begins to prey upon his nerves.

'Why is it,' I remember my cousin Clarence saying, after he had been about a year in the business, 'that all these misfits want to be photographed? Why do men with faces which you would have thought they would be anxious to hush up wish to be strewn about the country on whatnots and in albums? I started out full of ardour and enthusiasm, and my eager soul is being crushed. This morning the Mayor of Tooting East came to make an appointment. He is coming tomorrow afternoon to be taken in his cocked hat and robes of office; and there is absolutely no excuse for a man with a face like that perpetuating his features. I wish to goodness I was one of those fellows who only take camera portraits of beautiful women.'

His dream was to come true sooner than he had imagined. Within a week the great test-case of Biggs *v.* Mulliner had raised my cousin Clarence from an obscure studio in West Kensington to the position of London's most famous photographer.

You possibly remember the case? The events that led up to it were, briefly, as follows:

Jno Horatio Biggs, OBE, the newly-elected Mayor of Tooting East, alighted from a cab at the door of Clarence Mulliner's studio at four-ten on the afternoon of June the seventeenth. At four-eleven he went in. And at four-sixteen and a half he was observed shooting out of a first-floor window, vigorously assisted by my cousin, who was prodding him in the seat of the trousers with the sharp end of a photographic tripod. Those who were in a position to see stated that Clarence's face was distorted by a fury scarcely human.

Naturally the matter could not be expected to rest there. A week later the case of Biggs *v.* Mulliner had begun, the plaintiff claiming damages to the extent of ten thousand pounds and a new pair of trousers. And at first things looked very black for Clarence.

It was the speech of Sir Joseph Bodger, KC, briefed for the defence, that turned the scale.

'I do not,' said Sir Joseph, addressing the jury on the second day, 'propose to deny the charges which have been brought against my client. We freely admit that on the seventeenth inst. we did jab the defendant with our tripod in a manner calculated to cause alarm and despondency. But, gentlemen, we plead justification. The whole case turns upon one question. Is a photographer entitled to assault – either with or, as the case may be, without a tripod – a sitter who, after being warned that his face is not up to the minimum standard requirements, insists upon remaining in the chair and moistening the lips with the tip of the tongue? Gentlemen, I say Yes!

'Unless you decide in favour of my client, gentlemen of the jury, photographers – debarred by law from the privilege of rejecting sitters – will be at the mercy of anyone who comes along with the price of a dozen photographs in his pocket. You have seen the plaintiff, Biggs. You have noted his broad, slab-like face, intolerable to any man of refinement and sensibility. You have observed his walrus moustache, his double chin, his protruding eyes. Take another look at him, and then tell me if my client was not justified in chasing him with a tripod out of that sacred temple of Art and Beauty, his studio.

'Gentlemen, I have finished. I leave my client's fate in your hands with every confidence that you will return the only verdict that can conceivably issue from twelve men of your obvious intelligence, your manifest sympathy, and your superb breadth of vision.'

Of course, after that there was nothing to it. The jury decided in Clarence's favour without leaving the box; and the crowd waiting outside to hear the verdict carried him shoulder-high to his house, refusing to disperse until he had made a speech and sung Photographers never, never, never shall be slaves. And next morning every paper in England came out with a leading article commending him for having so courageously established, as it had not been established since the days of Magna Charta, the fundamental principle of the Liberty of the Subject.

The effect of this publicity on Clarence's fortunes was naturally stupendous. He had become in a flash the best-known photographer in the United Kingdom, and was now in a position to realise that vision which he had of taking the pictures of none but the beaming and the beautiful. Every day the loveliest ornaments of Society and the Stage flocked to his studio; and it was with the utmost astonishment, therefore, that, calling upon him one morning on my return to England after an absence of two years in the East, I learned that Fame and Wealth had not brought him happiness.

I found him sitting moodily in his studio, staring with

dull eyes at a camera-portrait of a well-known actress in a bathing suit. He looked up listlessly as I entered.

'Clarence!' I cried, shocked at his appearance, for there were hard lines about his mouth and wrinkles on a forehead that once had been smooth as alabaster. 'What is wrong?'

'Everything,' he replied, 'I'm fed up.'

'What with?'

'Life. Beautiful women. This beastly photography business.'

I was amazed. Even in the East rumours of his success had reached me, and on my return to London I found that they had not been exaggerated. In every photographers' club in the Metropolis, from the Negative and Solution in Pall Mall to the humble public houses frequented by the men who do your pictures while you wait on the sands at seaside resorts, he was being freely spoken of as the logical successor to the Presidency of the Amalgamated Guild of Bulb-Squeezers.

'I can't stick it much longer,' said Clarence, tearing the camera-portrait into a dozen pieces with a dry sob and burying his face in his hands. 'Actresses nursing their dolls! Countesses simpering over kittens! Film stars among their books! In ten minutes I go to catch a train at Waterloo. I have been sent for by the Duchess of Hampshire to take some studies of Lady Monica Southbourne in the castle grounds.'

A shudder ran through him. I patted him on the shoulder. I understood now.

'She has the most brilliant smile in England,' he whispered.

'Come, come!'

'Coy yet roguish, they tell me.'

'It may not be true.'

'And I bet she will want to be taken offering a lump of sugar to her dog, and the picture will appear in *The Sketch* and *Tatler* as "Lady Monica Southbourne and Friend".'

'Clarence, this is morbid.'

He was silent for a moment.

'Ah, well,' he said, pulling himself together with a visible effort, 'I have made my sodium sulphite, and I must lie in it.'

I saw him off in a cab. The last view I had of him was of his pale, drawn profile. He looked, I thought, like an aristocrat of the French Revolution being borne off to his doom on a tumbril. How little he guessed that the only girl in the world lay waiting for him round the corner.

No, you are wrong. Lady Monica did not turn out to be the only girl in the world. If what I said caused you to expect that, I misled you. Lady Monica proved to be all his fancy had pictured her. In fact even more. Not only was her smile coy yet roguish, but she had a sort of coquettish droop of the left eyelid of which no one had warned him. And, in addition to her two dogs, which she was portrayed in the act of feeding with two lumps of sugar, she possessed a totally unforeseen pet monkey, of which he was compelled to take no fewer than eleven studies.

No, it was not Lady Monica who captured Clarence's heart, but a girl in a taxi whom he met on his way to the station.

It was in a traffic jam at the top of Whitehall that he first observed this girl. His cab had become becalmed in a sea of omnibuses, and, chancing to look to the right, he perceived within a few feet of him another taxi, which had been heading for Trafalgar Square. There was a face at its window. It turned towards him, and their eyes met.

To most men it would have seemed an unattractive face. To Clarence, surfeited with the coy, the beaming, and the delicately-chiselled, it was the most wonderful thing he had ever looked at. All his life, he felt, he had been searching for something on these lines. That snub nose – those freckles – that breadth of cheekbone – the squareness of that chin. And not a dimple in sight. He told me afterwards that his only feeling at first was one of incredulity. He had not believed that the world contained women like this. And then the traffic jam loosened up and he was carried away.

It was as he was passing the Houses of Parliament that the realisation came to him that the strange bubbly sensation that seemed to start from just above the lower left side-pocket of his waistcoat was not, as he had at first supposed, dyspepsia, but love. Yes, love had come at long last to Clarence Mulliner; and for all the good it was likely to do him, he reflected bitterly, it might just as well have been the dyspepsia for which he had mistaken it. He loved a girl whom he would probably never see again. He did not know her name or where she lived or anything about her. All he knew was that he would cherish her image in his heart for ever, and that the thought of going on with the old dreary round of photographing lovely women with coy yet roguish smiles was almost more than he could bear.

However, custom is strong; and a man who has once allowed the bulb-squeezing habit to get a grip of him cannot cast it off in a moment. Next day Clarence was back in his studio, diving into the velvet nosebag as of yore and telling peeresses to watch the little birdie just as if nothing had happened. And if there was now a strange, haunting look of pain in his eyes, nobody objected to that. Indeed, inasmuch as the grief which gnawed at his heart had the effect of deepening and mellowing his camera-side manner to an almost sacerdotal unctuousness, his private sorrows actually helped his professional prestige. Women told one another that being photographed by Clarence Mulliner was like undergoing some wonderful spiritual experience in a noble cathedral; and his appointment book became fuller than ever.

So great now was his reputation that to anyone who had had the privilege of being taken by him, either full face or in profile, the doors of Society opened automatically. It was whispered that his name was to appear in the next Birthday Honours List; and at the annual banquet of the Amalgamated Bulb-Squeezers, when Sir Godfrey Stooge, the retiring President, in proposing his health, concluded a glowingly eulogistic speech with the words, 'Gentlemen, I give you my destined successor, Mulliner the Liberator!' five hundred frantic photographers almost shivered the glasses on the table with their applause.

And yet he was not happy. He had lost the only girl he had ever loved, and without her what was Fame? What was Affluence? What were the Highest Honours in the Land?

These were the questions he was asking himself one night as he sat in his library, sombrely sipping a final whisky-and-soda before retiring. He had asked them once and was going to ask them again, when he was interrupted by the sound of someone ringing at the front-door bell.

He rose, surprised. It was late for callers. The domestic staff had gone to bed, so he went to the door and opened it. A shadowy figure was standing on the steps.

'Mr Mulliner?'

'I am Mr Mulliner.'

The man stepped past him into the hall. And, as he did so, Clarence saw that he was wearing over the upper half of his face a black velvet mask.

'I must apologise for hiding my face, Mr Mulliner,' the visitor said, as Clarence led him to the library.

'Not at all,' replied Clarence, courteously. 'No doubt it is all for the best.'

'Indeed?' said the other, with a touch of asperity. 'If you really want to know, I am probably as handsome a man as there is in London. But my mission is one of such extraordinary secrecy that I dare not run the risk of being recognised.' He paused, and Clarence saw his eyes glint through the holes in the mask as he directed a rapid gaze into each corner of the library. 'Mr Mulliner, have you any acquaintance with the ramifications of international secret politics?'

'I have.'

'And you are a patriot?'

'I am.'

'Then I can speak freely. No doubt you are aware, Mr Mulliner, that for some time past this country and a certain rival Power have been competing for the friendship and alliance of a certain other Power?'

'No,' said Clarence, 'they didn't tell me that.'

'Such is the case. And the President of this Power—'

'Which one?'

'The second one.'

'Call it B.'

'The President of Power B is now in London. He arrived incognito, travelling under the assumed name of J. J. Shubert: and the representatives of Power A, to the best of our knowledge, are not yet aware of his presence. This gives us just the few hours necessary to clinch this treaty with Power B before Power A can interfere. I ought to tell you, Mr Mulliner, that if Power B forms an alliance with this country, the supremacy of the Anglo-Saxon race will be secured for hundreds of years. Whereas if Power A gets hold of Power B, civilisation will be thrown into the melting pot. In the eyes of all Europe – and when I say all Europe I refer particularly to Powers C, D, and E – this nation would sink to the rank of a fourth-class Power.'

'Call it Power F,' said Clarence.

'It rests with you, Mr Mulliner, to save England.'

'Great Britain,' corrected Clarence. He was half Scotch on his mother's side. 'But how? What can I do about it?'

'The position is this. The President of Power B has an overwhelming desire to have his photograph taken by Clarence Mulliner. Consent to take it, and our difficulties will be at an end. Overcome with gratitude, he will sign the treaty, and the Anglo-Saxon race will be safe.'

Clarence did not hesitate. Apart from the natural gratification of feeling that he was doing the Anglo-Saxon race a bit of good, business was business; and if the President took a dozen of the large size finished in silver wash it would mean a nice profit.

'I shall be delighted,' he said.

'Your patriotism,' said the visitor, 'will not go unrewarded. It will be gratefully noted in the Very Highest Circles.'

Clarence reached for his appointment book.

'Now, let me see. Wednesday? – No, I'm full up Wednesday. Thursday? – No. Suppose the President looks in at my studio between four and five on Friday?'

The visitor uttered a gasp.

'Good heavens, Mr Mulliner,' he exclaimed, 'surely you do not imagine that, with the vast issues at stake, these things can be done openly and in daylight? If the devils in the pay of Power A were to learn that the President intended to have his photograph taken by you, I would not give a straw for your chances of living an hour.'

'Then what do you suggest?'

'You must accompany me now to the President's suite at the Milan Hotel. We shall travel in a closed car, and God send that these fiends did not recognise me as I came here. If they did, we shall never reach that car alive. Have you, by any chance, while we have been talking, heard the hoot of an owl?'

'No,' said Clarence. 'No owls.'

'Then perhaps they are nowhere near. The fiends always imitate the hoot of an owl.'

'A thing,' said Clarence, 'which I tried to do when I was a small boy and never seemed able to manage. The popular idea that owls say "Tu-whit, tu-whoo" is all wrong. The actual noise they make is something far more difficult and complex, and it was beyond me.'

'Quite so.' The visitor looked at his watch. 'However, absorbing as these reminiscences of your boyhood days are, time is flying. Shall we be making a start?'

'Certainly.'

'Then follow me.'

It appeared to be holiday time for fiends, or else the night shift had not yet come on, for they reached the car without being molested. Clarence stepped in, and his masked visitor, after a keen look up and down the street, followed him.

'Talking of my boyhood—' began Clarence.

The sentence was never completed. A soft wet pad was pressed over his nostrils: the air became a-reek with the sickly fumes of chloroform: and Clarence knew no more.

When he came to, he was no longer in the car. He found himself lying on a bed in a room in a strange house. It was a medium-sized room with scarlet wallpaper, simply furnished with a wash-hand stand, a chest of drawers, two cane-bottomed chairs, and a 'God Bless Our Home' motto framed in oak. He was conscious of a severe headache, and was about to rise and make for the water bottle on the wash-stand when, to his consternation, he discovered that his arms and legs were shackled with stout cord.

As a family, the Mulliners have always been noted for their reckless courage; and Clarence was no exception to the rule. But for an instant his heart undeniably beat a little faster. He saw now that his masked visitor had tricked him. Instead of being a representative of His Majesty's Diplomatic Service (a most respectable class of men), he had really been all along a fiend in the pay of Power A.

No doubt he and his vile associates were even now chuckling at the ease with which their victim had been duped. Clarence gritted his teeth and struggled vainly to loose the knots which secured his wrists. He had fallen back exhausted when he heard the sound of a key turning and the door opened. Somebody crossed the room and stood by the bed, looking down on him.

The newcomer was a stout man with a complexion that matched the wallpaper. He was puffing slightly, as if he had found the stairs trying. He had broad, slab-like features; and his face was split in the middle by a walrus moustache. Somewhere and in some place, Clarence was convinced, he had seen this man before.

And then it all came back to him. An open window with a pleasant summer breeze blowing in; a stout man in a cocked hat trying to climb through this window; and he, Clarence, doing his best to help him with the sharp end of a tripod. It was Jno Horatio Biggs, the Mayor of Tooting East.

A shudder of loathing ran through Clarence.

'Traitor!' he cried.

'Eh?' said the Mayor.

'If anybody had told me that a son of Tooting, nursed in the keen air of freedom which blows across the Common, would sell himself for gold to the enemies of his country, I would never have believed it. Well, you may tell your employers—'

'What employers?'

'Power A.'

'Oh, that?' said the Mayor. 'I am afraid my secretary, whom I instructed to bring you to this house, was obliged to romance a little in order to ensure your accompanying him, Mr Mulliner. All that about Power A and Power B was just his little joke. If you want to know why you were brought here—'

Clarence uttered a low groan.

'I have guessed your ghastly object, you ghastly object,' he said quietly. 'You want me to photograph you.'

The Mayor shook his head.

'Not myself. I realise that that can never be. My daughter.'

'Your daughter?'

'My daughter.'

'Does she take after you?'

'People tell me there is a resemblance.'

'I refuse,' said Clarence.

'Think well, Mr Mulliner.'

'I have done all the thinking that is necessary. England – or, rather, Great Britain – looks to me to photograph only her fairest and loveliest; and though, as a man, I admit that I loathe beautiful women, as a photographer I have a duty to consider that is higher than any personal feelings. History has yet to record an instance of a photographer playing his country false, and Clarence Mulliner is not the man to supply the first one. I decline your offer.'

'I wasn't looking on it exactly as an offer,' said the Mayor, thoughtfully. 'More as a command, if you get my meaning.'

'You imagine that you can bend a lens-artist to your will and make him false to his professional reputation?'

'I was thinking of having a try.'

'Do you realise that, if my incarceration here were known, ten thousand photographers would tear this house brick from brick and you limb from limb?'

'But it isn't,' the Mayor pointed out. 'And that, if you follow me, is the whole point. You came here by night in a closed car. You could stay here for the rest of your life, and no one would be any the wiser. I really think you had better reconsider, Mr Mulliner.'

'You have had my answer.'

'Well, I'll leave you to think it over. Dinner will be served at seven-thirty. Don't bother to dress.'

At half-past seven precisely the door opened again and the Mayor reappeared, followed by a butler bearing on a silver salver a glass of water and a small slice of bread. Pride urged Clarence to reject the refreshment, but hunger overcame pride. He swallowed the bread which the butler offered him in small bits in a spoon, and drank the water.

'At what hour would the gentleman desire breakfast, sir?' asked the butler.

'Now,' said Clarence, for his appetite, always healthy, seemed to have been sharpened by the trials which he had undergone.

'Let us say nine o'clock,' suggested the Mayor. 'Put aside another slice of that bread, Meadows. And no doubt Mr Mulliner would enjoy a glass of this excellent water.'

For perhaps half an hour after his host had left him, Clarence's mind was obsessed to the exclusion of all other thoughts by a vision of the dinner he would have liked to be enjoying. All we Mulliners have been good trenchermen, and to put a bit of bread into it after it had been unoccupied for a whole day was to offer to Clarence's stomach an insult which it resented with an indescribable bitterness. Clarence's only emotion for some considerable time, then, was that of hunger. His thoughts centred themselves on food. And it was to this fact, oddly enough, that he owed his release.

For, as he lay there in a sort of delirium, picturing himself getting outside a medium-cooked steak smothered in onions, with grilled tomatoes and floury potatoes on the side, it was suddenly borne in upon him that this steak did not taste quite so good as other steaks which he had eaten in the past. It was tough and lacked juiciness. It tasted just like rope.

And then, his mind clearing, he saw that it actually was rope. Carried away by the anguish of hunger, he had been chewing the cord which bound his hands; and he now discovered that he had bitten into it quite deeply.

A sudden flood of hope poured over Clarence Mulliner. Carrying on at this rate, he perceived, he would be able ere long to free himself. It only needed a little imagination. After a brief interval to rest his aching jaws, he put himself deliberately into that state of relaxation which is recommended by the apostles of Suggestion.

'I am entering the dining room of my club,' murmured Clarence. 'I am sitting down. The waiter is handing me the bill of fare. I have selected roast duck with green peas and new potatoes, lamb cutlets with Brussels sprouts, fricassee of chicken, porterhouse steak, boiled beef and carrots, leg of mutton, haunch of mutton, mutton chops, curried mutton, veal, kidneys *sauté*, spaghetti Caruso, and eggs and bacon, fried on both sides. The waiter is now bringing my order. I have taken up my knife and fork. I am beginning to eat.'

And, murmuring a brief grace, Clarence flung himself on the rope and set to.

Twenty minutes later he was hobbling about the room, restoring the circulation to his cramped limbs.

Just as he had succeeded in getting himself nicely limbered up, he heard the key turning in the door.

Clarence crouched for the spring. The room was quite dark now, and he was glad of it, for darkness well fitted the work which lay before him. His plans, conceived on the spur of the moment, were necessarily sketchy, but they included jumping on the Mayor's shoulders and pulling his head off. After that, no doubt, other modes of self-expression would suggest themselves.

The door opened. Clarence made his leap. And he was just about to start on the programme as arranged, when he discovered with a shock of horror that this was no OBE that he was being rough with, but a woman. And no photographer worthy of the name will ever lay a hand upon a woman, save to raise her chin and tilt it a little more to the left.

'I beg your pardon!' he cried.

'Don't mention it,' said his visitor, in a low voice. 'I hope I didn't disturb you.'

'Not at all,' said Clarence.

There was a pause.

'Rotten weather,' said Clarence, feeling that it was for him, as the male member of the sketch, to keep the conversation going.

'Yes, isn't it?'

'A lot of rain we've had this summer.'

'Yes. It seems to get worse every year.'

'Doesn't it?'

'So bad for tennis.'

'And cricket.'

'And polo.'

'And garden parties.'

'I hate rain.'

'So do I.'

'Of course, we may have a fine August.'

'Yes, there's always that.'

The ice was broken, and the girl seemed to become more at her ease.

'I came to let you out,' she said. 'I must apologise for my father. He loves me foolishly and has no scruples where my happiness is concerned. He has always yearned to have me photographed by you, but I cannot consent to allow a photographer to be coerced into abandoning his principles. If you will follow me, I will let you out by the front door.'

'It's awfully good of you,' said Clarence, awkwardly. As any man of nice sentiment would have been, he was embarrassed. He wished that he could have obliged this kind-hearted girl by taking her picture, but a natural delicacy restrained him from touching on this subject. They went down the stairs in silence.

On the first landing a hand was placed on his in the darkness and the girl's voice whispered in his ear.

'We are just outside father's study,' he heard her say. 'We must be as quiet as mice.'

'As what?' said Clarence.

'Mice.'

'Oh, rather,' said Clarence, and immediately bumped into what appeared to be a pedestal of some sort.

These pedestals usually have vases on top of them, and it was revealed to Clarence a moment later that this one was no exception. There was a noise like ten simultaneous dinner services coming apart in the hands of ten simultaneous parlourmaids; and then the door was flung open, the landing became flooded with light, and the Mayor of Tooting East stood before them. He was carrying a revolver and his face was dark with menace.

'Ha!' said the Mayor.

But Clarence was paying no attention to him. He was staring open-mouthed at the girl. She had shrunk back against the wall, and the light fell full upon her.

'You!' cried Clarence.

'This—' began the Mayor.

'You! At last!'

'This is a pretty—'

'Am I dreaming?'

'This is a pretty state of af—'

'Ever since that day I saw you in the cab I have been scouring London for you. To think that I have found you at last!'

'This is a pretty state of affairs,' said the Mayor, breathing on the barrel of his revolver and polishing it on the sleeve of his coat. 'My daughter helping the foe of her family to fly—'

'Flee, father,' corrected the girl, faintly.

'Flea or fly – this is no time for arguing about insects. Let me tell you—'

Clarence interrupted him indignantly.

'What do you mean,' he cried, 'by saying that she took after you?'

'She does.'

'She does not. She is the loveliest girl in the world, while you look like Lon Chaney made up for something. See for yourself.' Clarence led them to the large mirror at the head of the stairs. 'Your face – if you can call it that – is one of those beastly blobby squashy sort of faces—'

'Here!' said the Mayor.

'—whereas hers is simply divine. Your eyes are bulbous and goofy—'

'Hey!' said the Mayor.

'—while hers are sweet and soft and intelligent. Your ears—'

'Yes, yes,' said the Mayor, petulantly. 'Some other time, some other time. Then am I to take it, Mr Mulliner—'

'Call me Clarence.'

'I refuse to call you Clarence.'

'You will have to very shortly, when I am your son-in-law.'

The girl uttered a cry. The Mayor uttered a louder cry.

'My son-in-law!'

'That,' said Clarence, firmly, 'is what I intend to be – and speedily.' He turned to the girl. 'I am a man of volcanic passions, and now that love has come to me there is no power in heaven or earth that can keep me from the object of my love. It will be my never-ceasing task – er—'

'Gladys,' prompted the girl.

'Thank you. It will be my never-ceasing task, Gladys, to strive daily to make you return that love—'

'You need not strive, Clarence,' she whispered, softly. 'It is already returned.'

Clarence reeled.

'Already?' he gasped.

'I have loved you since I saw you in that cab. When we were torn asunder, I felt quite faint.'

'So did I. I was in a daze. I tipped my cabman at Waterloo three half-crowns. I was aflame with love.'

'I can hardly believe it.'

'Nor could I, when I found out. I thought it was threepence. And ever since that day—'

The Mayor coughed.

'Then am I to take it – er – Clarence,' he said, 'that your objections to photographing my daughter are removed?'

Clarence laughed happily.

'Listen,' he said, 'and I'll show you the sort of son-in-law I am. Ruin my professional reputation though it may, I will take a photograph of you too!'

'Me!'

'Absolutely. Standing beside her with the tips of your fingers on her shoulder. And what's more, you can wear your cocked hat.'

Tears had begun to trickle down the Mayor's cheeks.

'My boy!' he sobbed, brokenly. 'My boy!'

And so happiness came to Clarence Mulliner at last. He never became President of the Bulb-Squeezers, for he retired from business the next day, declaring that the hand that had snapped the shutter when taking the photograph of his dear wife should never snap it again for sordid profit. The wedding, which took place some six weeks later, was attended by almost everybody of any note in Society or on the Stage; and was the first occasion on which a bride and bridegroom had ever walked out of church beneath an arch of crossed tripods.

The Heart of a Goof

It was a morning when all nature shouted 'Fore!' The breeze, as it blew gently up from the valley, seemed to bring a message of hope and cheer, whispering of chip-shots holed and brassies landing squarely on the meat. The fairway, as yet unscarred by the irons of a hundred dubs, smiled greenly up at the azure sky; and the sun, peeping above the trees, looked like a giant golf-ball perfectly lofted by the mashie of some unseen god and about to drop dead by the pin of the eighteenth. It was the day of the opening of the course after the long winter, and a crowd of considerable dimensions had collected at the first tee. Plus fours gleamed in the sunshine, and the air was charged with happy anticipation.

In all that gay throng there was but one sad face. It belonged to the man who was waggling his driver over the new ball perched on its little hill of sand. This man seemed careworn, hopeless. He gazed down the fairway, shifted his feet, waggled, gazed down the fairway again, shifted the dogs once more, and waggled afresh. He waggled as Hamlet might have waggled, moodily, irresolutely. Then, at last, he swung, and, taking from his caddie the niblick which the intelligent lad had been holding in readiness from the moment when he had walked on to the tee, trudged wearily off to play his second.

The Oldest Member, who had been observing the scene

with a benevolent eye from his favourite chair on the terrace, sighed.

'Poor Jenkinson,' he said, 'does not improve.'

'No,' agreed his companion, a young man with open features and a handicap of six. 'And yet I happen to know that he has been taking lessons all the winter at one of those indoor places.'

'Futile, quite futile,' said the Sage with a shake of his snowy head. 'There is no wizard living who could make that man go round in an average of sevens. I keep advising him to give up the game.'

'You!' cried the young man, raising a shocked and startled face from the driver with which he was toying. '*You* told him to give up golf! Why I thought—'

'I understand and approve of your horror,' said the Oldest Member, gently. 'But you must bear in mind that Jenkinson's is not an ordinary case. You know and I know scores of men who have never broken a hundred and twenty in their lives, and yet contrive to be happy, useful members of society. However badly they may play, they are able to forget. But with Jenkinson it is different. He is not one of those who can take it or leave it alone. His only chance of happiness lies in complete abstinence. Jenkinson is a goof.'

'A what?'

'A goof,' repeated the Sage. 'One of those unfortunate beings who have allowed this noblest of sports to get too great a grip upon them, who have permitted it to eat into their souls, like some malignant growth. The goof, you must understand, is not like you and me. He broods. He becomes morbid. His goofery unfits him for the battles of life. Jenkinson, for example, was once a man with a glowing future in the hay, corn, and feed business, but a constant stream of hooks, tops, and slices gradually made him so diffident and mistrustful of himself, that he let opportunity after opportunity slip, with the result that other, sterner, hay, corn, and feed merchants passed him in the race. Every time he had the chance to carry through some big deal in hay, or to execute some flashing *coup* in corn and feed, the fatal diffidence generated by a hundred rotten rounds would undo him. I understand his bankruptcy may be expected at any moment.'

'My golly!' said the young man, deeply impressed. 'I hope I never become a goof. Do you mean to say there is really no cure except giving up the game?'

The Oldest Member was silent for a while.

'It is curious that you should have asked that question,' he said at last, 'for only this morning I was thinking of the one case in my experience where a goof was enabled to overcome his deplorable malady. It was owing to a girl, of course. The longer I live, the more I come to see that most things are. But you will, no doubt, wish to hear the story from the beginning.'

The young man rose with the startled haste of some wild creature, which, wandering through the undergrowth, perceives the trap in his path.

'I should love to,' he mumbled, 'only I shall be losing my place at the tee.'

'The goof in question,' said the Sage, attaching himself with quiet firmness to the youth's coat-button, 'was a man of about your age, by name Ferdinand Dibble. I knew him well. In fact, it was to me—'

'Some other time, eh?'

'It was to me,' proceeded the Sage, placidly, 'that he came for sympathy in the great crisis of his life, and I am not ashamed to say that when he had finished laying bare his soul to me there were tears in my eyes. My heart bled for the boy.'

'I bet it did. But—'

The Oldest Member pushed him gently back into his seat.

'Golf,' he said, 'is the Great Mystery. Like some capricious goddess—'

The young man, who had been exhibiting symptoms of feverishness, appeared to become resigned. He sighed softly.

'Did you ever read "The Ancient Mariner"?' he said.

'Many years ago,' said the Oldest Member. 'Why do you ask?'

'Oh, I don't know,' said the young man. 'It just occurred to me.'

Golf (resumed the Oldest Member) is the Great Mystery. Like some capricious goddess, it bestows its favours with what would appear an almost fatheaded lack of method and discrimination. On every side we see big two-fisted he-men floundering round in three figures, stopping every few minutes to let through little shrimps with knock knees and hollow cheeks, who are tearing off snappy seventy-fours. Giants of finance have to accept a stroke per from their junior clerks. Men capable of governing empires fail to control a small, white ball, which presents no difficulties whatever to others with one ounce more brain than a cuckoo-clock. Mysterious, but there it is. There was no apparent reason why Ferdinand Dibble should not have been a competent golfer. He had strong wrists and a good eye. Nevertheless, the fact remains that he was a dub. And on a certain evening in June I realised that he was also a goof. I found it out quite suddenly as the result of a conversation which we had on this very terrace.

I was sitting here that evening thinking of this and that, when by the corner of the clubhouse I observed young Dibble in conversation with a girl in white. I could not see who she was, for her back was turned. Presently they parted and Ferdinand came slowly across to where I sat. His air was dejected. He had had the boots licked off him earlier in the afternoon by Jimmy Fothergill, and it was to this that I attributed his gloom. I was to find out in a few moments that I was partly but not entirely correct in this surmise. He took the next chair to mine, and for several minutes sat staring moodily down into the valley.

'I've just been talking to Barbara Medway,' he said, suddenly breaking the silence.

'Indeed?' I said. 'A delightful girl.'

'She's going away for the summer to Marvis Bay.'

'She will take the sunshine with her.'

'You bet she will!' said Ferdinand Dibble, with extraordinary warmth, and there was another long silence.

Presently Ferdinand uttered a hollow groan.

'I love her, dammit!' he muttered brokenly. 'Oh, golly, how I love her!'

I was not surprised at his making me the recipient of his confidences like this. Most of the young folk in the place brought their troubles to me sooner or later.

'And does she return your love?'

'I don't know. I haven't asked her.'

'Why not? I should have thought the point not without its interest for you.'

Ferdinand gnawed the handle of his putter distractedly.

'I haven't the nerve,' he burst out at length. 'I simply can't summon up the cold gall to ask a girl, least of all an angel like her, to marry me. You see, it's like this. Every time I work myself up to the point of having a dash at it, I go out and get trimmed by someone giving me a stroke a hole. Every time I feel I've mustered up enough pep to propose, I take ten on a bogey three. Every time I think I'm in good mid-season form for putting my fate to the test, to win or lose it all, something goes all blooey with my swing, and I slice into the rough at every tee. And then my self-confidence leaves me. I become nervous, tongue-tied, diffident. I wish to goodness I knew the man who invented this infernal game. I'd strangle him. But I suppose he's been dead for ages. Still, I could go and jump on his grave.'

It was at this point that I understood all, and the heart within me sank like lead. The truth was out. Ferdinand Dibble was a goof.

'Come, come, my boy,' I said, though feeling the uselessness of any words. 'Master this weakness.'

'I can't.'

'Try!'

'I have tried.'

He gnawed his putter again.

'She was asking me just now if I couldn't manage to come to Marvis Bay, too,' he said.

'That surely is encouraging? It suggests that she is not entirely indifferent to your society.'

'Yes, but what's the use? Do you know,' a gleam coming into his eyes for a moment, 'I have a feeling that if I could ever beat some really fairly good player – just once – I could bring the thing off.' The gleam faded. 'But what chance is there of that?'

It was a question which I did not care to answer. I merely patted his shoulder sympathetically, and after a little while he left me and walked away. I was still sitting there, thinking over his hard case, when Barbara Medway came out of the clubhouse.

She, too, seemed grave and preoccupied, as if there was something on her mind. She took the chair which Ferdinand had vacated, and sighed wearily.

'Have you ever felt,' she asked, 'that you would like to bang a man on the head with something hard and heavy? With knobs on?'

I said I had sometimes experienced such a desire, and asked if she had any particular man in mind. She seemed to hesitate for a moment before replying, then, apparently, made up her mind to confide in me. My advanced years carry with them certain pleasant compensations, one of which is that nice girls often confide in me. I frequently find myself enrolled as a father-confessor on the most intimate matters by beautiful creatures from whom many a younger man would give his eye-teeth to get a friendly word. Besides, I had known Barbara since she was a child. Frequently – though not recently – I had given her her evening bath. These things form a bond.

'Why are men such chumps?' she exclaimed.

'You still have not told me who it is that has caused these harsh words. Do I know him?'

'Of course you do. You've just been talking to him.'

'Ferdinand Dibble? But why should you wish to bang Ferdinand Dibble on the head with something hard and heavy with knobs on?'

'Because he's such a goop.'

'You mean a goof?' I queried, wondering how she could have penetrated the unhappy man's secret.

'No, a goop. A goop is a man who's in love with a girl and won't tell her so. I am as certain as I am of anything that Ferdinand is fond of me.'

'Your instinct is unerring. He has just been confiding in me on that very point.'

'Well, why doesn't he confide in *me,* the poor fish?' cried the high-spirited girl, petulantly flicking a pebble at a passing grasshopper. 'I can't be expected to fling myself into his arms unless he gives some sort of a hint that he's ready to catch me.'

'Would it help if I were to repeat to him the substance of this conversation of ours?'

'If you breathe a word of it, I'll never speak to you again,' she cried. 'I'd rather die an awful death than have any man think I wanted him so badly that I had to send relays of messengers begging him to marry me.'

I saw her point.

'Then I fear,' I said, gravely, 'that there is nothing to be done. One can only wait and hope. It may be that in the years to come Ferdinand Dibble will acquire a nice lissom, wristy swing, with the head kept rigid and the right leg firmly braced and—'

'What are you talking about?'

'I was toying with the hope that some sunny day Ferdinand Dibble would cease to be a goof.'

'You mean a goop?'

'No, a goof. A goof is a man who—' And I went on to explain the peculiar psychological difficulties which lay in the way of any declaration of affection on Ferdinand's part.

'But I never heard of anything so ridiculous in my life,' she ejaculated. 'Do you mean to say that he is waiting till he is good at golf before he asks me to marry him?'

'It is not quite so simple as that,' I said sadly. 'Many bad golfers marry, feeling that a wife's loving solicitude may improve their game. But they are rugged, thick-skinned men, not sensitive and introspective, like Ferdinand. Ferdinand has allowed himself to become morbid. It is one of the chief merits of golf that non-success at the game induces a certain amount of decent humility, which keeps a man from pluming himself too much on any petty triumphs he may achieve in other walks of life; but in all things there is a happy mean, and with Ferdinand this humility has gone too far. It has taken all the spirit out of him. He feels crushed and worthless. He is grateful to caddies when they accept a tip instead of drawing themselves up to their full height and flinging the money in his face.'

'Then do you mean that things have got to go on like this for ever?'

I thought for a moment.

'It is a pity,' I said, 'that you could not have induced Ferdinand to go to Marvis Bay for a month or two.'

'Why?'

'Because it seems to me, thinking the thing over, that it is just possible that Marvis Bay might cure him. At the hotel there he would find collected a mob of golfers – I used the term in its broadest sense, to embrace the paralytics and the men who play left-handed – whom even he would be able to beat. When I was last at Marvis Bay, the hotel links were a sort of Sargasso Sea into which had drifted all the pitiful flotsam and jetsam of golf. I have seen things done on that course at which I shuddered and averted my eyes – and I am not a weak man. If Ferdinand can polish up his game so as to go round in a fairly steady hundred and five, I fancy there is hope. But I understand he is not going to Marvis Bay.'

'Oh yes, he is,' said the girl.

'Indeed! He did not tell me that when we were talking just now.'

'He didn't know it then. He will when I have had a few words with him.'

And she walked with firm steps back into the clubhouse.

It has been well said that there are many kinds of golf, beginning at the top with the golf of professionals and the best amateurs and working down through the golf of ossified men to that of Scotch University professors. Until recently this last was looked upon as the lowest possible depth; but nowadays, with the growing popularity of summer hotels, we are able to add a brand still lower, the golf you find at places like Marvis Bay.

To Ferdinand Dibble, coming from a club where the standard of play was rather unusually high, Marvis Bay was a revelation, and for some days after his arrival there he went about dazed, like a man who cannot believe it is really true. To go out on the links at this summer resort was like entering a new world. The hotel was full of stout, middle-aged men, who, after a misspent youth devoted to making money, had taken to a game at which real proficiency can only be acquired by those who start playing in their cradles and keep their weight down. Out on the course each morning you could see representatives of every nightmare style that was ever invented. There was the man who seemed to be attempting to deceive his ball and lull it into a false security by looking away from it and then making a lightning slash in the apparent hope of catching it off its guard. There was the man who wielded his mid-iron like one killing snakes. There was the man who addressed his ball as if he were stroking a cat, the man who drove as if he were cracking a whip, the man who brooded over each shot like one whose heart is bowed down by bad news from home, and the man who scooped with his mashie as if he were ladling soup. By the end of the first week Ferdinand Dibble was the acknowledged champion of the place. He had gone through the entire menagerie like a bullet through a cream puff.

First, scarcely daring to consider the possibility of success, he had taken on the man who tried to catch his ball off its guard and had beaten him five up and four to play. Then, with gradually growing confidence, he tackled in turn the Cat-Stroker, the Whip-Cracker, the Heart Bowed Down, and the Soup-Scooper, and walked all over their faces with spiked shoes. And as these were the leading local amateurs, whose prowess the octogenarians and the men who went round in bath chairs vainly strove to emulate, Ferdinand Dibble was faced on the eighth morning of his visit by the startling fact that he had no more worlds to conquer. He was monarch of all he surveyed, and, what is more, had won his first trophy, the prize in the great medal-play handicap tournament, in which he had nosed in ahead of the field by two strokes, edging out his nearest rival, a venerable old gentleman, by means of a brilliant and unexpected four on the last hole. The prize was a handsome pewter mug, about the size of the old oaken bucket, and Ferdinand used to go to his room immediately after dinner to croon over it like a mother over her child.

You are wondering, no doubt, why, in these circumstances, he did not take advantage of the new spirit of exhilarated pride which had replaced his old humility and instantly propose to Barbara Medway. I will tell you. He did not propose to Barbara because Barbara was not there. At the last moment she had been detained at home to nurse a sick parent and had been compelled to postpone her visit for a couple of weeks. He could, no doubt, have proposed in one of the daily letters which he wrote to her, but somehow, once he started writing, he found that he used up so much space describing his best shots on the links that day that it was difficult to squeeze in a declaration of undying passion. After all, you can hardly cram that sort of thing into a postscript.

He decided, therefore, to wait till she arrived, and meanwhile pursued his conquering course. The longer he waited the better, in one way, for every morning and afternoon that passed was adding new layers to his self-esteem. Day by day in every way he grew chestier and chestier.

Meanwhile, however, dark clouds were gathering. Sullen mutterings were to be heard in corners of the hotel lounge, and the spirit of revolt was abroad. For Ferdinand's chestiness had not escaped the notice of his defeated rivals. There is nobody so chesty as a normally unchesty man who suddenly becomes chesty, and I am sorry to say that the chestiness which had come to Ferdinand was the aggressive type of chestiness which breeds enemies. He had developed a habit of holding the game up in order to give his opponent advice. The Whip-Cracker had not forgiven, and never would forgive, his well-meant but galling criticism of his backswing. The Scooper, who had always scooped since the day when, at the age of sixty-four, he subscribed to the Correspondence Course which was to teach him golf in twelve lessons by mail, resented being told by a snip of a boy that the mashie-stroke should be a smooth, unhurried swing. The Snake-Killer— But I need not weary you with a detailed recital of these men's grievances; it is enough to say that they all had it in for Ferdinand, and one night, after dinner, they met in the lounge to decide what was to be done about it.

A nasty spirit was displayed by all.

'A mere lad telling me how to use my mashie!' growled the Scooper. 'Smooth and unhurried my left eyeball! I get it up, don't I? Well, what more do you want?'

'I keep telling him that mine is the old, full St Andrews swing,' muttered the Whip-Cracker, between set teeth, 'but he won't listen to me.'

'He ought to be taken down a peg or two,' hissed the Snake-Killer. It is not easy to hiss a sentence without a single 's' in it, and the fact that he succeeded in doing so shows to what a pitch of emotion the man had been goaded by Ferdinand's maddening air of superiority.

'Yes, but what can we do?' queried an octogenarian, when this last remark had been passed on to him down his ear-trumpet.

'That's the trouble,' sighed the Scooper. 'What can we do?' And there was a sorrowful shaking of heads.

'I know!' exclaimed the Cat-Stroker, who had not hitherto spoken. He was a lawyer, and a man of subtle and sinister mind. 'I have it! There's a boy in my office – young Parsloe – who could beat this man Dibble hollow. I'll wire him to come down here and we'll spring him on this fellow and knock some of the conceit out of him.'

There was a chorus of approval.

'But are you sure he can beat him?' asked the Snake-Killer, anxiously. 'It would never do to make a mistake.'

'Of course I'm sure,' said the Cat-Stroker. 'George Parsloe once went round in ninety-four.'

'Many changes there have been since ninety-four,' said the octogenarian, nodding sagely. 'Ah, many, many changes. None of these motor-cars then, tearing about and killing—'

Kindly hands led him off to have an egg-and-milk, and the remaining conspirators returned to the point at issue with bent brows.

'Ninety-four?' said the Scooper, incredulously. 'Do you mean counting every stroke?'

'Counting every stroke.'

'Not conceding himself any putts?'

'Not one.'

'Wire him to come at once,' said the meeting with one voice.

That night the Cat-Stroker approached Ferdinand, smooth, subtle, lawyer-like.

'Oh, Dibble,' he said, 'just the man I wanted to see. Dibble, there's a young friend of mine coming down here who goes in for golf a little. George Parsloe is his name. I was wondering if you could spare time to give him a game. He is just a novice, you know.'

'I shall be delighted to play a round with him,' said Ferdinand, kindly.

'He might pick up a pointer or two from watching you,' said the Cat-Stroker.

'True, true,' said Ferdinand.

'Then I'll introduce you when he shows up.'

'Delighted,' said Ferdinand.

He was in excellent humour that night, for he had had a letter from Barbara saying that she was arriving on the next day but one.

It was Ferdinand's healthy custom of a morning to get up in good time and take a dip in the sea before breakfast. On the morning of the day of Barbara's arrival, he arose, as usual, donned his flannels, took a good look at the cup, and started out. It was a fine, fresh morning, and he glowed both externally and internally. As he crossed the links, for the nearest route to the water was through the fairway of the seventh, he was whistling happily and rehearsing in his mind the opening sentences of his proposal. For it was his firm resolve that night after dinner to ask Barbara to marry him. He was proceeding over the smooth turf without a care in the world, when there was a sudden cry of 'Fore!' and the next moment a golf-ball, missing him by inches, sailed up the fairway and came to a rest fifty yards from where he stood. He looked round and observed a figure coming towards him from the tee.

The distance from the tee was fully a hundred and thirty yards. Add fifty to that, and you have a hundred and eighty yards. No such drive had been made on the Marvis Bay links since their foundation, and such is the generous spirit of the true golfer that Ferdinand's first emotion, after the not inexcusable spasm of panic caused by the hum of the ball past his ear, was one of cordial admiration. By some kindly miracle, he supposed, one of his hotel acquaintances had been permitted for once in his life to time a drive right. It was only when the other man came up that there began to steal over him a sickening apprehension. The faces of all those who hewed divots on the hotel course were familiar to him, and the fact that this fellow was a stranger seemed to point with dreadful certainty to his being the man he had agreed to play.

'Sorry,' said the man. He was a tall, strikingly handsome youth, with brown eyes and a dark moustache.

'Oh, that's all right,' said Ferdinand. 'Er – do you always drive like that?'

'Well, I generally get a bit longer ball, but I'm off my drive this morning. It's lucky I came out and got this practice. I'm playing a match tomorrow with a fellow named Dibble, who's a local champion, or something.'

'Me,' said Ferdinand, humbly.

'Eh? Oh, you?' Mr Parsloe eyed him appraisingly. 'Well, may the best man win.'

As this was precisely what Ferdinand was afraid was

going to happen, he nodded in a sickly manner and tottered off to his bathe. The magic had gone out of the morning. The sun still shone, but in a silly, feeble way; and a cold and depressing wind had sprung up. For Ferdinand's inferiority complex, which had seemed cured for ever, was back again, doing business at the old stand.

How sad it is in this life that the moment to which we have looked forward with the most glowing anticipation so often turns out on arrival, flat, cold, and disappointing. For ten days Barbara Medway had been living for that meeting with Ferdinand, when, getting out of the train, she would see him popping about on the horizon with the love-light sparkling in his eyes and words of devotion trembling on his lips. The poor girl never doubted for an instant that he would unleash his pent-up emotions inside the first five minutes, and her only worry was lest he should give an embarrassing publicity to the sacred scene by falling on his knees on the station platform.

'Well, here I am at last,' she cried gaily.

'Hullo!' said Ferdinand, with a twisted smile.

The girl looked at him, chilled. How could she know that his peculiar manner was due entirely to the severe attack of cold feet resultant upon his meeting with George Parsloe that morning? The interpretation which she placed upon it was that he was not glad to see her. If he had behaved like this before, she would, of course, have put it down to ingrowing goofery, but now she had his written statements to prove that for the last ten days his golf had been one long series of triumphs.

'I got your letters,' she said, persevering bravely.

'I thought you would,' said Ferdinand, absently.

'You seem to have been doing wonders.'

'Yes.'

There was a silence.

'Have a nice journey?' said Ferdinand.

'Very,' said Barbara.

She spoke coldly, for she was madder than a wet hen. She saw it all now. In the ten days since they had parted, his love, she realised, had waned. Some other girl, met in the romantic surroundings of this picturesque resort, had supplanted her in his affections. She knew how quickly Cupid gets off the mark at a summer hotel, and for an instant she blamed herself for ever having been so ivory-skulled as to let him come to this place alone. Then regret was swallowed up in wrath, and she became so glacial that Ferdinand, who had been on the point of telling her the secret of his gloom, retired into his shell and conversation during the drive to the hotel never soared above a certain level. Ferdinand said the sunshine was nice and Barbara said yes, it was nice, and Ferdinand said it looked pretty on the water, and Barbara said yes, it did look pretty on the water, and Ferdinand said he hoped it was not going to rain, and Barbara said yes, it would be a pity if it rained. And then there was another lengthy silence.

'How is my uncle?' asked Barbara at last.

I omitted to mention that the individual to whom I have referred as the Cat-Stroker was Barbara's mother's brother, and her host at Marvis Bay.

'Your uncle?'

'His name is Tuttle. Have you met him?'

'Oh yes. I've seen a good deal of him. He has got a friend staying with him,' said Ferdinand, his mind returning to the matter nearest his heart. 'A fellow named Parsloe.'

'Oh, is George Parsloe here? How jolly!'

'Do you know him?' barked Ferdinand, hollowly. He would not have supposed that anything could have added to his existing depression, but he was conscious now of having slipped a few rungs farther down the ladder of gloom. There had been a horribly joyful ring in her voice. Ah, well, he reflected morosely, how like life it all was! We never know what the morrow may bring forth. We strike a good patch and are beginning to think pretty well of ourselves, and along comes a George Parsloe.

'Of course I do,' said Barbara. 'Why, there he is.'

The cab had drawn up at the door of the hotel, and on the porch George Parsloe was airing his graceful person. To Ferdinand's fevered eye he looked like a Greek god, and his inferiority complex began to exhibit symptoms of elephantiasis. How could he compete at love or golf with a fellow who looked as if he had stepped out of the movies and considered himself off his drive when he did a hundred and eighty yards?

'Geor-gee!' cried Barbara, blithely. 'Hullo, George!'

'Why, hullo, Barbara!'

They fell into pleasant conversation, while Ferdinand hung miserably about in the offing. And presently, feeling that his society was not essential to their happiness, he slunk away.

George Parsloe dined at the Cat-Stroker's table that night, and it was with George Parsloe that Barbara roamed in the moonlight after dinner. Ferdinand, after a profitless hour at the billiard table, went early to his room. But not even the rays of the moon, glinting on his cup, could soothe the fever in his soul. He practised putting sombrely into his tooth-glass for a while; then, going to bed, fell at last into a troubled sleep.

Barbara slept late the next morning and breakfasted in her room. Coming down towards noon, she found a strange emptiness in the hotel. It was her experience of summer hotels that a really fine day like this one was the cue for half the inhabitants to collect in the lounge, shut all the windows, and talk about conditions in the jute industry. To her surprise, though the sun was streaming down from a cloudless sky, the only occupant of the lounge was the octogenarian with the ear-trumpet. She observed that he was chuckling to himself in a senile manner.

'Good morning,' she said, politely, for she had made his acquaintance on the previous evening.

'Hey?' said the octogenarian, suspending his chuckling and getting his trumpet into position.

'I said "Good morning!"' roared Barbara into the receiver.

'Hey?'

'Good morning!'

'Ah! Yes, it's a very fine morning, a very fine morning. If it wasn't for missing my bun and glass of milk at twelve sharp,' said the octogenarian, 'I'd be down on the links. That's where I'd be, down on the links. If it wasn't for missing my bun and glass of milk.'

This refreshment arriving at this moment, he dismantled the radio outfit and began to restore his tissues.

'Watching the match,' he explained, pausing for a moment in his bun-mangling.

'What match?'

The octogenarian sipped his milk.

'What match?' repeated Barbara.

'Hey?'

'What match?'

The octogenarian began to chuckle again and nearly swallowed a crumb the wrong way.

'Take some of the conceit out of him,' he gurgled.

'Out of who?' asked Barbara, knowing perfectly well that she should have said 'whom.'

'Yes,' said the octogenarian.

'Who is conceited?'

'Ah! This young fellow, Dibble. Very conceited. I saw it in his eye from the first, but nobody would listen to me. Mark my words, I said, that boy needs taking down a peg or two. Well, he's going to be this morning. Your uncle wired to young Parsloe to come down, and he's arranged a match between them. Dibble—' Here the octogenarian choked again and had to rinse himself out with milk, 'Dibble doesn't know that Parsloe once went round in ninety-four!'

'What?'

Everything seemed to go black to Barbara. Through a murky mist she appeared to be looking at a negro octogenarian, sipping ink. Then her eyes cleared, and she found herself clutching for support at the back of a chair. She understood now. She realised why Ferdinand had been so distrait, and her whole heart went out to him in a spasm of maternal pity. How she had wronged him!

'Take some of the conceit out of him,' the octogenarian was mumbling, and Barbara felt a sudden sharp loathing for the old man. For two pins she could have dropped a beetle in his milk. Then the need for action roused her. What action? She did not know. All she knew was that she must act.

'Oh!' she cried.

'Hey?' said the octogenarian, bringing his trumpet to the ready.

But Barbara had gone.

It was not far to the links, and Barbara covered the distance on flying feet. She reached the clubhouse, but the course was empty except for the Scooper, who was preparing to drive off the first tee. In spite of the fact that something seemed to tell her subconsciously that this was one of the sights she ought not to miss, the girl did not wait to watch. Assuming that the match had started soon after breakfast, it must by now have reached one of the holes on the second nine. She ran down the hill, looking to left and right, and was presently aware of a group of spectators clustered about a green in the distance. As she hurried towards them they moved away, and now she could see Ferdinand advancing to the next tee. With a thrill that shook her whole body she realised that he had the honour. So he must have won one hole, at any rate. Then she saw her uncle.

'How are they?' she gasped.

Mr Tuttle seemed moody. It was apparent that things were not going altogether to his liking.

'All square at the fifteenth,' he replied, gloomily.

'All square!'

'Yes. Young Parsloe,' said Mr Tuttle with a sour look in the direction of that lissom athlete, 'doesn't seem to be able to do a thing right on the greens. He has been putting like a sheep with the botts.'

From the foregoing remark of Mr Tuttle you will, no doubt, have gleaned at least a clue to the mystery of how Ferdinand Dibble had managed to hold his long-driving adversary up to the fifteenth green, but for all that you will probably consider that some further explanation of this amazing state of affairs is required. Mere bad putting on the part of George Parsloe is not, you feel, sufficient to cover the matter entirely. You are right. There was another very important factor in the situation – to wit, that by some extraordinary chance Ferdinand Dibble had started right off from the first tee, playing the game of a lifetime. Never had he made such drives, never chipped his chips so shrewdly.

About Ferdinand's driving there was as a general thing a fatal stiffness and over-caution which prevented success. And with his chip-shots he rarely achieved accuracy owing to his habit of rearing his head like the lion of the jungle just before the club struck the ball. But today he had been swinging with a careless freedom, and his chips had been true and clean. The thing had puzzled him all the way round. It had not elated him, for, owing to Barbara's aloofness and the way in which she had gambolled about George Parsloe, like a young lamb in the springtime, he was in too deep a state of dejection to be elated by anything. And now, suddenly, in a flash of clear vision, he perceived the reason why he had been playing so well today. It was just because he was not elated. It was simply because he was so profoundly miserable.

That was what Ferdinand told himself as he stepped off the sixteenth, after hitting a screamer down the centre of the fairway, and I am convinced that he was right. Like so many indifferent golfers, Ferdinand Dibble had always made the game hard for himself by thinking too much. He was a deep student of the works of the masters, and whenever he prepared to play a stroke he had a complete mental list of all the mistakes which it was possible to make. He would remember how Taylor had warned against dipping the right shoulder, how Vardon had inveighed against any movement of the head; he would recall how Ray had mentioned the tendency to snatch back the club, how Braid had spoken sadly of those who sin against their better selves by stiffening the muscles and heaving.

The consequence was that when, after waggling in a frozen manner till mere shame urged him to take some definite course of action, he eventually swung, he invariably proceeded to dip his right shoulder, stiffen his muscles, heave, and snatch back the club, at the same time raising his head sharply as in the illustrated plate ('Some Frequent Faults of Beginners – No. 3 – Lifting the Bean') facing page thirty-four of James Braid's *Golf Without Tears.* Today he had been so preoccupied with his broken heart that he had made his shots absently, almost carelessly, with the result that at least one in every three had been a lallapaloosa.

Meanwhile, George Parsloe had driven off and the match was progressing. George was feeling a little flustered by now. He had been given to understand that this bird Dibble was a hundred-at-his-best man, and all the way round the fellow had been reeling off fives in great profusion, and had once actually got a four. True, there had been an occasional six, and even a seven, but that did not alter the main fact that the man was making the dickens of a game of it. With the haughty spirit of one who had once done a ninety-four, George Parsloe had anticipated being at least three up at the turn. Instead of which he had been two down, and had had to fight strenuously to draw level.

Nevertheless, he drove steadily and well, and would certainly have won the hole had it not been for his weak and sinful putting. The same defect caused him to halve the seventeenth, after being on in two, with Ferdinand wandering in the desert and only reaching the green with his fourth. Then, however, Ferdinand holed out from a distance of seven yards, getting a five; which George's three putts just enabled him to equal.

Barbara had watched the proceedings with a beating heart. At first she had looked on from afar; but now, drawn as by a magnet, she approached the tee. Ferdinand was driving off. She held her breath. Ferdinand held his breath. And all around one could see their respective breaths being held by George Parsloe, Mr Tuttle, and the enthralled crowd of spectators. It was a moment of the acutest tension, and it was broken by the crack of Ferdinand's driver as it met the ball and sent it hopping along the ground for a mere thirty yards. At this supreme crisis in the match Ferdinand Dibble had topped.

George Parsloe teed up his ball. There was a smile of quiet satisfaction on his face. He snuggled the driver in his hands, and gave it a preliminary swish. This, felt George Parsloe, was where the happy ending came. He could drive as he had never driven before. He would so drive that it would take his opponent at least three shots to catch up with him. He drew back his club with infinite caution, poised it at the top of the swing—

'I always wonder—' said a clear, girlish voice, ripping the silence like the explosion of a bomb.

George Parsloe started. His club wobbled. It descended. The ball trickled into the long grass in front of the tee. There was a grim pause.

'You were saying, Miss Medway—' said George Parsloe, in a small, flat voice.

'Oh, I'm so sorry,' said Barbara. 'I'm afraid I put you off.'

'A little, perhaps. Possibly the merest trifle. But you were saying you wondered about something. Can I be of any assistance?'

'I was only saying,' said Barbara, 'that I always wonder why tees are called tees.'

George Parsloe swallowed once or twice. He also blinked a little feverishly. His eyes had a dazed, staring expression.

'I am afraid I cannot tell you off-hand,' he said, 'but I will make a point of consulting some good encyclopædia at the earliest opportunity.'

'Thank you so much.'

'Not at all. It will be a pleasure. In case you were thinking of inquiring at the moment when I am putting why greens are called greens, may I venture the suggestion now that it is because they are green?'

And, so saying, George Parsloe stalked to his ball and found it nestling in the heart of some shrub of which, not being a botanist, I cannot give you the name. It was a close-knit, adhesive shrub, and it twined its tentacles so lovingly around George Parsloe's niblick that he missed his first shot altogether. His second made the ball rock, and his third dislodged it. Playing a full swing with his brassie and being by now a mere cauldron of seething emotions he missed his fourth. His fifth came to within a few inches of Ferdinand's drive, and he picked it up and hurled it from him into the rough as if it had been something venomous.

'Your hole and match,' said George Parsloe, thinly.

Ferdinand Dibble sat beside the glittering ocean. He had hurried off the course with swift strides the moment George Parsloe had spoken those bitter words. He wanted to be alone with his thoughts.

They were mixed thoughts. For a moment joy at the reflection that he had won a tough match came irresistibly to the surface, only to sink again as he remembered that life, whatever its triumphs, could hold nothing for him now that Barbara Medway loved another.

'Mr Dibble!'

He looked up. She was standing at his side. He gulped and rose to his feet.

'Yes?'

There was a silence.

'Doesn't the sun look pretty on the water?' said Barbara.

Ferdinand groaned. This was too much.

'Leave me,' he said, hollowly. 'Go back to your Parsloe, the man with whom you walked in the moonlight beside this same water.'

'Well, why shouldn't I walk with Mr Parsloe in the moonlight beside this same water?' demanded Barbara, with spirit.

'I never said,' replied Ferdinand, for he was a fair man at heart, 'that you shouldn't walk with Mr Parsloe beside this same water. I simply said you did walk with Mr Parsloe beside this same water.'

'I've a perfect right to walk with Mr Parsloe beside this same water,' persisted Barbara. 'He and I are old friends.'

Ferdinand groaned again.

'Exactly! There you are! As I suspected. Old friends. Played together as children, and what not, I shouldn't wonder.'

'No, we didn't. I've only known him five years. But he is engaged to be married to my greatest chum, so that draws us together.'

Ferdinand uttered a strangled cry.

'Parsloe engaged to be married!'

'Yes. The wedding takes place next month.'

'But look here.' Ferdinand's forehead was wrinkled. He was thinking tensely. 'Look here,' said Ferdinand, a close reasoner. 'If Parsloe's engaged to your greatest chum, he can't be in love with *you.*'

'No.'

'And you aren't in love with him?'

'No.'

'Then, by gad,' said Ferdinand, 'how about it?'

'What do you mean?'

'Will you marry me?' bellowed Ferdinand.

'Yes.'

'You will?'

'Of course I will.'

'Darling!' cried Ferdinand.

*

'There is only one thing that bothers me a bit,' said Ferdinand, thoughtfully, as they strolled together over the scented meadows, while in the trees above them a thousand birds trilled Mendelssohn's Wedding March.

'What is that?'

'Well, I'll tell you,' said Ferdinand. 'The fact is, I've just discovered the great secret of golf. You can't play a really hot game unless you're so miserable that you don't worry over your shots. Take the case of a chip-shot, for instance. If you're really wretched, you don't care where the ball is going and so you don't raise your head to see. Grief automatically prevents pressing and over-swinging. Look at the top-notchers. Have you ever seen a happy pro?'

'No. I don't think I have.'

'Well, then!'

'But pros are all Scotchmen,' argued Barbara.

'It doesn't matter. I'm sure I'm right. And the darned thing is that I'm going to be so infernally happy all the rest of my life that I suppose my handicap will go up to thirty or something.'

Barbara squeezed his hand lovingly. 'Don't worry, precious,' she said, soothingly. 'It will be all right. I am a woman, and, once we are married, I shall be able to think of at least a hundred ways of snootering you to such an extent that you'll be fit to win the Amateur Championship.'

'You will?' said Ferdinand, anxiously. 'You're sure?'

'Quite, quite sure, dearest,' said Barbara.

'My angel!' said Ferdinand.

He folded her in his arms, using the interlocking grip.

Best Seller

A sharp snort, plainly emanating from a soul in anguish, broke the serene silence that brooded over the bar-parlour of the Angler's Rest. And, looking up, we perceived Miss Postlethwaite, our sensitive barmaid, dabbing at her eyes with a dishcloth.

'Sorry you were troubled,' said Miss Postlethwaite, in answer to our concerned gaze, 'but he's just gone off to India, leaving her standing tight-lipped and dry-eyed in the moonlight outside the old Manor. And her little dog has crawled up and licked her hand, as if he understood and sympathised.'

We stared at one another blankly. It was Mr Mulliner who, with his usual clear insight, penetrated to the heart of the mystery.

'Ah,' said Mr Mulliner, 'you have been reading *Rue for Remembrance*, I see. How did you like it?'

''Slovely,' said Miss Postlethwaite. 'It lays the soul of Woman bare as with a scalpel.'

'You do not consider that there is any falling off from the standard of its predecessors? You find it as good as *Parted Ways*?'

'Better.'

'Oh!' said a Stout and Bitter, enlightened. 'You're reading a novel?'

'The latest work,' said Mr Mulliner, 'from the pen of

the authoress of *Parted Ways*, which, as no doubt you remember, made so profound a sensation some years ago. I have a particular interest in this writer's work, as she is my niece.'

'Your niece?'

'By marriage. In private life she is Mrs Egbert Mulliner.' He sipped his hot Scotch and lemon, and mused a while.

'I wonder,' he said, 'if you would care to hear the story of my nephew Egbert and his bride? It is a simple little story, just one of those poignant dramas of human interest which are going on in our midst every day. If Miss Postlethwaite is not too racked by emotion to replenish my glass, I shall be delighted to tell it to you.'

I will ask you (said Mr Mulliner) to picture my nephew Egbert standing at the end of the pier at the picturesque little resort of Burwash Bay one night in June, trying to nerve himself to ask Evangeline Pembury the question that was so near his heart. A hundred times he had tried to ask it, and a hundred times he had lacked the courage. But tonight he was feeling in particularly good form, and he cleared his throat and spoke.

'There is something,' he said in a low, husky voice, 'that I want to ask you.'

He paused. He felt strangely breathless. The girl was looking out across the moonlit water. The night was very still. From far away in the distance came the faint strains of the town band, as it picked its way through the Star of Eve song from *Tannhäuser* – somewhat impeded by the second trombone, who had got his music sheets mixed and was playing 'The Wedding of the Painted Doll'.

'Something,' said Egbert, 'that I want to ask you.'

'Go on,' she whispered.

Again he paused. He was afraid. Her answer meant so much to him.

Egbert Mulliner had come to this quiet seaside village for a rest cure. By profession he was an assistant editor, attached to the staff of the *Weekly Booklover*; and, as every statistician knows, assistant editors of literary weeklies are ranked high up among the Dangerous Trades. The strain of interviewing female novelists takes toll of the physique of all but the very hardiest.

For six months, week in and week out, Egbert Mulliner had been listening to female novelists talking about Art and their Ideals. He had seen them in cosy corners in their boudoirs, had watched them being kind to dogs and happiest when among their flowers. And one morning the proprietor of the *Booklover,* finding the young man sitting at his desk with little flecks of foam about his mouth and muttering over and over again in a dull, toneless voice the words, 'Aurelia McGoggin, she draws her inspiration from the scent of white lilies!' had taken him straight off to a specialist.

'Yes,' the specialist had said, after listening at Egbert's chest for a while through a sort of telephone, 'we are a little run down, are we not? We see floating spots, do we not, and are inclined occasionally to bark like a seal from pure depression of spirit? Precisely. What we need is to augment the red corpuscles in our bloodstream.'

And this augmentation of red corpuscles had been effected by his first sight of Evangeline Pembury. They had met at a picnic. As Egbert rested for a moment from the task of trying to dredge the sand from a plateful of chicken salad, his eyes had fallen on a divine girl squashing a wasp with a teaspoon. And for the first time since he had tottered out of the offices of the *Weekly Booklover* he had ceased to feel like something which a cat, having dragged from an ash-can, has inspected and rejected with a shake of the head as unfit for feline consumption. In an instant his interior had become a sort of Jamboree of red corpuscles. Millions of them were splashing about and calling gaily to other millions, still hesitating on the bank: 'Come on in! The blood's fine!'

Ten minutes later he had reached the conclusion that life without Evangeline Pembury would be a blank.

And yet he had hesitated before laying his heart at her feet. She looked all right. She seemed all right. Quite possibly she *was* all right. But before proposing he had to be sure. He had to make certain that there was no danger of her suddenly producing a manuscript fastened in the top left corner with pink silk and asking his candid opinion of it. Everyone has his pet aversion. Some dislike slugs, others cockroaches. Egbert Mulliner disliked female novelists.

And so now, as they stood together in the moonlight, he said:

'Tell me, have you ever written a novel?'

She seemed surprised.

'A novel? No.'

'Short stories, perhaps?'

'No.'

Egbert lowered his voice.

'Poems?' he whispered, hoarsely.

'No.'

Egbert hesitated no longer. He produced his soul like a conjurer extracting a rabbit from a hat and slapped it down before her. He told her of his love, stressing its depth, purity, and lasting qualities. He begged, pleaded, rolled his eyes, and clasped her little hand in his. And when, pausing for a reply, he found that she had been doing a lot of thinking along the same lines and felt much the same about him as he did about her, he nearly fell over backwards. It seemed to him that his cup of joy was full.

It is odd how love will affect different people. It caused Egbert next morning to go out on the links and do the first nine in one over bogey. Whereas Evangeline, finding herself filled with a strange ferment which demanded immediate outlet, sat down at a little near-Chippendale table, ate five marshmallows, and began to write a novel.

Three weeks of the sunshine and ozone of Burwash Bay had toned up Egbert's system to the point where his medical adviser felt that it would be safe for him to go back to London and resume his fearful trade. Evangeline followed him a month later. She arrived home at four-fifteen on a sunny afternoon, and at four-sixteen-and-a-half Egbert shot through the door with the lovelight in his eyes.

'Evangeline!'

'Egbert!'

But we will not dwell on the ecstasies of the reunited lovers. We will proceed to the point where Evangeline raised her head from Egbert's shoulder and uttered a little giggle. One would prefer to say that she gave a light laugh. But it was not a light laugh. It was a giggle – a furtive, sinister, shamefaced giggle, which froze Egbert's blood with a nameless fear. He stared at her, and she giggled again.

'Egbert,' she said, 'I want to tell you something.'

'Yes?' said Egbert.

Evangeline giggled once more.

'I know it sounds too silly for words,' she said, 'but—'

'Yes? Yes?'

'I've written a novel, Egbert.'

In the old Greek tragedies it was a recognised rule that any episode likely to excite the pity and terror of the audience to too great an extent must be enacted behind the scenes. Strictly speaking, therefore, this scene should be omitted. But the modern public can stand more than the ancient Greeks, so it had better remain on the records.

The room stopped swimming before Egbert Mulliner's tortured eyes. Gradually the piano, the chairs, the pictures, and the case of stuffed birds on the mantelpiece resumed their normal positions. He found speech.

'You've written a novel?' he said, dully.

'Well, I've got to chapter twenty-four.'

'You've got to chapter twenty-four?'

'And the rest will be easy.'

'The rest will be easy?'

Silence fell for a space – a silence broken only by Egbert's laboured breathing. Then Evangeline spoke impulsively.

'Oh, Egbert!' she cried. 'I really do think some of it is rather good. I'll read it to you now.'

How strange it is, when some great tragedy has come upon us, to look back at the comparatively mild beginnings of our misfortunes and remember how we thought then that Fate had done its worst. Egbert, that afternoon, fancied that he had plumbed the lowest depths of misery and anguish. Evangeline, he told himself, had fallen from the pedestal on which he had set her. She had revealed herself as a secret novel-writer. It was the limit, he felt, the extreme edge. It put the tin hat on things.

It was, alas! nothing of the kind. It bore the same resemblance to the limit that the first drop of rain bears to the thunderstorm.

The mistake was a pardonable one. The acute agony which he suffered that afternoon was more than sufficient excuse for Egbert Mulliner's blunder in supposing that he had drained the bitter cup to the dregs. He writhed, as he listened to this thing which she had entitled *Parted Ways*, unceasingly. It tied his very soul in knots.

Evangeline's novel was a horrible, an indecent production. Not in the sense that it would be likely to bring a blush to any cheek but his, but because she had put on paper in bald words every detail of the only romance that had ever come under her notice – her own. There it was, his entire courtship, including the first holy kiss and not omitting the quarrel which they had had within two days of the engagement. In the novel she had elaborated this quarrel, which in fact had lasted twenty-three minutes, into a ten years' estrangement – thus justifying the title and preventing the story finishing in the first five thousand words. As for his proposal, that was inserted *verbatim;* and, as he listened, Egbert shuddered to think that he could have polluted the air with such frightful horseradish.

He marvelled, as many a man has done before and will again, how women can do these things. Listening to *Parted*

Ways made him, personally, feel as if he had suddenly lost his trousers while strolling along Piccadilly.

Something of these feelings he would have liked to put into words, but the Mulliners are famous for their chivalry. He would, he imagined, feel a certain shame if he ever hit Evangeline or walked on her face in thick shoes; but that shame would be as nothing to the shame he would feel if he spoke one millimetre of what he thought about *Parted Ways*.

'Great!' he croaked.

Her eyes were shining.

'Do you really think so?'

'Fine!'

He found it easier to talk in monosyllables.

'I don't suppose any publisher would buy it,' said Evangeline.

Egbert began to feel a little better. Nothing, of course, could alter the fact that she had written a novel; but it might be possible to hush it up.

'So what I am going to do is to pay the expenses of publication.'

Egbert did not reply. He was staring into the middle distance and trying to light a fountain pen with an unlighted match.

And Fate chuckled grimly, knowing that it had only just begun having fun with Egbert.

Once in every few publishing seasons there is an Event. For no apparent reason, the great heart of the Public gives a startled jump, and the public's great purse is emptied to secure copies of some novel which has stolen into the world without advance advertising and whose only claim to recognition is that the *Licensed Victuallers' Gazette* has stated in a two-line review that it is 'readable'.

The rising firm of Mainprice and Peabody published a first edition of three hundred copies of *Parted Ways*. And when they found, to their chagrin, that Evangeline was only going to buy twenty of these – somehow Mainprice, who was an optimist, had got the idea that she was good for a hundred ('You can sell them to your friends') their only interest in the matter was to keep an eye on the current quotations for waste paper. The book they were going to make their money on was Stultitia Bodwin's *Offal*, in connection with which they had arranged in advance for a newspaper discussion on 'The Growing Menace of the Sex Motive in Fiction: Is There to be no Limit?'

Within a month *Offal* was off the map. The newspaper discussion raged before an utterly indifferent public, which had made one of its quick changes and discovered that it had had enough of sex, and that what it wanted now was good, sweet, wholesome, tender tales of the pure love of a man for a maid, which you could leave lying about and didn't have to shove under the cushions of the chesterfield every time you heard your growing boys coming along. And the particular tale which it selected for its favour was Evangeline's *Parted Ways*.

It is these swift, unheralded changes of the public mind which make publishers stick straws in their hair and powerful young novelists rush round to the wholesale grocery firms to ask if the berth of junior clerk is still open. Up to the very moment of the Great Switch, sex had been the one safe card. Publishers' lists were congested with scarlet tales of Men Who Did and Women Who Shouldn't Have Done but Who Took a Pop at It. And now the bottom had dropped out of the market without a word of warning, and practically the only way in which readers could gratify their new-born taste for the pure and simple was by fighting for copies of *Parted Ways*.

They fought like tigers. The offices of Mainprice and Peabody hummed like a hive. Printing machines worked day and night. From the Butes of Kyle to the rock-bound coasts of Cornwall, a great cry went up for *Parted Ways*. In every home in Ealing West *Parted Ways* was found on the whatnot, next to the aspidistra and the family album. Clergymen preached about it, parodists parodied it, stock-brokers stayed away from Cochran's Revue to sit at home and cry over it.

Numerous paragraphs appeared in the Press concerning its probable adaptation into a play, a musical comedy, and a talking picture. Nigel Playfair was stated to have bought it for Sybil Thorndike, Sir Alfred Butt for Nellie Wallace. Laddie Cliff was reported to be planning a musical play based on it, starring Stanley Lupino and Leslie Henson. It was rumoured that Carnera was considering the part of 'Percy', the hero.

And on the crest of this wave, breathless but happy, rode Evangeline.

And Egbert? Oh, that's Egbert, spluttering down in the trough there. We can't be bothered about Egbert now.

Egbert, however, found ample time to be bothered about himself. He passed the days in a frame of mind which it would be ridiculous to call bewilderment. He was stunned, overwhelmed, sandbagged. Dimly he realised that considerably more than a hundred thousand perfect strangers were gloating over the most sacred secrecies of his private life, and that the exact words of his proposal of marriage were engraven on considerably over a hundred thousand minds. But, except that it made him feel as if he were being tarred and feathered in front of a large and interested audience, he did not mind that so much. What really troubled him was the alteration in Evangeline.

The human mind adjusts itself readily to prosperity. Evangeline's first phase, when celebrity was new and bewildering, soon passed. The stammering reception of the first reporter became a memory. At the end of two weeks she was talking to the Press with the easy nonchalance of a prominent politician, and coming back at notebook-bearing young men with words which they had to look up in the office Webster. Her art, she told them, was rhythmical rather than architectural, and she inclined, if anything, to the school of the surrealists.

She had soared above Egbert's low-browed enthusiasms. When he suggested motoring out to Addington and putting in a few holes of golf, she excused herself. She had letters to answer. People would keep writing to her, saying how much *Parted Ways* had helped them, and one had to be civil to one's public. Autographs, too. She really could not spare a moment.

He asked her to come with him to the Amateur Championship. She shook her head. The date, she said, clashed with her lecture to the East Dulwich Daughters of Minerva Literary and Progress Club on 'Some Tendencies of Modern Fiction'.

All these things Egbert might have endured, for, despite the fact that she could speak so lightly of the Amateur Championship, he still loved her dearly. But at this point there suddenly floated into his life like a cloud of poison gas the sinister figure of Jno Henderson Banks.

'Who,' he asked, suspiciously, one day, as she was giving him ten minutes before hurrying off to address the Amalgamated Mothers of Manchester on 'The Novel: Should It Teach?' – 'was that man I saw you coming down the street with?'

'That wasn't a man,' replied Evangeline. 'That was my literary agent.'

And so it proved. Jno Henderson Banks was now in control of Evangeline's affairs. This outstanding blot on the public weal was a sort of human *charlotte russe* with tortoiseshell-rimmed eye-glasses and a cooing, reverential manner towards his female clients. He had a dark, romantic face, a lissom figure, one of those beastly cravat things that go twice round the neck, and a habit of beginning his remarks with the words 'Dear lady'. The last man, in short, whom a fiancé would wish to have hanging about his betrothed. If Evangeline had to have a literary agent, the sort of literary agent Egbert would have selected for her would have been one of those stout, pie-faced literary agents who chew half-smoked cigars and wheeze as they enter the editorial sanctum.

A jealous frown flitted across his face.

'Looked a bit of a Gawd-help-us to me,' he said, critically.

'Mr Banks,' retorted Evangeline, 'is a superb man of business.'

'Oh, yeah?' said Egbert, sneering visibly.

And there for a time the matter rested.

But not for long. On the following Monday morning Egbert called Evangeline up on the telephone and asked her to lunch.

'I am sorry,' said Evangeline. 'I am engaged to lunch with Mr Banks.'

'Oh?' said Egbert.

'Yes,' said Evangeline.

'Ah!' said Egbert.

Two days later Egbert called Evangeline up on the telephone and invited her to dinner.

'I am sorry,' said Evangeline. 'I am dining with Mr Banks.'

'Ah?' said Egbert.

'Yes,' said Evangeline.

'Oh!' said Egbert.

Three days after that Egbert arrived at Evangeline's flat with tickets for the theatre.

'I am sorry—' began Evangeline.

'Don't say it,' said Egbert. 'Let me guess. You are going to the theatre with Mr Banks?'

'Yes, I am. He has seats for the first night of Tchekov's *Six Corpses in Search of an Undertaker*.'

'He has, has he?'

'Yes, he has.'

'He *has*, eh?'

'Yes, he has.'

Egbert took a couple of turns about the room, and for

a space there was silence except for the sharp grinding of his teeth. Then he spoke.

'Touching lightly on this gumboil Banks,' said Egbert, 'I am the last man to stand in the way of your having a literary agent. If you must write novels, that is a matter between you and your God. And, if you do see fit to write novels, I suppose you must have a literary agent. But – and this is where I want you to follow me very closely – I cannot see the necessity of employing a literary agent who looks like Lord Byron; a literary agent who coos in your left ear, a literary agent who not only addresses you as "Dear lady", but appears to find it essential to the conduct of his business to lunch, dine, and go to the theatre with you daily.'

'I—'

Egbert held up a compelling hand.

'I have not finished,' he said. 'Nobody,' he proceeded, 'could call me a narrow-minded man. If Jno Henderson Banks looked a shade less like one of the great lovers of history, I would have nothing to say. If, when he talked business to a client, Jno Henderson Banks's mode of vocal delivery were even slightly less reminiscent of a nightingale trilling to its mate, I would remain silent. But he doesn't, and it isn't. And such being the case, and taking into consideration the fact that you are engaged to me, I feel it my duty to instruct you to see this drooping flower far more infrequently. In fact, I would advocate expunging him altogether. If he wishes to discuss business with you, let him do it over the telephone. And I hope he gets the wrong number.'

Evangeline had risen, and was facing him with flashing eyes.

'Is that so?' she said.

'That,' said Egbert, 'is so.'

'Am I a serf?' demanded Evangeline.

'A what?' said Egbert.

'A serf. A slave. A peon. A creature subservient to your lightest whim.'

Egbert considered the point.

'No,' he said. 'I shouldn't think so.'

'No,' said Evangeline, 'I am not. And I refuse to allow you to dictate to me in the choice of my friends.'

Egbert stared blankly.

'You mean, after all I have said, that you intend to let this blighted chrysanthemum continue to frisk round?'

'I do.'

'You seriously propose to continue chummy with this revolting piece of cheese?'

'I do.'

'You absolutely and literally decline to give this mistake of Nature the push?'

'I do.'

'Well!' said Egbert.

A pleading note came into his voice.

'But, Evangeline, it is your Egbert who speaks.'

The haughty girl laughed a hard, bitter laugh.

'Is it?' she said. She laughed again. 'Do you imagine that we are still engaged?'

'Aren't we?'

'We certainly aren't. You have insulted me, outraged my finest feelings, given an exhibition of malignant tyranny which makes me thankful that I have realised in time the sort of man you are. Goodbye, Mr Mulliner!'

'But listen—' began Egbert.

'Go!' said Evangeline. 'Here is your hat.'

She pointed imperiously to the door. A moment later she had banged it behind him.

It was a grim-faced Egbert Mulliner who entered the elevator, and a grimmer-faced Egbert Mulliner who strode down Sloane Street. His dream, he realised, was over. He laughed harshly as he contemplated the fallen ruins of the castle which he had built in the air.

Well, he still had his work.

In the offices of the *Weekly Booklover* it was whispered that a strange change had come over Egbert Mulliner. He seemed a stronger, tougher man. His editor, who since Egbert's illness had behaved towards him with a touching humanity, allowing him to remain in the office and write paragraphs about Forthcoming Books while others, more robust, were sent off to interview the female novelists, now saw in him a right-hand man on whom he could lean.

When a column on 'Myrtle Bootle Among Her Books' was required, it was Egbert whom he sent out into the No Man's Land of Bloomsbury. When young Eustace Johnson, a novice who ought never to have been entrusted with such a dangerous commission, was found walking round in circles and bumping his head against the railings of Regent's Park after twenty minutes with Laura La Motte Grindlay, the great sex novelist, it was Egbert who was flung into the breach. And Egbert came through, wan but unscathed.

It was during this period that he interviewed Mabelle Grangerson and Mrs Goole-Plank on the same afternoon – a feat which is still spoken of with bated breath in the offices of the *Weekly Booklover*. And not only in the *Booklover* offices. To this day 'Remember Mulliner!' is the slogan with which every literary editor encourages the fainthearted who are wincing and hanging back.

'Was Mulliner afraid?' they say. 'Did Mulliner quail?'

And so it came about that when a 'Chat with Evangeline Pembury' was needed for the big Christmas Special Number, it was of Egbert that his editor thought first. He sent for him.

'Ah, Mulliner!'

'Well, chief?'

'Stop me if you've heard this one before,' said the editor, 'but it seems there was once an Irishman, a Scotsman, and a Jew—'

Then, the formalities inseparable from an interview between editor and assistant concluded, he came down to business.

'Mulliner,' he said, in that kind, fatherly way of his which endeared him to all his staff, 'I am going to begin by saying that it is in your power to do a big thing for the dear old paper. But after that I must tell you that, if you wish, you can refuse to do it. You have been through a hard time lately, and if you feel yourself unequal to this task, I shall understand. But the fact is, we have got to have a "Chat with Evangeline Pembury" for our Christmas Special.'

He saw the young man wince, and nodded sympathetically.

'You think it would be too much for you? I feared as much. They say she is the worst of the lot. Rather haughty and talks about uplift. Well, never mind. I must see what I can do with young Johnson. I hear he has quite recovered now, and is anxious to re-establish himself. Quite. I will send Johnson.'

Egbert Mulliner was himself again now.

'No, chief,' he said. 'I will go.'

'You will?'

'I will.'

'We shall need a column and a half.'

'You shall have a column and a half.'

The editor turned away, to hide a not unmanly emotion.

'Do it now, Mulliner,' he said, 'and get it over.'

A strange riot of emotion seethed in Egbert Mulliner's soul as he pressed the familiar bell which he had thought never to press again. Since their estrangement he had seen Evangeline once or twice, but only in the distance. Now he was to meet her face to face. Was he glad or sorry? He could not say. He only knew he loved her still.

He was in the sitting room. How cosy it looked, how impregnated with her presence. There was the sofa on which he had so often sat, his arm about her waist—

A footstep behind him warned him that the time had come to don the mask. Forcing his features into an interviewer's hard smile, he turned.

'Good afternoon,' he said.

She was thinner. Either she had found success wearing, or she had been on the eighteen-day diet. Her beautiful face seemed drawn, and, unless he was mistaken, careworn.

He fancied that for an instant her eyes had lit up at the sight of him, but he preserved the formal detachment of a stranger.

'Good afternoon, Miss Pembury,' he said. 'I represent

the *Weekly Booklover*. I understand that my editor has been in communication with you and that you have kindly consented to tell us a few things which may interest our readers regarding your art and aims.'

She bit her lip.

'Will you take a seat, Mr—?'

'Mulliner,' said Egbert.

'Mr Mulliner,' said Evangeline. 'Do sit down. Yes, I shall be glad to tell you anything you wish.'

Egbert sat down.

'Are you fond of dogs, Miss Pembury?' he asked.

'I adore them,' said Evangeline.

'I should like, a little later, if I may,' said Egbert, 'to secure a snapshot of you being kind to a dog. Our readers appreciate these human touches, you understand.'

'Oh, quite,' said Evangeline. 'I will send out for a dog. I love dogs – and flowers.'

'You are happiest among your flowers, no doubt?'

'On the whole, yes.'

'You sometimes think they are the souls of little children who have died in their innocence?'

'Frequently.'

'And now,' said Egbert, licking the tip of his pencil, 'perhaps you would tell me something about your ideals. How are the ideals?'

Evangeline hesitated.

'Oh, they're fine,' she said.

'The novel,' said Egbert, 'has been described as among this age's greatest instruments for uplift? How do you check up on *that*?'

'Oh, yes.'

'Of course, there are novels and novels.'

'Oh, yes.'

'Are you contemplating a successor to *Parted Ways*?'

'Oh, yes.'

'Would it be indiscreet, Miss Pembury, to inquire to what extent it has progressed?'

'Oh, Egbert!' said Evangeline.

There are some speeches before which dignity melts like ice in August, resentment takes the full count, and the milk of human kindness surges back into the aching heart as if the dam had burst. Of these, 'Oh, Egbert!', especially when accompanied by tears, is one of the most notable.

Evangeline's 'Oh, Egbert!' had been accompanied by a Niagara of tears. She had flung herself on the sofa and was now chewing the cushion in an ecstasy of grief. She gulped like a bull-pup swallowing a chunk of steak. And, on the instant, Egbert Mulliner's adamantine reserve collapsed as if its legs had been knocked from under it. He dived for the sofa. He clasped her hand. He stroked her hair. He squeezed her waist. He patted her shoulder. He massaged her spine.

'Evangeline!'

'Oh, Egbert!'

The only flaw in Egbert Mulliner's happiness, as he knelt beside her, babbling comforting words, was the gloomy conviction that Evangeline would certainly lift the entire scene, dialogue and all, and use it in her next novel. And it was for this reason that, when he could manage it, he censored his remarks to some extent.

But, as he warmed to his work, he forgot caution altogether. She was clinging to him, whispering his name piteously. By the time he had finished, he had committed himself to about two thousand words of a nature calculated to send Mainprice and Peabody screaming with joy about their office.

He refused to allow himself to worry about it. What of it? He had done his stuff, and if it sold a hundred thousand copies – well, let it sell a hundred thousand copies. Holding Evangeline in his arms, he did not care if he was copyrighted in every language, including the Scandinavian.

'Oh, Egbert!' said Evangeline.

'My darling!'

'Oh, Egbert, I'm in such trouble.'

'My angel! What is it?'

Evangeline sat up and tried to dry her eyes.

'It's Mr Banks.'

A savage frown darkened Egbert Mulliner's face. He told himself that he might have foreseen this. A man who wore a tie that went twice round the neck was sure, sooner or later, to inflict some hideous insult on helpless womanhood. Add tortoiseshell-rimmed glasses, and you had what practically amounted to a fiend in human shape.

'I'll murder him,' he said. 'I ought to have done it long ago, but one keeps putting these things off. What has he done? Did he force his loathsome attentions on you? Has that tortoiseshell-rimmed satyr been trying to kiss you, or something?'

'He has been fixing me up solid.'

Egbert blinked.

'Doing what?'

'Fixing me up solid. With the magazines. He has arranged

for me to write three serials and I don't know how many short stories.'

'Getting you contracts, you mean?'

Evangeline nodded tearfully.

'Yes. He seems to have fixed me up solid with almost everybody. And they've been sending me cheques in advance – hundreds of them. What am I to do? Oh, what am I to do?'

'Cash them,' said Egbert.

'But afterwards?'

'Spend the money.'

'But after that?'

Egbert reflected.

'Well, it's a nuisance, of course,' he said, 'but after that I suppose you'll have to write the stuff.'

Evangeline sobbed like a lost soul.

'But I can't! I've been trying for weeks, and I can't write anything. And I never shall be able to write anything. I don't want to write anything. I hate writing. I don't know what to write about. I wish I were dead.'

She clung to him.

'I got a letter from him this morning. He has just fixed me up solid with two more magazines.'

Egbert kissed her tenderly. Before he had become an assistant editor, he, too, had been an author, and he understood. It is not the being paid money in advance that jars the sensitive artist: it is the having to work.

'What shall I do?' cried Evangeline.

'Drop the whole thing,' said Egbert. 'Evangeline, do you remember your first drive at golf? I wasn't there, but I bet it travelled about five hundred yards and you wondered what people meant when they talked about golf being a difficult game. After that, for ages, you couldn't do anything right. And then, gradually, after years of frightful toil, you began to get the knack of it. It is just the same with writing. You've had your first drive, and it has been some smite. Now, if you're going to stick to it, you've got to do the frightful toil. What's the use? Drop it.'

'And return the money?'

Egbert shook his head.

'No,' he said, firmly. 'There you go too far. Stick to the money like glue. Clutch it with both hands. Bury it in the garden and mark the spot with a cross.'

'But what about the stories? Who is going to write them?'

Egbert smiled a tender smile.

'I am,' he said. 'Before I saw the light, I, too, used to write stearine bilge just like *Parted Ways*. When we are married, I shall say to you, if I remember the book of words correctly, "With all my worldly goods I thee endow." They will include three novels I was never able to kid a publisher into printing, and at least twenty short stories no editor would accept. I give them to you freely. You can have the first of the novels tonight, and we will sit back and watch Mainprice and Peabody sell half a million copies.'

'Oh, Egbert!' said Evangeline.

'Evangeline!' said Egbert.

Gala Night

The bar-parlour of the Angler's Rest was fuller than usual. Our local race meeting had been held during the afternoon, and this always means a rush of custom. In addition to the *habitués,* that faithful little band of listeners which sits nightly at the feet of Mr Mulliner, there were present some half a dozen strangers. One of these, a fair-haired young Stout and Mild, wore the unmistakable air of a man who has not been fortunate in his selections. He sat staring before him with dull eyes and a drooping jaw, and nothing that his companions could do seemed able to cheer him up.

A genial Sherry and Bitters, one of the regular patrons, eyed the sufferer with bluff sympathy.

'What your friend appears to need, gentlemen,' he said, 'is a dose of Mulliner's Buck-U-Uppo.'

'What's Mulliner's Buck-U-Uppo?' asked one of the strangers, a Whisky Sour, interested. 'Never heard of it myself.'

Mr Mulliner smiled indulgently.

'He is referring,' he explained, 'to a tonic invented by my brother Wilfred, the well-known analytical chemist. It is not often administered to human beings, having been designed primarily to encourage elephants in India to conduct themselves with an easy nonchalance during the tiger hunts which are so popular in that country. But occasionally human beings do partake of it, with impressive results. I was telling the company here not long ago of the remarkable effect it had on my nephew Augustine, the curate.'

'It bucked him up?'

'It bucked him up very considerably. It acted on his bishop, too, when he tried it, in a similar manner. It is undoubtedly a most efficient tonic, strong and invigorating.'

'How is Augustine, by the way?' asked the Sherry and Bitters.

'Extremely well. I received a letter from him only this morning. I am not sure if I told you, but he is a vicar now, at Walsingford-below-Chiveney-on-Thames. A delightful resort, mostly honeysuckle and apple-cheeked villagers.'

'Anything been happening to him lately?'

'It is strange that you should ask that,' said Mr Mulliner, finishing his hot Scotch and lemon and rapping gently on the table. 'In this letter to which I allude he has quite an interesting story to relate. It deals with the loves of Ronald Bracy-Gascoigne and Hypatia Wace. Hypatia is a school-friend of my nephew's wife. She has been staying at the vicarage, nursing her through a sharp attack of mumps. She is also the niece and ward of Augustine's superior of the Cloth, the Bishop of Stortford.'

'Was that the bishop who took the Buck-U-Uppo?'

'The same,' said Mr Mulliner. 'As for Ronald Bracy-Gascoigne, he is a young man of independent means who resides in the neighbourhood. He is, of course, one of the Berkshire Bracy-Gascoignes.'

'Ronald,' said a Lemonade and Angostura thoughtfully. 'Now, there's a name I never cared for.'

'In that respect,' said Mr Mulliner, 'you differ from Hypatia Wace. She thought it swell. She loved Ronald Bracy-Gascoigne with all the fervour of a young girl's heart, and they were provisionally engaged to be married. Provisionally, I say, because, before the firing squad could actually be assembled, it was necessary for the young couple to obtain the consent of the Bishop of Stortford. Mark that, gentlemen. Their engagement was subject to the Bishop of Stortford's consent. This was the snag that protruded jaggedly from the middle of the primrose path of their happiness, and for quite a while it seemed as if Cupid must inevitably stub his toe on it.'

I will select as the point at which to begin my tale (said Mr Mulliner), a lovely evening in June, when all Nature seemed to smile and the rays of the setting sun fell like molten gold upon the picturesque garden of the vicarage at Walsingford-below-Chiveney-on-Thames. On a rustic bench beneath a spreading elm, Hypatia Wace and Ronald Bracy-Gascoigne watched the shadows lengthening across the smooth lawn: and to the girl there appeared something symbolical and ominous about this creeping blackness. She shivered. To her, it was as if the sunbathed lawn represented her happiness and the shadows the doom that was creeping upon it.

'Are you doing anything at the moment, Ronnie?' she asked.

'Eh?' said Ronald Bracy-Gascoigne. 'What? Doing anything? Oh, you mean doing anything? No, I'm not doing anything.'

'Then kiss me,' cried Hypatia.

'Right ho,' said the young man. 'I see what you mean. Rather a scheme. I will.'

He did so: and for some moments they clung together in a close embrace. Then Ronald, releasing her gently, began to slap himself between the shoulder-blades.

'Beetle or something down my back,' he explained. 'Probably fell off the tree.'

'Kiss me again,' whispered Hypatia.

'In one second, old girl,' said Ronald. 'The instant I've dealt with this beetle or something. Would you mind just fetching me a whack on about the fourth knob of the spine, reading from the top downwards. I fancy that would make it think a bit.'

Hypatia uttered a sharp exclamation.

'Is this a time,' she cried passionately, 'to talk of beetles?'

'Well, you know, don't you know,' said Ronald, with a touch of apology in his voice, 'they seem rather to force themselves on your attention when they get down your back. I daresay you've had the same experience yourself. I don't suppose in the ordinary way I mention beetles half a dozen times a year, but . . . I should say the fifth knob would be about the spot now. A good, sharp slosh with plenty of follow-through ought to do the trick.'

Hypatia clenched her hands. She was seething with that febrile exasperation which, since the days of Eve, has come upon women who find themselves linked to a cloth-head.

'You poor sap,' she said tensely. 'You keep babbling about beetles, and you don't appear to realise that, if you want to kiss me, you'd better cram in all the kissing you can now, while the going is good. It doesn't seem to have occurred to you that after tonight you're going to fade out of the picture.'

'Oh, I say, no! Why?'

'My Uncle Percy arrives this evening.'

'The Bishop?'

'Yes. And my Aunt Priscilla.'

'And you think they won't be any too frightfully keen on me?'

'I know they won't. I wrote and told them we were engaged, and I had a letter this afternoon saying you wouldn't do.'

'No, I say, really? Oh, I say, dash it!'

'"Out of the question", my uncle said. And underlined it.'

'Not really? Not absolutely underlined it?'

'Yes. Twice. In very black ink.'

A cloud darkened the young man's face. The beetle had begun to try out a few tentative dance steps on the small of his back, but he ignored it. A Tiller troupe of beetles could not have engaged his attention now.

'But what's he got against me?'

'Well, for one thing he has heard that you were sent down from Oxford.'

'But all the best men are. Look at What's-his-name. Chap who wrote poems. Shellac, or some such name.'

'And then he knows that you dance a lot.'

'What's wrong with dancing? I'm not very well up in these things, but didn't David dance before Saul? Or am I thinking of a couple of other fellows? Anyway, I know that somebody danced before somebody and was extremely highly thought of in consequence.'

'David . . .'

'I'm not saying it *was* David, mind you. It may quite easily have been Samuel.'

'David . . .'

'Or even Nimshi, the son of Bimshi, or somebody like that.'

'David, or Samuel, or Nimshi the son of Bimshi,' said Hypatia, 'did not dance at the Home from Home.'

Her allusion was to the latest of those frivolous night-clubs which spring up from time to time on the reaches of the Thames which are within a comfortable distance from London. This one stood some half a mile from the vicarage gates.

'Is *that* what the Bish is beefing about?' demanded Ronald, genuinely astonished. 'You don't mean to tell me he really objects to the Home from Home? Why, a cathedral couldn't be more rigidly respectable. Does he realise that the place has only been raided five times in the whole course of its existence? A few simple words of explanation will put all this right. I'll have a talk with the old boy.'

Hypatia shook her head.

'No,' she said. 'It's no use talking. He has made his mind up. One of the things he said in his letter was that, rather than countenance my union to a worthless worldling like you, he would gladly see me turned into a pillar of salt like Lot's wife, Genesis 19, 26. And nothing could be fairer than that, could it? So what I would suggest is that you start in immediately to fold me in your arms and cover my face with kisses. It's the last chance you'll get.'

The young man was about to follow her advice, for he could see that there was much in what she said: but at this moment there came from the direction of the house the sound of a manly voice trolling the Psalm for the Second Sunday after Septuagesima. And an instant later their host, the Rev. Augustine Mulliner, appeared in sight. He saw them and came hurrying across the garden, leaping over the flower beds with extraordinary lissomness.

'Amazing elasticity that bird has, both physical and mental,' said Ronald Bracy-Gascoigne, eyeing Augustine, as he approached, with a gloomy envy. 'How does he get that way?'

'He was telling me last night,' said Hypatia. 'He has a tonic which he takes regularly. It is called Mulliner's Buck-U-Uppo, and acts directly upon the red corpuscles.'

'I wish he would give the Bish a swig of it,' said Ronald moodily. A sudden light of hope came into his eyes. 'I say, Hyp, old girl,' he exclaimed. 'That's rather a notion. Don't you think it's rather a notion? It looks to me like something of an idea. If the Bish were to dip his beak into the stuff, it might make him take a brighter view of me.'

Hypatia, like all girls who intend to be good wives, made it a practice to look on any suggestions thrown out by her future lord and master as fatuous and futile.

'I never heard anything so silly,' she said.

'Well, I wish you would try it. No harm in trying it, what?'

'Of course I shall do nothing of the kind.'

'Well, I do think you might try it,' said Ronald. 'I mean, try it, don't you know.'

He could speak no further on the matter, for now they were no longer alone. Augustine had come up. His kindly face looked grave.

'I say, Ronnie, old bloke,' said Augustine, 'I don't want

to hurry you, but I think I ought to inform you that the Bishes, male and female, are even now on their way up from the station. I should be popping, if I were you. The prudent man looketh well to his going. Proverbs, 14, 15.'

'All right,' said Ronald sombrely. 'I suppose,' he added, turning to the girl, 'you wouldn't care to sneak out tonight and come and have one final spot of shoe-slithering at the Home from Home? It's a Gala Night. Might be fun, what? Give us a chance of saying goodbye properly, and all that.'

'I never heard anything so silly,' said Hypatia, mechanically. 'Of course I'll come.'

'Right ho. Meet you down the road about twelve then,' said Ronald Bracy-Gascoigne.

He walked swiftly away, and presently was lost to sight behind the shrubbery. Hypatia turned with a choking sob, and Augustine took her hand and squeezed it gently.

'Cheer up, old onion,' he urged. 'Don't lose hope. Remember, many waters cannot quench love. Song of Solomon, 8, 7.'

'I don't see what quenching love has got to do with it,' said Hypatia peevishly. 'Our trouble is that I've got an uncle complete with gaiters and a hat with bootlaces on it who can't see Ronnie with a telescope.'

'I know.' Augustine nodded sympathetically. 'And my heart bleeds for you. I've been through all this sort of thing myself. When I was trying to marry Jane, I was stymied by a father-in-law-to-be who had to be seen to be believed. A chap, I assure you, who combined chronic shortness of temper with the ability to bend pokers round his biceps. Tact was what won him over, and tact is what I propose to employ in your case. I have an idea at the back of my mind. I won't tell you what it is, but you may take it from me it's the real tabasco.'

'How kind you are, Augustine!' sighed the girl.

'It comes from mixing with Boy Scouts. You may have noticed that the village is stiff with them. But don't you worry, old girl. I owe you a lot for the way you've looked after Jane these last weeks, and I'm going to see you through. If I can't fix up your little affair, I'll eat my *Hymns Ancient and Modern*. And uncooked at that.'

And with these brave words Augustine Mulliner turned two handsprings, vaulted over the rustic bench, and went about his duties in the parish.

Augustine was rather relieved, when he came down to dinner that night, to find that Hypatia was not to be among those present. The girl was taking her meal on a tray with Jane, his wife, in the invalid's bedroom, and he was consequently able to embark with freedom on the discussion of her affairs. As soon as the servants had left the room, accordingly he addressed himself to the task.

'Now listen, you two dear good souls,' he said. 'What I want to talk to you about, now that we are alone, is this business of Hypatia and Ronald Bracy-Gascoigne.'

The Lady Bishopess pursed her lips, displeased. She was a woman of ample and majestic build. A friend of Augustine's, who had been attached to the Tank Corps during the War, had once said that he knew nothing that brought the old days back more vividly than the sight of her. All she needed, he maintained, was a steering wheel and a couple of machine guns, and you could have moved her up into any front line and no questions asked.

'Please, Mr Mulliner!' she said coldly.

Augustine was not to be deterred. Like all the Mulliners, he was at heart a man of reckless courage.

'They tell me you are thinking of bunging a spanner into the works,' he said. 'Not true, I hope?'

'Quite true, Mr Mulliner. Am I not right, Percy?'

'Quite,' said the Bishop.

'We have made careful inquiries about the young man, and are satisfied that he is entirely unsuitable.'

'Would you say that?' said Augustine. 'A pretty good egg, I've always found him. What's your main objection to the poor lizard?'

The Lady Bishopess shivered.

'We learn that he is frequently to be seen dancing at an advanced hour, not only in gilded London night-clubs but even in what should be the purer atmosphere of Walsingford-below-Chiveney-on-Thames. There is a resort in this neighbourhood known, I believe, as the Home from Home.'

'Yes, just down the road,' said Augustine. 'It's a Gala Night tonight, if you cared to look in. Fancy dress optional.'

'I understand that he is to be seen there almost nightly. Now, against dancing *qua* dancing,' proceeded the Lady Bishopess, 'I have nothing to say. Properly conducted, it is a pleasing and innocuous pastime. In my own younger days I myself was no mean exponent of the polka, the *schottische* and the Roger de Coverley. Indeed, it was at a Dance in Aid of the Distressed Daughters of Clergymen of the Church of England Relief Fund that I first met my husband.'

'Really?' said Augustine. 'Well, cheerio!' he said, draining his glass of port.

'But dancing, as the term is understood nowadays, is another matter. I have no doubt that what you call a Gala Night would prove, on inspection, to be little less than one of those orgies where perfect strangers of both sexes unblushingly throw coloured celluloid balls at one another and in other ways behave in a manner more suitable to the Cities of the Plain than to our dear England. No, Mr Mulliner, if this young man Ronald Bracy-Gascoigne is in the habit of frequenting places of the type of the Home from Home, he is not a fit mate for a pure young girl like my niece Hypatia. Am I not correct, Percy?'

'Perfectly correct, my dear.'

'Oh, right ho, then,' said Augustine philosophically, and turned the conversation to the forthcoming Pan-Anglican synod.

Living in the country had given Augustine Mulliner the excellent habit of going early to bed. He had a sermon to compose on the morrow, and in order to be fresh and at his best in the morning he retired shortly before eleven. And, as he had anticipated an unbroken eight hours of refreshing sleep, it was with no little annoyance that he became aware, towards midnight, of a hand on his shoulder, shaking him. Opening his eyes, he found that the light had been switched on and that the Bishop of Stortford was standing at his bedside.

'Hullo!' said Augustine. 'Anything wrong?'

The Bishop smiled genially, and hummed a bar or two of the hymn for those of riper years at sea. He was plainly in excellent spirits.

'Nothing, my dear fellow,' he replied. 'In fact, very much the reverse. How are you, Mulliner?'

'I feel fine, Bish.'

'I'll bet you two chasubles to a hassock you don't feel as fine as I do,' said the Bishop. 'It must be something in the air of this place. I haven't felt like this since Boat-Race Night of the year 1893. Wow!' he continued. 'Whoopee! How goodly are thy tents, O Jacob, and thy tabernacles, O Israel! Numbers, 44, 5.' And, gripping the rail of the bed, he endeavoured to balance himself on his hands with his feet in the air.

Augustine looked at him with growing concern. He could not rid himself of a curious feeling that there was something sinister behind this ebullience. Often before, he had seen his guest in a mood of dignified animation, for the robust cheerfulness of the other's outlook was famous in ecclesiastical circles. But here, surely, was something more than dignified animation.

'Yes,' proceeded the Bishop, completing his gymnastics and sitting down on the bed, 'I feel like a fighting cock, Mulliner. I am full of beans. And the idea of wasting the golden hours of the night in bed seemed so silly that I had to get up and look in on you for a chat. Now, this is what I want to speak to you about, my dear fellow. I wonder if you recollect writing to me – round about Epiphany, it would have been – to tell me of the hit you made in the Boy Scouts pantomime here? You played Sindbad the Sailor, if I am not mistaken?'

'That's right.'

'Well, what I came here to ask, my dear Mulliner, was

this. Can you, by any chance, lay your hand on that Sindbad costume? I want to borrow it, if I may.'

'What for?'

'Never mind what for, Mulliner. Sufficient for you to know that motives of the soundest churchmanship render it essential for me to have that suit.'

'Very well, Bish. I'll find it for you tomorrow.'

'Tomorrow will not do. This dilatory spirit of putting things off, this sluggish attitude of *laissez-faire* and procrastination,' said the Bishop, frowning, 'are scarcely what I expected to find in you, Mulliner. But there,' he added, more kindly, 'let us say no more. Just dig up that Sindbad costume and look slippy about it, and we will forget the whole matter. What does it look like?'

'Just an ordinary sailor suit, Bish.'

'Excellent. Some species of headgear goes with it, no doubt?'

'A cap with HMS *Blotto* on the band.'

'Admirable. Then, my dear fellow,' said the Bishop, beaming, 'if you will just let me have it, I will trouble you no further tonight. Your day's toil in the vineyard has earned repose. The sleep of the labouring man is sweet. Ecclesiastes, 5, 12.'

As the door closed behind his guest, Augustine was conscious of a definite uneasiness. Only once before had he seen his spiritual superior in quite this exalted condition. That had been two years ago, when they had gone down to Harchester College to unveil the statue of Lord Hemel of Hempstead. On that occasion, he recollected, the Bishop, under the influence of an overdose of Buck-U-Uppo, had not been content with unveiling the statue. He had gone out in the small hours of the night and painted it pink. Augustine could still recall the surge of emotion which had come upon him when, leaning out of the window, he had observed the prelate climbing up the waterspout on his way back to his room. And he still remembered the sorrowful pity with which he had listened to the other's lame explanation that he was a cat belonging to the cook.

Sleep, in the present circumstances, was out of the question. With a pensive sigh, Augustine slipped on a dressing gown and went downstairs to his study. It would ease his mind, he thought, to do a little work on that sermon of his.

Augustine's study was on the ground floor, looking on to the garden. It was a lovely night, and he opened the French windows, the better to enjoy the soothing scents of the flowers beyond. Then, seating himself at his desk, he began to work.

The task of composing a sermon which should practically make sense and yet not be above the heads of his rustic flock was always one that caused Augustine Mulliner to concentrate tensely. Soon he was lost in his labour and oblivious to everything but the problem of how to find a word of one syllable that meant Supralapsarianism. A glaze of preoccupation had come over his eyes, and the tip of his tongue, protruding from the left corner of his mouth, revolved in slow circles.

From this waking trance he emerged slowly to the realisation that somebody was speaking his name and that he was no longer alone in the room.

Seated in his armchair, her lithe young body wrapped in a green dressing gown, was Hypatia Wace.

'Hullo!' said Augustine, staring. 'You here?'

'Hullo,' said Hypatia. 'Yes, I'm here.'

'I thought you had gone to the Home from Home to meet Ronald.'

Hypatia shook her head.

'We never made it,' she said. 'Ronnie rang up to say that he had had a private tip that the place was to be raided tonight. So we thought it wasn't safe to start anything.'

'Quite right,' said Augustine approvingly. 'Prudence first. Whatsoever thou takest in hand, remember the end and thou shalt never do amiss. Ecclesiastes, 7, 36.'

Hypatia dabbed at her eyes with her handkerchief.

'I couldn't sleep, and I saw the light, so I came down. I'm so miserable, Augustine.'

'About this Ronnie business?'

'Yes.'

'There, there. Everything's going to be hotsy-totsy.'

'I don't see how you make that out. Have you heard Uncle Percy and Aunt Priscilla talk about Ronnie? They couldn't be more off the poor, unfortunate fish if he were the Scarlet Woman of Babylon.'

'I know. I know. But, as I hinted this afternoon, I have a little plan. I have been giving your case a good deal of thought, and I think you will agree with me that it is your Aunt Priscilla who is the real trouble. Sweeten her, and the Bish will follow her lead. What she thinks today, he always thinks tomorrow. In other words, if we can win her over, he will give his consent in a minute. Am I wrong or am I right?'

Hypatia nodded.

'Yes,' she said. 'That's right, as far as it goes. Uncle Percy always does what Aunt Priscilla tells him to. But how are you going to sweeten her?'

'With Mulliner's Buck-U-Uppo. You remember how often I have spoken to you of the properties of that admirable tonic. It changes the whole mental outlook like magic. We have only to slip a few drops into your Aunt Priscilla's hot milk tomorrow night, and you will be amazed at the results.'

'You really guarantee that?'

'Absolutely.'

'Then that's fine,' said the girl, brightening visibly, 'because that's exactly what I did this evening. Ronnie was suggesting it when you came up this afternoon, and I thought I might as well try it. I found the bottle in the cupboard in here, and I put some in Aunt Priscilla's hot milk and, in order to make a good job of it, some in Uncle Percy's toddy, too.'

An icy hand seemed to clutch at Augustine's heart. He began to understand the inwardness of the recent scene in his bedroom.

'How much?' he gasped.

'Oh, not much,' said Hypatia. 'I didn't want to poison the dear old things. About a tablespoonful apiece.'

A shuddering groan came raspingly from Augustine's lips.

'Are you aware,' he said in a low, toneless voice, 'that the medium dose for an adult elephant is one teaspoonful?'

'No!'

'Yes. The most fearful consequences result from anything in the nature of an overdose.' He groaned. 'No wonder the Bishop seemed a little strange in his manner just now.'

'Did he seem strange in his manner?'

Augustine nodded dully.

'He came into my room and did handsprings on the end of the bed and went away in my Sindbad the Sailor suit.'

'What did he want that for?'

Augustine shuddered.

'I scarcely dare to face the thought,' he said, 'but can he have been contemplating a visit to the Home from Home? It is Gala Night, remember.'

'Why, of course,' said Hypatia. 'And that must have been why Aunt Priscilla came to me about an hour ago and asked me if I could lend her my Columbine costume.'

'She did!' cried Augustine.

'Certainly she did. I couldn't think what she wanted it for. But now, of course, I see.'

Augustine uttered a moan that seemed to come from the depths of his soul.

'Run up to her room and see if she is still there,' he said. 'If I'm not very much mistaken, we have sown the wind and we shall reap the whirlwind. Hosea, 8, 7.'

The girl hurried away, and Augustine began to pace the floor feverishly. He had completed five laps and was beginning a sixth, when there was a noise outside the French windows and a sailorly form shot through and fell panting into the armchair.

'Bish!' cried Augustine.

The Bishop waved a hand, to indicate that he would be with him as soon as he had attended to this matter of taking in a fresh supply of breath, and continued to pant. Augustine watched him, deeply concerned. There was a shop-soiled look about his guest. Part of the Sindbad costume had been torn away as if by some irresistible force, and the hat was missing. His worst fears appeared to have been realised.

'Bish!' he cried. 'What has been happening?'

The Bishop sat up. He was breathing more easily now, and a pleased, almost complacent, look had come into his face.

'Woof!' he said. 'Some binge!'

'Tell me what happened,' pleaded Augustine, agitated.

The Bishop reflected, arranging his facts in chronological order.

'Well,' he said, 'when I got to the Home from Home, everybody was dancing. Nice orchestra. Nice tune. Nice floor. So I danced, too.'

'You danced?'

'Certainly I danced, Mulliner,' replied the Bishop with a dignity that sat well upon him. A hornpipe. I consider it the duty of the higher clergy on these occasions to set an example. You didn't suppose I would go to a place like the Home from Home to play solitaire? Harmless relaxation is not forbidden, I believe?'

'But can you dance?'

'*Can* I dance?' said the Bishop. 'Can I *dance,* Mulliner? Have you ever heard of Nijinsky?'

'Yes.'

'My stage name,' said the Bishop.

Augustine swallowed tensely.

'Who did you dance with?' he asked.

'At first,' said the Bishop, 'I danced alone. But then, most fortunately, my dear wife arrived, looking perfectly charming in some sort of filmy material, and we danced together.'

'But wasn't she surprised to see you there?'

'Not in the least. Why should she be?'

'Oh, I don't know.'

'Then why did you put the question?'

'I wasn't thinking.'

'Always think before you speak, Mulliner,' said the Bishop reprovingly.

The door opened, and Hypatia hurried in.

'She's not—' She stopped. 'Uncle!' she cried.

'Ah, my dear,' said the Bishop. 'But I was telling you, Mulliner. After we had been dancing for some time, a most annoying thing occurred. Just as we were enjoying ourselves – everybody cutting up and having a good time – who should come in but a lot of interfering policemen. A most brusque and unpleasant body of men. Inquisitive, too. One of them kept asking me my name and address. But I soon put a stop to all that sort of nonsense. I plugged him in the eye.'

'You plugged him in the eye?'

'I plugged him in the eye, Mulliner. That's when I got this suit torn. The fellow was annoying me intensely. He ignored my repeated statement that I gave my name and address only to my oldest and closest friends, and had the audacity to clutch me by what I suppose a costumier would describe as the slack of my garment. Well, naturally I plugged him in the eye. I come of a fighting line, Mulliner. My ancestor, Bishop Odo, was famous in William the Conqueror's day for his work with the battleaxe. So I biffed this bird. And did he take a toss? Ask me!' said the Bishop, chuckling contentedly.

Augustine and Hypatia exchanged glances.

'But, Uncle—' began Hypatia.

'Don't interrupt, my child,' said the Bishop. 'I cannot marshal my thoughts if you persist in interrupting. Where was I? Ah, yes. Well, then the already existing state of confusion grew intensified. The whole *tempo* of the proceedings became, as it were, quickened. Somebody turned out the lights, and somebody else upset a table and I decided to come away.' A pensive look flitted over his face. 'I trust,' he said, 'that my dear wife also contrived to leave without undue inconvenience. The last I saw of her, she was diving through one of the windows in a manner which, I thought, showed considerable lissomness and resource. Ah, here she is, and looking none the worse for her adventures. Come in, my dear. I was just telling Hypatia and our good host here of our little evening from home.'

The Lady Bishopess stood breathing heavily. She was not in the best of training. She had the appearance of a Tank which is missing on one cylinder.

'Save me, Percy,' she gasped.

'Certainly, my dear,' said the Bishop cordially. 'From what?'

In silence the Lady Bishopess pointed at the window. Through it, like some figure of doom, was striding a policeman. He, too, was breathing in a laboured manner, like one touched in the wind.

The Bishop drew himself up.

'And what, pray,' he asked coldly, 'is the meaning of this intrusion?'

'Ah!' said the policeman.

He closed the windows and stood with his back against them.

It seemed to Augustine that the moment had arrived for a man of tact to take the situation in hand.

'Good evening, constable,' he said genially. 'You appear to have been taking exercise. I have no doubt that you would enjoy a little refreshment.'

The policeman licked his lips, but did not speak.

'I have an excellent tonic here in my cupboard,' proceeded Augustine, 'and I think you will find it most restorative. I will mix it with a little seltzer.'

The policeman took the glass, but in a preoccupied manner. His attention was still riveted on the Bishop and his consort.

'Caught you, have I?' he said.

'I fail to understand you, officer,' said the Bishop frigidly.

'I've been chasing her,' said the policeman, pointing to the Lady Bishopess, 'a good mile it must have been.'

'Then you acted,' said the Bishop severely, 'in a most offensive and uncalled-for way. On her physician's recommendation, my dear wife takes a short cross-country run each night before retiring to rest. Things have come to a sorry pass if she cannot follow her doctor's orders without being pursued – I will use a stronger word – chivvied – by the constabulary.'

'And it was by her doctor's orders that she went to the Home from Home, eh?' said the policeman keenly.

'I shall be vastly surprised to learn,' said the Bishop, 'that my dear wife has been anywhere near the resort you mention.'

'And you were there, too. I saw you.'

'Absurd!'

'I saw you punch Constable Booker in the eye.'

'Ridiculous!'

'If you weren't there,' said the policeman, 'what are you doing wearing that sailor suit?'

The Bishop raised his eyebrows.

'I cannot permit my choice of costume,' he said, 'arrived at – I need scarcely say – only after much reflection and meditation, to be criticised by a man who habitually goes about in public in a blue uniform and a helmet. What, may I enquire, is it that you object to in this sailor suit? There is nothing wrong, I venture to believe, nothing degrading in a sailor suit. Many of England's greatest men have worn sailor suits. Nelson . . . Admiral Beatty—'

'And Arthur Prince,' said Hypatia.

'And, as you say, Arthur Prince.'

The policeman was scowling darkly. As a dialectician, he seemed to be feeling he was outmatched. And yet, he appeared to be telling himself, there must be some answer even to the apparently unanswerable logic to which he had just been listening. To assist thought, he raised the glass of Buck-U-Uppo and seltzer in his hand, and drained it at a draught.

And, as he did so, suddenly, abruptly, as breath fades from steel, the scowl passed from his face, and in its stead there appeared a smile of infinite kindliness and goodwill. He wiped his moustache, and began to chuckle to himself, as at some diverting memory.

'Made me laugh, that did,' he said. 'When old Booker went head over heels that time. Don't know when I've seen a nicer punch. Clean, crisp . . . Don't suppose it travelled more than six inches, did it? I reckon you've done a bit of boxing in your time, sir.'

At the sight of the constable's smiling face, the Bishop had relaxed the austerity of his demeanour. He no longer looked like Savonarola rebuking the sins of the people. He was his old genial self once more.

'Quite true, officer,' he said, beaming. 'When I was a somewhat younger man than I am at present, I won the Curates' Open Heavyweight Championship two years in succession. Some of the ancient skill still lingers, it would seem.'

The policeman chuckled again.

'I should say it does, sir. But,' he continued, a look of annoyance coming into his face, 'what all the fuss was about is more than I can say. Our fatheaded Inspector says, "You go and raid that Home from Home, chaps, see?" he says, and so we went and done it. But my heart wasn't in it, no more was any of the other fellers' hearts in it. What's wrong with a little rational enjoyment? That's what I say. What's wrong with it?'

'Precisely, officer.'

'That's what I say. What's wrong with it? Let people enjoy themselves how they like is what I say. And if the police come interfering – well, punch them in the eye, I say, same as you did Constable Booker. That's what I say.'

'Exactly,' said the Bishop. He turned to his wife. 'A fellow of considerable intelligence, this, my dear.'

'I liked his face right from the beginning,' said the Lady Bishopess. 'What is your name, officer?'

'Smith, lady. But call me Cyril.'

'Certainly,' said the Lady Bishopess. 'It will be a pleasure to do so. I used to know some Smiths in Lincolnshire years ago, Cyril. I wonder if they were any relation.'

'Maybe, lady. It's a small world.'

'Though, now I come to think of it, their name was Robinson.'

'Well, that's life, lady, isn't it?' said the policeman.

'That's just about what it is, Cyril,' agreed the Bishop. 'You never spoke a truer word.'

Into this love-feast, which threatened to become more glutinous every moment, there cut the cold voice of Hypatia Wace.

'Well, I must say,' said Hypatia, 'that you're a nice lot!'

'Who's a nice lot, lady?' asked the policeman.

'These two,' said Hypatia. 'Are you married, officer?'

'No, lady. I'm just a solitary chip drifting on the river of life.'

'Well, anyway, I expect you know what it feels like to be in love.'

'Too true, lady.'

'Well, I'm in love with Mr Bracy-Gascoigne. You've met him, probably. Wouldn't you say he was a person of the highest character?'

'The whitest man I know, lady.'

'Well, I want to marry him, and my uncle and aunt here won't let me, because they say he's worldly. Just because he goes out dancing. And all the while they are dancing the soles of their shoes through. I don't call it fair.'

She buried her face in her hands with a stifled sob. The Bishop and his wife looked at each other in blank astonishment.

'I don't understand,' said the Bishop.

'Nor I,' said the Lady Bishopess. 'My dear child, what is all this about our not consenting to your marriage with

Mr Bracy-Gascoigne? However did you get that idea into your head? Certainly, as far as I am concerned, you may marry Mr Bracy-Gascoigne. And I think I speak for my dear husband?'

'Quite,' said the Bishop. 'Most decidedly.'

Hypatia uttered a cry of joy.

'Good egg! May I really?'

'Certainly you may. You have no objection, Cyril?'

'None whatever, lady.'

Hypatia's face fell.

'Oh, dear!' she said.

'What's the matter?'

'It just struck me that I've got to wait hours and hours before I can tell him. Just think of having to wait hours and hours!'

The Bishop laughed his jolly laugh.

'Why wait hours and hours, my dear? No time like the present.'

'But he's gone to bed.'

'Well, rout him out,' said the Bishop heartily. 'Here is what I suggest that we should do. You and I and Priscilla – and you, Cyril? – will all go down to his house and stand under his window and shout.'

'Or throw gravel at the window,' suggested the Lady Bishopess.

'Certainly, my dear, if you prefer it.'

'And when he sticks his head out,' said the policeman, 'how would it be to have the garden hose handy and squirt him? Cause a lot of fun and laughter, that would.'

'My dear Cyril,' said the Bishop, 'you think of everything. I shall certainly use any influence I may possess with the authorities to have you promoted to a rank where your remarkable talents will enjoy greater scope. Come, let us be going. You will accompany us, my dear Mulliner?'

Augustine shook his head.

'Sermon to write, Bish.'

'Just as you say, Mulliner. Then if you will be so good as to leave the window open, my dear fellow, we shall be able to return to our beds at the conclusion of our little errand of goodwill without disturbing the domestic staff.'

'Right ho, Bish.'

'Then, for the present, pip-pip, Mulliner.'

'Toodle-oo, Bish,' said Augustine.

He took up his pen, and resumed his composition. Out in the sweet-scented night he could hear the four voices dying away in the distance. They seemed to be singing an old English part-song. He smiled benevolently.

'A merry heart doeth good like a medicine. Proverbs 17, 22,' murmured Augustine.

July

Trouble Down at Tudsleigh

Two Eggs and a couple of Beans were having a leisurely spot in the smoking room of the Drones Club, when a Crumpet came in and asked if anybody present wished to buy a practically new copy of Tennyson's poems. His manner, as he spoke, suggested that he had little hope that business would result. Nor did it. The two Beans and one of the Eggs said No. The other Egg merely gave a short, sardonic laugh.

The Crumpet hastened to put himself right with the Company.

'It isn't mine. It belongs to Freddie Widgeon.'

The senior of the two Beans drew his breath in sharply, genuinely shocked.

'You aren't telling us Freddie Widgeon bought a Tennyson?'

The junior Bean said that this confirmed a suspicion which had long been stealing over him. Poor old Freddie was breaking up.

'Not at all,' said the Crumpet. 'He had the most excellent motives. The whole thing was a strategic move, and in my opinion a jolly fine strategic move. He did it to boost his stock with the girl.'

'What girl?'

'April Carroway. She lived at a place called Tudsleigh down in Worcestershire. Freddie went there for the fishing, and the day he left London he happened to run into his uncle, Lord Blicester, and the latter, learning that he was to be in those parts, told him on no account to omit to look in at Tudsleigh Court and slap his old friend, Lady Carroway, on the back. So Freddie called there on the afternoon of his arrival, to get the thing over: and as he was passing through the garden on his way out he suddenly heard a girl's voice proceeding from the interior of a summer-house. And so musical was it that he edged a bit closer and shot a glance through the window. And, as he did so, he reeled and came within a toucher of falling.'

From where he stood he could see the girl plainly, and she was, he tells me, the absolute ultimate word, the last bubbling cry. She could not have looked better to him if he had drawn up the specifications personally. He was stunned. He had had no idea that there was anything like this on the premises. There and then he abandoned his scheme of spending the next two weeks fishing: for day by day in every way, he realised, he must haunt Tudsleigh Court from now on like a resident spectre.

He had now recovered sufficiently for his senses to function once more, and he gathered that what the girl was doing was reading some species of poetry aloud to a small, grave female kid with green eyes and turned-up nose who sat at her side. And the idea came to him that it would be a pretty sound scheme if he could find out what this bilge was. For, of course, when it comes to wooing, it's simply half the battle to get a line on the adored object's favourite literature. Ascertain what it is and mug it up and decant an excerpt or two in her presence, and before you can say 'What ho!' she is looking on you as a kindred soul and is all over you.

And it was at this point that he had a nice little slice of luck. The girl suddenly stopped reading: and, placing the volume face down on her lap, sat gazing dreamily nor'-nor'-east for a space, as I believe girls frequently do when they strike a particularly juicy bit halfway through a poem. And the next moment Freddie was hareing off to the local post office to wire to London for a *Collected Works of Alfred, Lord Tennyson.* He was rather relieved, he tells me, because, girls being what they are, it might quite easily have been Shelley or even Browning.

Well, Freddie lost no time in putting into operation his scheme of becoming the leading pest at Tudsleigh Court. On the following afternoon he called there again, met Lady Carroway once more, and was introduced to this girl, April, and to the green-eyed kid, who, he learned, was her young sister Prudence. So far, so good. But just as he was starting to direct at April a respectfully volcanic look which would give her some rough kind of preliminary intimation that here came old Colonel Romeo in person, his hostess went on to say something which sounded like 'Captain Bradbury', and he perceived with a nasty shock that he was not the only visitor. Seated in a chair with a cup of tea in one hand and half a muffin in the other was an extraordinarily large and beefy bird in tweeds.

'Captain Bradbury, Mr Widgeon,' said Lady Carroway.

'Captain Bradbury is in the Indian Army. He is home on leave and has taken a house up the river.'

'Oh?' said Freddie, rather intimating by his manner that this was just the dirty sort of trick he would have imagined the other would have played.

'Mr Widgeon is the nephew of my old friend, Lord Blicester.'

'Ah?' said Captain Bradbury, hiding with a ham-like hand a yawn that seemed to signify that Freddie's foul antecedents were of little interest to him. It was plain that this was not going to be one of those sudden friendships. Captain Bradbury was obviously feeling that a world fit for heroes to live in should contain the irreducible minimum of Widgeons: while, as for Freddie, the last person he wanted hanging about the place at this highly critical point in his affairs was a richly tanned military man with deep-set eyes and a natty moustache.

However, he quickly rallied from his momentary agitation. Once that volume of Tennyson came, he felt, he would pretty soon put this bird where he belonged. A natty moustache is not everything. Nor is a rich tan. And the same may be said of deep-set eyes. What bungs a fellow over with a refined and poetical girl is Soul. And in the course of the next few days Freddie expected to have soul enough for six. He exerted himself, accordingly, to be the life of the party, and so successful were his efforts that, as they were leaving, Captain Bradbury drew him aside and gave him the sort of look he would have given a Pathan discovered pinching the old regiment's rifles out on the North-Western Frontier. And it was only now that Freddie really began to appreciate the other's physique. He had had no notion that they were making the soldiery so large nowadays.

'Tell me, Pridgeon . . .'

'Widgeon,' said Freddie, to keep the records straight.

'Tell me, Widgeon, are you making a long stay in these parts?'

'Oh, yes. Fairly longish.'

'I shouldn't.'

'You wouldn't?'

'Not if I were you.'

'But I like the scenery.'

'If you got both eyes bunged up, you wouldn't be able to see the scenery.'

'Why should I get both eyes bunged up?'

'You might.'

'But why?'

'I don't know. You just might. These things happen. Well, good evening, Widgeon,' said Captain Bradbury and hopped into his two-seater like a performing elephant alighting on an upturned barrel. And Freddie made his way to the Blue Lion in Tudsleigh village, where he had established his headquarters.

It would be idle to deny that this little chat gave Frederick Widgeon food for thought. He brooded on it over his steak and French fries that night, and was still brooding on it long after he had slid between the sheets and should have been in a restful sleep. And when morning brought its eggs and bacon and coffee he began to brood on it again.

He's a pretty astute sort of chap, Freddie, and he had

not failed to sense the threatening note in the Captain's remarks. And he was somewhat dubious as to what to do for the best. You see, it was the first time anything of this sort had happened to him. I suppose, all in all, Freddie Widgeon has been in love at first sight with possibly twenty-seven girls in the course of his career: but hitherto everything had been what you might call plain sailing. I mean, he would flutter round for a few days and then the girl, incensed by some floater on his part or possibly merely unable to stand the sight of him any longer, would throw him out on his left ear, and that would be that. Everything pleasant and agreeable and orderly, as you might say. But this was different. Here he had come up against a new element, the jealous rival, and it was beginning to look not so good.

It was the sight of Tennyson's poems that turned the scale. The volume had arrived early on the previous day, and already he had mugged up two-thirds of the 'Lady of Shalott'. And the thought that, if he were to oil out now, all this frightful sweat would be so much dead loss, decided the issue. That afternoon he called once more at Tudsleigh Court, prepared to proceed with the matter along the lines originally laid out. And picture his astonishment and delight when he discovered that Captain Bradbury was not among those present.

There are very few advantages about having a military man as a rival in your wooing, but one of these is that every now and then such a military man has to pop up to London to see the blokes at the War Office. This Captain Bradbury had done today, and it was amazing what a difference his absence made. A gay confidence seemed to fill

Freddie as he sat there wolfing buttered toast. He had finished the 'Lady of Shalott' that morning and was stuffed to the tonsils with good material. It was only a question of time, he felt, before some chance remark would uncork him and give him the cue to do his stuff.

And presently it came. Lady Carroway, withdrawing to write letters, paused at the door to ask April if she had any message for her Uncle Lancelot.

'Give him my love,' said April, 'and say I hope he likes Bournemouth.'

The door closed. Freddie coughed.

'He's moved then?' he said.

'I beg your pardon?'

'Just a spot of persiflage. Lancelot, you know. Tennyson, you know. You remember in the "Lady of Shalott" Lancelot was putting in most of his time at Camelot.'

The girl stared at him, dropping a slice of bread-and-butter in her emotion.

'You don't mean to say you read Tennyson, Mr Widgeon?'

'Me?' said Freddie. 'Tennyson? Read Tennyson? Me read Tennyson? Well, well, well! Bless my soul! Why, I know him by heart – some of him.'

'So do I! "Break, break, break, on your cold grey stones, oh Sea . . ."'

'Quite. Or take the "Lady of Shalott".'

'"I hold it truth with him who sings . . ."'

'So do I, absolutely. And then, again, there's the "Lady of Shalott". Dashed extraordinary that you should like Tennyson, too.'

'I think he's wonderful.'

'What a lad! That "Lady of Shalott"! Some spin on the ball there.'

'It's so absurd, the way people sneer at him nowadays.'

'The silly bounders. Don't know what's good for them.'

'He's my favourite poet.'

'Mine, too. Any bird who could write the "Lady of Shalott" gets the cigar or coconut, according to choice, as far as I'm concerned.'

They gazed at one another emotionally.

'Well, I'd never have thought it,' said April.

'Why not?'

'I mean, you gave me the impression of being . . . well, rather the dancing, night-club sort of man.'

'What! Me? Night clubs? Good gosh! Why, my idea of a happy evening is to curl up with Tennyson's latest.'

'Don't you love "Locksley Hall"?'

'Oh, rather. And the "Lady of Shalott".'

'And "Maud"?'

'Aces,' said Freddie. 'And the "Lady of Shalott".'

'How fond you seem of the "Lady of Shalott"!'

'Oh, I am.'

'So am I, of course. The river here always reminds me so much of that poem.'

'Why, of course it does!' said Freddie. 'I've been trying to think all the time why it seemed so dashed familiar. And, talking of the river, I suppose you wouldn't care for a row up it tomorrow?'

The girl looked doubtful.

'Tomorrow?'

'My idea was to hire a boat, sling in a bit of chicken and ham and a Tennyson . . .'

'But I had promised to go to Birmingham tomorrow with Captain Bradbury to help him choose a fishing rod. Still, I suppose, really, any other day would do for that, wouldn't it?'

'Exactly.'

'We could go later on.'

'Positively,' said Freddie. 'A good deal later on. Much later on. In fact, the best plan would be to leave it quite open. One o'clock tomorrow, then, at the Town Bridge? Right. Fine. Splendid. Topping. I'll be there with my hair in a braid.'

All through the rest of the day Freddie was right in the pink. Walked on air, you might say. But towards nightfall, as he sat in the bar of the Blue Lion, sucking down a whisky and splash and working his way through 'Locksley Hall', a shadow fell athwart the table and, looking up, he perceived Captain Bradbury.

'Good evening, Widgeon,' said Captain Bradbury.

There is only one word, Freddie tells me, to describe the gallant C.'s aspect at this juncture. It was sinister. His eyebrows had met across the top of his nose, his chin was sticking out from ten to fourteen inches, and he stood there flexing the muscles of his arms, making the while a low sound like the rumbling of an only partially extinct volcano. The impression Freddie received was that at any moment molten lava might issue from the man's mouth, and he wasn't absolutely sure that he liked the look of things.

However, he tried to be as bright as possible.

'Ah, Bradbury!' he replied, with a lilting laugh.

Captain Bradbury's right eyebrow had now become so closely entangled with his left that there seemed no hope of ever extricating it without the aid of powerful machinery.

'I understand that you called at Tudsleigh Court today'

'Oh, rather. We missed you, of course, but, nevertheless, a pleasant time was had by all.'

'So I gathered. Miss Carroway tells me that you have invited her to picnic up the river with you tomorrow.'

'That's right. Up the river. The exact spot.'

'You will, of course, send her a note informing her that you are unable to go, as you have been unexpectedly called back to London.'

'But nobody's called me back to London.'

'Yes, they have. I have.'

Freddie tried to draw himself up. A dashed difficult thing to do, of course, when you're sitting down, and he didn't make much of a job of it.

'I fail to understand you, Bradbury.'

'Let me make it clearer,' said the Captain. 'There is an excellent train in the mornings at twelve-fifteen. You will catch it tomorrow.'

'Oh, yes?'

'I shall call here at one o'clock. If I find that you have not gone, I shall . . . Did I ever happen to mention that I won the Heavyweight Boxing Championship of India last year?'

Freddie swallowed a little thoughtfully.

'You did?'

'Yes.'

Freddie pulled himself together.

'The Amateur Championship?'

'Of course.'

'I used to go in quite a lot for amateur boxing,' said Freddie with a little yawn. 'But I got bored with it. Not enough competition. Too little excitement. So I took on pros. But I found them so extraordinarily brittle that I chucked the whole thing. That was when Bulldog Whacker had to go to hospital for two months after one of our bouts. I collect old china now.'

Brave words, of course, but he watched his visitor depart with emotions that were not too fearfully bright. In fact, he tells me, he actually toyed for a moment with the thought that there might be a lot to be said for that twelve-fifteen train.

It was but a passing weakness. The thought of April Carroway soon strengthened him once more. He had invited her to this picnic, and he intended to keep the tryst even if it meant having to run like a rabbit every time Captain Bradbury hove in sight. After all, he reflected, it was most improbable that a big heavy fellow like that would be able to catch him.

His frame of mind, in short, was precisely that of the old Crusading Widgeons when they heard that the Paynim had been sighted in the offing.

The next day, accordingly, found Freddie seated in a hired rowboat at the landing stage by the Town Bridge. It was a lovely summer morning with all the fixings, such as blue skies, silver wavelets, birds, bees, gentle breezes and what not. He had stowed the luncheon basket in the stern, and was whiling away the time of waiting by brushing up his 'Lady of Shalott', when a voice spoke from the steps. He looked up and perceived the kid Prudence gazing down at him with her grave, green eyes.

'Oh, hullo,' he said.

'Hullo,' said the child.

Since his entry to Tudsleigh Court, Prudence Carroway had meant little or nothing in Freddie's life. He had seen her around, of course, and had beamed at her in a benevolent sort of way, it being his invariable policy to beam benevolently at all relatives and connections of the adored object, but he had scarcely given her a thought. As always on these occasions, his whole attention had been earmarked for the adored one. So now his attitude was rather that of a bloke who wonders to what he is indebted for the honour of this visit.

'Nice day,' he said, tentatively.

'Yes,' said the kid. 'I came to tell you that April can't come.'

The sun, which had been shining with exceptional brilliance, seemed to Freddie to slip out of sight like a diving duck.

'You don't mean that!'

'Yes, I do.'

'Can't come?'

'No. She told me to tell you she's awfully sorry, but some friends of Mother's have phoned that they are passing through and would like lunch, so she's got to stay on and help cope with them.'

'Oh, gosh!'

'So she wants you to take me instead, and she's going to try to come on afterwards. I told her we would lunch near Griggs's Ferry.'

Something of the inky blackness seemed to Freddie to pass from the sky. It was ajar, of course, but still, if the girl was going to join him later . . . And, as for having this kid along, well, even that had its bright side. He could see that it would be by no means a bad move to play the hearty host to the young blighter. Reports of the lavishness of his hospitality and the suavity of his demeanour would get round to April and might do him quite a bit of good. It is a recognised fact that a lover is never wasting his time when he lushes up the little sister.

'All right,' he said. 'Hop in.'

So the kid hopped, and they shoved off. There wasn't anything much in the nature of intellectual conversation for the first ten minutes or so, because there was a fairish amount of traffic on the river at this point and the kid, who had established herself at the steering apparatus, seemed to have a rather sketchy notion of the procedure. As she explained to Freddie after they had gone about halfway through a passing barge, she always forgot which of the ropes it was that you pulled when you wanted to go to the right. However, the luck of the Widgeons saw them through and eventually they came, still afloat, to the unfrequented upper portions of the stream. Here in some mysterious way the rudder fell off, and after that it was all much easier. And it was at this point that the kid, having no longer anything to occupy herself with, reached out and picked up the book.

'Hullo! Are you reading Tennyson?'

'I was before we started, and I shall doubtless dip into him again later on. You will generally find me having a pop at the bard under advisement when I get a spare five minutes.'

'You don't mean to say you like him?'

'Of course I do. Who doesn't?'

'I don't. April's been making me read him, and I think he's soppy.'

'He is not soppy at all. Dashed beautiful.'

'But don't you think his girls are awful blisters?'

Apart from his old crony, the Lady of Shalott, Freddie had not yet made the acquaintance of any of the women in Tennyson's poems, but he felt very strongly that if they were good enough for April Carroway they were good enough for a green-eyed child with freckles all over her nose, and he said as much, rather severely.

'Tennyson's heroines,' said Freddie, 'are jolly fine specimens of pure, sweet womanhood, so get that into your nut, you soulless kid. If you behaved like a Tennyson heroine, you would be doing well.'

'Which of them?'

'Any of them. Pick 'em where you like. You can't go wrong. How much further to this Ferry place?'

'It's round the next bend.'

It was naturally with something of a pang that Freddie tied the boat up at their destination. Not only was this Griggs's Ferry a lovely spot, it was in addition completely deserted. There was a small house through the trees, but it showed no signs of occupancy. The only living thing for miles around appeared to be an elderly horse which was taking a snack on the river bank. In other words, if only April had been here and the kid hadn't, they would have been alone together with no human eye to intrude upon their sacred solitude. They could have read Tennyson to each other till they were blue in the face, and not a squawk from a soul.

A saddening thought, of course. Still, as the row had given him a nice appetite, he soon dismissed these wistful yearnings and started unpacking the luncheon basket. And at the end of about twenty minutes, during which period nothing had broken the stillness but the sound of champing jaws, he felt that it would not be amiss to chat with his little guest.

'Had enough?' he asked.

'No,' said the kid. 'But there isn't any more.'

'You seem to tuck away your food all right.'

'The girls at school used to call me Teresa the Tapeworm,' said the kid with a touch of pride.

It suddenly struck Freddie as a little odd that with July only half over this child should be at large. The summer holidays, as he remembered it, always used to start round about the first of August.

'Why aren't you at school now?'

'I was bunked last month.'

'Really?' said Freddie, interested. 'They gave you the push, did they? What for?'

'Shooting pigs.'

'Shooting pigs?'

'With a bow and arrow. One pig, that is to say. Percival. He belonged to Miss Maitland, the headmistress. Do you ever pretend to be people in books?'

'Never. And don't stray from the point at issue. I want to get to the bottom of this thing about the pig.'

'I'm not straying from the point at issue. I was playing William Tell.'

'The old apple-knocker, you mean?'

'The man who shot an apple off his son's head. I tried to get one of the girls to put the apple on her head, but she wouldn't, so I went down to the pigsty and put it on Percival's. And the silly goop shook it off and started to eat it just as I was shooting, which spoiled my aim and I got him on the left ear. He was rather vexed about it. So was Miss Maitland. Especially as I was supposed to be in disgrace at the time, because I had set the dormitory on fire the night before.'

Freddie blinked a bit.

'You set the dormitory on fire?'

'Yes.'

'Any special reason, or just a passing whim?'

'I was playing Florence Nightingale.'

'Florence Nightingale?'

'The Lady with the Lamp. I dropped the lamp.'

'Tell me,' said Freddie. 'This Miss Maitland of yours. What colour is her hair?'

'Grey.'

'I thought as much. And now, if you don't mind, switch off the childish prattle for the nonce. I feel a restful sleep creeping over me.'

'My Uncle Joe says that people who sleep after lunch have got fatty degeneration of the heart.'

'Your Uncle Joe is an ass,' said Freddie.

How long it was before Freddie awoke, he could not have said. But when he did the first thing that impressed itself upon him was that the kid was no longer in sight, and this worried him a bit. I mean to say, a child who, on her own showing, plugged pigs with arrows and set fire to dormitories was not a child he was frightfully keen on having roaming about the countryside at a time when he was supposed to be more or less in charge of her. He got up, feeling somewhat perturbed, and started walking about and bellowing her name.

Rather a chump it made him feel, he tells me, because a fellow all by himself on the bank of a river shouting 'Prudence! Prudence!' is apt to give a false impression to any passer-by who may hear him. However, he didn't have to bother about that long, for at this point, happening to glance at the river, he saw her body floating in it.

'Oh, dash it!' said Freddie.

Well, I mean, you couldn't say it was pleasant for him. It put him in what you might call an invidious position. Here he was, supposed to be looking after this kid, and when he got home April Carroway would ask him if he had had a jolly day and he would reply: 'Topping, thanks, except that young Prudence went and got drowned, regretted by all except possibly Miss Maitland.' It wouldn't go well, and he could see it wouldn't go well, so on the chance of a last-minute rescue he dived in. And he was considerably surprised, on arriving at what he had supposed to be a drowning child, to discover that it was merely the outer husk. In other words, what was floating there was not the kid in person but only her frock. And why a frock that had a kid in it should suddenly have become a kidless frock was a problem beyond him.

Another problem, which presented itself as he sloshed

ashore once more, was what the dickens he was going to do now. The sun had gone in and a nippy breeze was blowing, and it looked to him as if only a complete change of costume could save him from pneumonia. And as he stood there wondering where this change of costume was to come from he caught sight of that house through the trees.

Now, in normal circs Freddie would never dream of calling on a bird to whom he had never been introduced and touching him for a suit of clothes. He's scrupulously rigid on points like that and has been known to go smokeless through an entire night at the theatre rather than ask a stranger for a match. But this was a special case. He didn't hesitate. A quick burst across country, and he was at the front door, rapping the knocker and calling 'I say!' And when at the end of about three minutes nobody had appeared he came rather shrewdly to the conclusion that the place must be deserted.

Well, this, of course, fitted in quite neatly with his plans. He much preferred to nip in and help himself rather than explain everything at length to someone who might very easily be one of those goops who are not quick at grasping situations. Observing that the door was not locked, accordingly he pushed in and toddled up the stairs to the bedroom on the first floor.

Everything was fine. There was a cupboard by the bed, and in it an assortment of clothes which left him a wide choice. He fished out a neat creation in checked tweed, located a shirt, a tie, and a sweater in the chest of drawers and, stripping off his wet things, began to dress.

As he did so, he continued to muse on this mystery of

the child Prudence. He wondered what Sherlock Holmes would have made of it, or Lord Peter Wimsey, for that matter. The one thing certain was that the moment he was clothed he must buzz out and scour the countryside for her. So with all possible speed he donned the shirt, the tie, and the sweater, and had just put on a pair of roomy but serviceable shoes when his eye, roving aimlessly about the apartment, fell upon a photograph on the mantelpiece.

It represented a young man of powerful physique seated in a chair in flimsy garments. On his face was a rather noble expression, on his lap a massive silver cup, and on his hands boxing-gloves. And in spite of the noble expression he had no difficulty in recognising the face as that of his formidable acquaintance, Captain Bradbury.

And at this moment, just as he had realised that Fate, after being tolerably rough with him all day, had put the lid on it by leading him into his rival's lair, he heard a sound of footsteps in the garden below. And, leaping to the window, he found his worst fears confirmed. The Captain, looking larger and tougher than ever, was coming up the gravel path to the front door. And that door, Freddie remembered with considerable emotion, he had left open.

Well, Freddie, as you know, has never been the dreamy meditative type. I would describe him as essentially the man of action. And he acted now as never before. He tells me he doubts if a chamois of the Alps, unless at the end of a most intensive spell of training, could have got down those stairs quicker than he did. He says the whole thing rather resembled an effort on the part of one of those Indian fakirs who bung their astral bodies about all over the place, going into thin air in Bombay and reassembling the parts two minutes later in Darjheeling. The result being that he reached the front door just as Captain Bradbury was coming in, and slammed it in his face. A hoarse cry, seeping through the woodwork, caused him to shoot both bolts and prop a small chair against the lower panel.

And he was just congratulating himself on having done all that man could do and handled a difficult situation with energy and tact, when a sort of scrabbling noise to the south-west came to his ears, and he realised with a sickening sinking of the heart what it means to be up against one of these Indian Army strategists, trained from early youth to do the dirty on the lawless tribes of the North-Western Frontier. With consummate military skill, Captain Bradbury, his advance checked at the front door, was trying to outflank him by oozing in through the sitting room window.

However, most fortunately it happened that whoever washed and brushed up this house had left a mop in the hall. It was a good outsize mop, and Freddie whisked it up in his stride and shot into the sitting room. He arrived just in time to see a leg coming over the sill. Then a face came into view, and Freddie tells me that the eyes into which he found himself gazing have kept him awake at night ever since.

For an instant, they froze him stiff, like a snake's. Then reason returned to her throne and, recovering himself with a strong effort, he rammed the mop home, sending his adversary base over apex into a bed of nasturtiums. This done, he shut the window and bolted it.

You might have thought that with a pane of glass in between them Captain Bradbury's glare would have lost in volume. This, Freddie tells me, was not the case. As he had now recognised his assailant, it had become considerably more above proof. It scorched Freddie like a death ray.

But the interchange of glances did not last long. These Indian Army men do not look, they act. And it has been well said of them that, while you may sometimes lay them a temporary stymie, you cannot baffle them permanently. The Captain suddenly turned and began to gallop round the corner of the house. It was plainly his intention to resume the attack from another and a less well-guarded quarter. This, I believe, is a common manoeuvre on the North-West Frontier. You get your Afghan shading his eyes and looking out over the *maidan*, and then you sneak up the *pahar* behind him and catch him bending.

This decided Freddie. He simply couldn't go on indefinitely, leaping from spot to spot, endeavouring with a mere mop to stem the advance of a foe as resolute as this Bradbury. The time had come for a strategic retreat. Not ten seconds, accordingly, after the other had disappeared, he was wrenching the front door open.

He was taking a risk, of course. There was the possibility that he might be walking into an ambush. But all seemed well. The Captain had apparently genuinely gone round to the back, and Freddie reached the gate with the comfortable feeling that in another couple of seconds he would be out in the open and in a position to leg it away from the danger zone.

All's well that ends well, felt Freddie.

It was at this juncture that he found that he had no trousers on.

*

I need scarcely enlarge upon the agony of spirit which this discovery caused poor old Freddie. Apart from being the soul of modesty, he is a chap who prides himself on always being well and suitably dressed for both town and country. In a costume which would have excited remark at the Four Arts Ball in Paris, he writhed with shame and embarrassment. And he was just saying: 'This is the end!' when what should he see before him but a two-seater car, which he recognised as the property of his late host.

And in the car was a large rug.

It altered the whole aspect of affairs. From neck to waist, you will recall, Freddie was adequately, if not neatly, clad. The garments which he had borrowed from Captain Bradbury were a good deal too large, but at least they covered the person. In a car with that rug over his lap his outward appearance would be virtually that of the Well-Dressed Man.

He did not hesitate. He had never pinched a car before, but he did it now with all the smoothness of a seasoned professional. Springing into the driving seat, he tucked the rug about his knees, trod on the self-starter, and was off.

His plans were all neatly shaped. It was his intention to make straight for the Blue Lion. Arrived there, a swift dash would take him through the lobby and up the stairs to his room, where no fewer than seven pairs of trousers awaited his choice. And as the lobby was usually deserted except for the growing boy who cleaned the knives and boots, a lad who could be relied on merely to give a cheery guffaw and then dismiss the matter from his mind, he anticipated no further trouble.

But you never know. You form your schemes and run

them over in your mind and you can't see a flaw in them, and then something happens out of a blue sky which dishes them completely. Scarcely had Freddie got half a mile down the road when a girlish figure leaped out of some bushes at the side, waving its arms, and he saw that it was April Carroway.

If you had told Freddie only a few hours before that a time would come when he would not be pleased to see April Carroway, he would have laughed derisively. But it was without pleasure that he looked upon her now. Nor, as he stopped the car and was enabled to make a closer inspection of the girl, did it seem as if she were pleased to see him. Why this should be so he could not imagine, but beyond a question she was not looking chummy. Her face was set, and there was an odd, stony expression in her eyes.

'Oh, hullo!' said Freddie. 'So you got away from your lunch party all right.'

'Yes.'

Freddie braced himself to break the bad news. The whole subject of the kid Prudence and her mysterious disappearance was one on which he would have preferred not to touch, but obviously it had to be done. I mean, you can't go about the place mislaying girls' sisters and just not mention it. He coughed.

'I say,' he said, 'a rather rummy thing has occurred. Odd, you might call it. With the best intentions in the world, I seem to have lost your sister Prudence.'

'So I gathered. Well, I've found her.'

'Eh?'

At this moment, a disembodied voice suddenly came

from inside one of the bushes, causing Freddie to shoot a full two inches out of his seat. He tells me he remembered a similar experience having happened to Moses in the Wilderness, and he wondered if the prophet had taken it as big as he had done.

'I'm in here!'

Freddie gaped. 'Was that Prudence?' he gurgled.

'That was Prudence,' said April coldly.

'But what's she doing there?'

'She is obliged to remain in those bushes, because she has nothing on.'

'Nothing on? No particular engagements, you mean?'

'I mean no clothes. The horse kicked hers into the river.'

Freddie blinked. He could make nothing of this.

'A horse kicked the clothes off her?'

'It didn't kick them off me,' said the voice. 'They were lying on the bank in a neat bundle. Miss Maitland always taught us to be neat with our clothes. You see, I was playing Lady Godiva, as you advised me to.'

Freddie clutched at his brow. He might have known, he told himself, that the moment he dropped off for a few minutes' refreshing sleep this ghastly kid would be up to something frightful. And he might also have known, he reflected, that she would put the blame on him. He had studied Woman, and he knew that when Woman gets into a tight place her first act is to shovel the blame off on to the nearest male.

'When did I ever advise you to play Lady Godiva?'

'You told me I couldn't go wrong in imitating any of Tennyson's heroines.'

'You appear to have encouraged her and excited her

imagination,' said April, giving him a look which, while it was of a different calibre from Captain Bradbury's, was almost as unpleasant to run up against. 'I can't blame the poor child for being carried away.'

Freddie did another spot of brow-clutching. No wooer, he knew, makes any real progress with the girl he loves by encouraging her young sister to ride horses about the countryside in the nude.

'But, dash it . . .'

'Well, we need not go into that now. The point is that she is in those bushes with only a small piece of sacking over her, and is likely to catch cold. Perhaps you will be kind enough to drive her home?'

'Oh, rather. Of course. Certainly.'

'And put that rug over her,' said April Carroway. 'It may save her from a bad chill.'

The world reeled about Freddie. The voice of a donkey braying in a neighbouring meadow seemed like the mocking laughter of demons. The summer breeze was still murmuring through the tree-tops and birds still twittered in the hedgerows, but he did not hear them.

He swallowed a couple of times.

'I'm sorry . . .'

April Carroway was staring at him incredulously. It was as if she could not believe her ears.

'You don't mean to say that you refuse to give up your rug to a child who is sneezing already?'

'I'm sorry . . .'

'Do you realise . . .'

'I'm sorry . . . Cannot relinquish rug . . . Rheumatism . . . Bad . . . In the knee-joints . . . Doctor's orders . . .'

'Mr Widgeon,' said April Carroway imperiously, 'give me that rug immediately!'

An infinite sadness came into Frederick Widgeon's eyes. He gave the girl one long, sorrowful look – a look in which remorse, apology, and a lifelong devotion were nicely blended. Then, without a word, he put the clutch in and drove on, out into the sunset.

Somewhere on the outskirts of Wibbleton-in-the-Vale, when the dusk was falling and the air was fragrant with the evening dew, he managed to sneak a pair of trousers from a scarecrow in a field. Clad in these, he drove to London. He is now living down in the suburbs somewhere, trying to grow a beard in order to foil possible pursuit from Captain Bradbury.

And what he told me to say was that, if anybody cares to have an only slightly soiled copy of the works of Alfred, Lord Tennyson, at a sacrifice price, he is in the market. Not only has he taken an odd dislike to this particular poet, but he had a letter from April Carroway this morning, the contents of which have solidified his conviction that the volume to which I allude is of no further use to owner.

Fixing it for Freddie

'Jeeves,' I said, looking in on him one afternoon on my return from the club, 'I don't want to interrupt you.'

'No, sir?'

'But I would like a word with you.'

'Yes, sir?'

He had been packing a few of the Wooster necessaries in the old kit-bag against our approaching visit to the seaside, and he now rose and stood bursting with courteous zeal.

'Jeeves,' I said, 'a somewhat disturbing situation has arisen with regard to a pal of mine.'

'Indeed, sir?'

'You know Mr Bullivant?'

'Yes, sir.'

'Well, I slid into the Drones this morning for a bite of lunch, and found him in a dark corner of the smoking room looking like the last rose of summer. Naturally I was surprised. You know what a bright lad he is as a rule. The life and soul of every gathering he attends.'

'Yes, sir.'

'Quite the little lump of fun, in fact.'

'Precisely, sir.'

'Well, I made inquiries, and he told me that he had had a quarrel with the girl he's engaged to. You knew he was engaged to Miss Elizabeth Vickers?'

'Yes, sir. I recall reading the announcement in the *Morning Post.*'

'Well, he isn't any longer. What the row was about he didn't say, but the broad facts, Jeeves, are that she has scratched the fixture. She won't let him come near her, refuses to talk on the phone, and sends back his letters unopened.'

'Extremely trying, sir.'

'We ought to do something, Jeeves. But what?'

'It is somewhat difficult to make a suggestion, sir.'

'Well, what I'm going to do for a start is to take him down to Marvis Bay with me. I know these birds who have been handed their hat by the girl of their dreams, Jeeves. What they want is a complete change of scene.'

'There is much in what you say, sir.'

'Yes. Change of scene is the thing. I heard of a man. Girl refused him. Man went abroad. Two months later girl wired him "Come back, Muriel." Man started to write out a reply; suddenly found that he couldn't remember girl's surname; so never answered at all, and lived happily ever after. It may well be, Jeeves, that after Freddie Bullivant has had a few weeks of Marvis Bay he will get completely over it.'

'Very possibly, sir.'

'And, if not, it is quite likely that, refreshed by sea air and good simple food, you will get a brainwave and think up some scheme for bringing these two misguided blighters together again.'

'I will do my best, sir.'

'I knew it, Jeeves, I knew it. Don't forget to put in plenty of socks.'

'No, sir.'

'Also of tennis shirts not a few.'

'Very good, sir.'

I left him to his packing, and a couple of days later we started off for Marvis Bay, where I had taken a cottage for July and August.

I don't know if you know Marvis Bay? It's in Dorsetshire; and, while not what you would call a fiercely exciting spot, has many good points. You spend the day there bathing and sitting on the sands, and in the evening you stroll out on the shore with the mosquitoes. At nine p.m. you rub ointment on the wounds and go to bed. It was a simple, healthy life, and it seemed to suit poor old Freddie absolutely. Once the moon was up and the breeze sighing in the trees, you couldn't drag him from that beach with ropes. He became quite a popular pet with the mosquitoes. They would hang round waiting for him to come out, and would give a miss to perfectly good strollers just so as to be in good condition for him.

It was during the day that I found Freddie, poor old chap, a trifle heavy as a guest. I suppose you can't blame a bloke whose heart is broken, but it required a good deal of fortitude to bear up against this gloom-crushed exhibit during the early days of our little holiday. When he wasn't chewing a pipe and scowling at the carpet, he was sitting at the piano, playing 'The Rosary' with one finger. He couldn't play anything except 'The Rosary', and he couldn't play much of that. However firmly and confidently he started off, somewhere around the third bar a fuse would blow out and he would have to start all over again.

He was playing it as usual one morning when I came in from bathing: and it seemed to me that he was extracting more hideous melancholy from it even than usual. Nor had my senses deceived me.

'Bertie,' he said in a hollow voice, skidding on the fourth crotchet from the left as you enter the second bar and producing a distressing sound like the death-rattle of a sand eel, 'I've seen her!'

'Seen her?' I said. 'What, Elizabeth Vickers? How do you mean, you've seen her? She isn't down here.'

'Yes, she is. I suppose she's staying with relations or something. I was down at the post office, seeing if there were any letters, and we met in the doorway.'

'What happened?'

'She cut me dead.'

He started 'The Rosary' again, and stubbed his finger on a semi-quaver.

'Bertie,' he said, 'you ought never to have brought me here. I must go away.'

'Go away? Don't talk such rot. This is the best thing that could have happened. It's a most amazing bit of luck, her being down here. This is where you come out strong.'

'She cut me.'

'Never mind. Be a sportsman. Have another dash at her.'

'She looked clean through me.'

'Well, don't mind that. Stick at it. Now, having got her down here, what you want,' I said, 'is to place her under some obligation to you. What you want is to get her timidly thanking you. What you want—'

'What's she going to thank me timidly for?'

I thought for a while. Undoubtedly he had put his finger on the nub of the problem. For some moments I was at a loss, not to say nonplussed. Then I saw the way.

'What you want,' I said, 'is to look out for a chance and save her from drowning.'

'I can't swim.'

That was Freddie Bullivant all over. A dear old chap in a thousand ways, but no help to a fellow, if you know what I mean.

He cranked up the piano once more, and I legged it for the open.

I strolled out on the beach and began to think this thing over. I would have liked to consult Jeeves, of course, but Jeeves had disappeared for the morning. There was no doubt that it was hopeless expecting Freddie to do anything for himself in this crisis. I'm not saying that dear old Freddie hasn't got his strong qualities. He is good at polo, and I have heard him spoken of as a coming man at snooker-pool. But apart from this you couldn't call him a man of enterprise.

Well, I was rounding some rocks, thinking pretty tensely, when I caught sight of a blue dress, and there was the girl in person. I had never met her, but Freddie had sixteen photographs of her sprinkled round his bedroom, and I knew I couldn't be mistaken. She was sitting on the sand, helping a small, fat child to build a castle. On a chair close by was an elderly female reading a novel. I heard the girl call her 'aunt'. So, getting the reasoning faculties to work, I deduced that the fat child must be her cousin. It struck me that if Freddie had been there he would probably have tried to work up some sentiment about the kid on the strength of it. I couldn't manage this. I don't think I ever saw a kid who made me feel less sentimental. He was one of those round, bulging kids.

After he had finished his castle he seemed to get bored with life and began to cry. The girl, who seemed to read him like a book, took him off to where a fellow was selling sweets at a stall. And I walked on.

Now, those who know me, if you ask them, will tell you that I'm a chump. My Aunt Agatha would testify to this effect. So would my Uncle Percy and many more of my nearest and – if you like to use the expression – dearest. Well, I don't mind. I admit it. I *am* a chump. But what I do say – and I should like to lay the greatest possible stress on this – is that every now and then, just when the populace has given up hope that I will ever show any real human intelligence – I get what it is idle to pretend is not an inspiration. And that's what happened now. I doubt if the idea that came to me at this juncture would have occurred to a single one of any dozen of the largest-brained blokes in history. Napoleon might have got it, but I'll bet Darwin and Shakespeare and Thomas Hardy wouldn't have thought of it in a thousand years.

It came to me on my return journey. I was walking back along the shore, exercising the old bean fiercely, when I saw the fat child meditatively smacking a jellyfish with a spade. The girl wasn't with him. The aunt wasn't with him. In fact, there wasn't anybody else in sight. And the solution of the whole trouble between Freddie and his Elizabeth suddenly came to me in a flash.

From what I had seen of the two, the girl was evidently fond of this kid: and, anyhow, he was her cousin, so what I said to myself was this: If I kidnap this young heavyweight for a brief space of time: and if, when the girl has got frightfully anxious about where he can have got to, dear old Freddie suddenly appears leading the infant by the hand and telling a story to the effect that he found him wandering at large about the country and practically saved his life, the girl's gratitude is bound to make her chuck hostilities and be friends again.

So I gathered up the kid and made off with him.

Freddie, dear old chap, was rather slow at first in getting on to the fine points of the idea. When I appeared at the cottage, carrying the child, and dumped him down in the sitting room, he showed no joy whatever. The child had started to bellow by this time, not thinking much of the thing, and Freddie seemed to find it rather trying.

'What the devil's all this?' he asked, regarding the little visitor with a good deal of loathing.

The kid loosed off a yell that made the windows rattle, and I saw that this was a time for strategy. I raced to the kitchen and fetched a pot of honey. It was the right idea. The kid stopped bellowing and began to smear his face with the stuff.

'Well?' said Freddie, when silence had set in.

I explained the scheme. After a while it began to strike him. The careworn look faded from his face, and for the first time since his arrival at Marvis Bay he smiled almost happily.

'There's something in this, Bertie.'

'It's the goods.'

'I think it will work,' said Freddie.

And, disentangling the child from the honey, he led him out.

'I expect Elizabeth will be on the beach somewhere,' he said.

What you might call a quiet happiness suffused me, if that's the word I want. I was very fond of old Freddie, and it was jolly to think that he was shortly about to click once more. I was leaning back in a chair on the veranda, smoking a peaceful cigarette, when down the road I saw the old boy returning, and, by George, the kid was still with him.

'Hallo!' I said. 'Couldn't you find her?'

I then perceived that Freddie was looking as if he had been kicked in the stomach.

'Yes, I found her,' he replied, with one of those bitter, mirthless laughs you read about.

'Well, then—?'

He sank into a chair and groaned.

'This isn't her cousin, you idiot,' he said. 'He's no relation at all – just a kid she met on the beach. She had never seen him before in her life.'

'But she was helping him build a sandcastle.'

'I don't care. He's a perfect stranger.'

It seemed to me that, if the modern girl goes about building sandcastles with kids she has only known for five minutes and probably without a proper introduction at that, then all that has been written about her is perfectly true. Brazen is the word that seems to meet the case.

I said as much to Freddie, but he wasn't listening.

'Well, who is this ghastly child, then?' I said.

'I don't know. O Lord, I've had a time! Thank goodness you will probably spend the next few years of your life in Dartmoor for kidnapping. That's my only consolation. I'll come and jeer at you through the bars on visiting days.'

'Tell me all, old man,' I said.

He told me all. It took him a good long time to do it, for he broke off in the middle of nearly every sentence to call me names, but I gradually gathered what had happened. The girl Elizabeth had listened like an iceberg while he worked off the story he had prepared, and then – well, she didn't actually call him a liar in so many words, but she gave him to understand in a general sort of way that he was a worm and an outcast. And then he crawled off with the kid, licked to a splinter.

'And mind,' he concluded, 'this is your affair. I'm not mixed up in it at all. If you want to escape your sentence – or anyway get a portion of it remitted – you'd better go and find the child's parents and return him before the police come for you.'

'Who are his parents?'

'I don't know.'

'Where do they live?'

'I don't know.'

The kid didn't seem to know, either. A thoroughly vapid and uninformed infant. I got out of him the fact that he had a father, but that was as far as he went. It didn't seem ever to have occurred to him, chatting of an evening with the old man, to ask him his name and address. So, after a wasted ten minutes, out we went into the great world, more or less what you might call at random.

I give you my word that, until I started to tramp the place with this child, I never had a notion that it was such a difficult job restoring a son to his parents. How kidnappers ever get caught is a mystery to me. I searched Marvis Bay like a bloodhound, but nobody came forward to claim the infant. You would have thought, from the lack of interest in him, that he was stopping there all by himself in a cottage of his own. It wasn't till, by another inspiration, I thought to ask the sweet-stall man that I got on the track. The sweet-stall man, who seemed to have seen a lot of him, said that the child's name was Kegworthy, and that his parents lived at a place called Ocean Rest.

It then remained to find Ocean Rest. And eventually, after visiting Ocean View, Ocean Prospect, Ocean Breeze, Ocean Cottage, Ocean Bungalow, Ocean Nook and Ocean Homestead, I trailed it down.

I knocked at the door. Nobody answered. I knocked again. I could hear movements inside, but nobody appeared. I was just going to get to work with that knocker in such a way that it would filter through these people's heads that I wasn't standing there just for the fun of the thing, when a voice from somewhere above shouted 'Hi!'

I looked up and saw a round, pink face, with grey whiskers east and west of it, staring down at me from an upper window.

'Hi!' it shouted again. 'You can't come in.'

'I don't want to come in.'

'Because— Oh, is that Tootles?'

'My name is not Tootles. Are you Mr Kegworthy? I've brought back your son.'

'I see him. Peep-bo, Tootles, Dadda can see 'oo.'

The face disappeared with a jerk. I could hear voices. The face reappeared.

'Hi!'

I churned the gravel madly. This blighter was giving me the pip.

'Do you live here?' asked the face.

'I have taken a cottage here for a few weeks.'

'What's your name?'

'Wooster.'

'Fancy that! Do you spell it W-o-r-c-e-s-t-e-r or W-o-o-s-t-e-r?'

'W-o-o—'

'I ask because I once knew a Miss Wooster, spelled W-o-o—'

I had had about enough of this spelling-bee.

'Will you open the door and take this child in?'

'I mustn't open the door. This Miss Wooster that I knew married a man named Spenser. Was she any relation?'

'She is my Aunt Agatha,' I replied, and I spoke with a good deal of bitterness, trying to suggest by my manner that he was exactly the sort of man, in my opinion, who would know my Aunt Agatha.

He beamed down at me.

'This is most fortunate. We were wondering what to do with Tootles. You see, we have mumps here. My daughter Bootles has just developed mumps. Tootles must not be exposed to the risk of infection. We could not think what to do with him. It was most fortunate, your finding the dear child. He strayed from his nurse. I would hesitate to trust him to a stranger, but you are different. Any nephew of Mrs Spenser's has my complete confidence. You must take Tootles into your house. It will be an ideal arrangement. I have written to my brother in London to come and fetch him. He may be here in a few days.'

'May!'

'He is a busy man, of course; but he should certainly be here within a week. Till then Tootles can stop with you. It is an excellent plan. Very much obliged to you. Your wife will like Tootles.'

'I haven't got a wife!' I yelled; but the window had closed with a bang, as if the man with the whiskers had found a germ trying to escape and had headed it off just in time.

I breathed a deep breath and wiped the old forehead.

The window flew up again.

'Hi!'

A package weighing about a ton hit me on the head and burst like a bomb.

'Did you catch it?' said the face, reappearing. 'Dear me, you missed it. Never mind. You can get it at the grocer's. Ask for Bailey's Granulated Breakfast Chips. Tootles takes them for breakfast with a little milk. Not cream. Milk. Be sure to get Bailey's.'

'Yes, but—'

The face disappeared, and the window was banged down again. I lingered a while, but nothing else happened, so, taking Tootles by the hand, I walked slowly away.

And as we turned up the road we met Freddie's Elizabeth.

'Well, baby?' she said, sighting the kid. 'So Daddy found you again, did he? Your little son and I made great friends on the beach this morning,' she said to me.

This was the limit. Coming on top of that interview with the whiskered lunatic, it so utterly unnerved me that she had nodded goodbye and was halfway down the road before I caught up with my breath enough to deny the charge of being the infant's father.

I hadn't expected Freddie to sing with joy when he saw me looming up with child complete, but I did think he might have showed a little more manly fortitude, a little more of the old British bulldog spirit. He leaped up when we came in, glared at the kid and clutched his head. He didn't speak for a long time; but, to make up for it, when he began he did not leave off for a long time.

'Well,' he said, when he had finished the body of his remarks, 'say something! Heavens, man, why don't you say something?'

'If you'll give me a chance, I will,' I said, and shot the bad news.

'What are you going to do about it?' he asked. And it would be idle to deny that his manner was peevish.

'What can we do about it?'

'We? What do you mean, we? I'm not going to spend my time taking turns as a nursemaid to this excrescence. I'm going back to London.'

'Freddie!' I cried. 'Freddie, old man!' My voice shook. 'Would you desert a pal at a time like this?'

'Yes, I would.'

'Freddie,' I said, 'you've got to stand by me. You must. Do you realise that this child has to be undressed, and bathed, and dressed again? You wouldn't leave me to do all that single-handed?'

'Jeeves can help you.'

'No, sir,' said Jeeves, who had just rolled in with lunch; 'I must, I fear, disassociate myself completely from the matter.' He spoke respectfully but firmly. 'I have had little or no experience with children.'

'Now's the time to start,' I urged.

'No, sir; I am sorry to say that I cannot involve myself in any way.'

'Then you must stand by me, Freddie.'

'I won't.'

'You must. Reflect, old man! We have been pals for years. Your mother likes me.'

'No, she doesn't.'

'Well, anyway, we were at school together and you owe me a tenner.'

'Oh, well,' he said in a resigned sort of voice.

'Besides, old thing,' I said, 'I did it all for your sake, you know.'

He looked at me in a curious way, and breathed rather hard for some moments.

'Bertie,' he said, 'one moment. I will stand a good deal, but I will not stand being expected to be grateful.'

Looking back at it, I can see that what saved me from Colney Hatch in this crisis was my bright idea in buying up most of the contents of the local sweetshop. By serving out sweets to the kid practically incessantly we managed to get through the rest of that day pretty satisfactorily. At eight o'clock he fell asleep in a chair; and, having undressed him by unbuttoning every button in sight and, where there were no buttons, pulling till something gave, we carried him up to bed.

Freddie stood looking at the pile of clothes on the floor with a sort of careworn wrinkle between his eyes, and I knew what he was thinking. To get the kid undressed had been simple – a mere matter of muscle. But how were we to get him into his clothes again? I stirred the heap with my foot. There was a long linen arrangement which might have been anything. Also a strip of pink flannel which was like nothing on earth. All most unpleasant.

But in the morning I remembered that there were children in the next bungalow but one, and I went there before breakfast and borrowed their nurse. Women are wonderful, by Jove they are! This nurse had all the spare parts assembled and in the right places in about eight minutes, and there was the kid dressed and looking fit to go to a garden party at Buckingham Palace. I showered wealth upon her, and she promised to come in morning and evening. I sat down to breakfast almost cheerful again. It was the first bit of silver lining that had presented itself to date.

'And, after all,' I said, 'there's lots to be argued in favour of having a child about the place, if you know what I mean. Kind of cosy and domestic, what?'

Just then the kid upset the milk over Freddie's trousers, and when he had come back after changing he lacked sparkle.

It was shortly after breakfast that Jeeves asked if he could have a word in my ear.

Now, though in the anguish of recent events I had rather tended to forget what had been the original idea in bringing Freddie down to this place, I hadn't forgotten it altogether; and I'm bound to say that, as the days went by, I had found myself a little disappointed in Jeeves. The scheme had been, if you recall, that he should refresh himself with sea-air and simple food and, having thus got his brain into prime working order, evolve some means of bringing Freddie and his Elizabeth together again.

And what had happened? The man had eaten well and he had slept well, but not a step did he appear to have taken towards bringing about the happy ending. The only move that had been made in that direction had been made by me, alone and unaided; and, though I freely admit that it had turned out a good deal of a bloomer, still the fact remains that I had shown zeal and enterprise. Consequently I received him with a bit of hauteur when he blew in. Slightly cold. A trifle frosty.

'Yes, Jeeves?' I said. 'You wished to speak to me?'

'Yes, sir.'

'Say on, Jeeves,' I said.

'Thank you, sir. What I desired to say, sir, was this: I attended a performance at the local cinema last night.'

I raised the eyebrows. I was surprised at the man.

With life in the home so frightfully tense and the young master up against it to such a fearful extent, I disapproved of him coming toddling in and prattling about his amusements.

'I hope you enjoyed yourself,' I said in rather a nasty manner.

'Yes, sir, thank you. The management was presenting a super-super-film in seven reels, dealing with life in the wilder and more feverish strata of New York Society, featuring Bertha Blevitch, Orlando Murphy and Baby Bobbie. I found it most entertaining, sir.'

'That's good,' I said. 'And if you have a nice time this morning on the sands with your spade and bucket, you will come and tell me all about it, won't you? I have so little on my mind just now that it's a treat to hear all about your happy holiday.'

Satirical, if you see what I mean. Sarcastic. Almost bitter, as a matter of fact, if you come right down to it.

'The title of the film was *Tiny Hands*, sir. And the father and mother of the character played by Baby Bobbie had unfortunately drifted apart—'

'Too bad,' I said.

'Although at heart they loved each other still, sir.'

'Did they really? I'm glad you told me that.'

'And so matters went on, sir, till came a day when—'

'Jeeves,' I said, fixing him with a dashed unpleasant eye, 'what the dickens do you think you're talking about? Do you suppose that, with this infernal child landed on me and the peace of the home practically shattered into a million bits, I want to hear—'

'I beg your pardon, sir. I would not have mentioned this cinema performance were it not for the fact that it gave me an idea, sir.'

'An idea!'

'An idea that will, I fancy, sir, prove of value in straightening out the matrimonial future of Mr Bullivant. To which end, if you recollect, sir, you desired me to—'

I snorted with remorse.

'Jeeves,' I said, 'I wronged you.'

'Not at all, sir.'

'Yes, I did. I wronged you. I had a notion that you had given yourself up entirely to the pleasures of the seaside and had chucked that business altogether. I might have known better. Tell me all, Jeeves.'

He bowed in a gratified manner. I beamed. And, while we didn't actually fall on each other's necks, we gave each other to understand that all was well once more.

'In this super-super-film, *Tiny Hands*, sir,' said Jeeves, 'the parents of the child had, as I say, drifted apart.'

'Drifted apart,' I said, nodding. 'Right! And then?'

'Came a day, sir, when their little child brought them together again.'

'How?'

'If I remember rightly, sir, he said, "Dadda, doesn't 'oo love Mummie no more?" '

'And then?'

'They exhibited a good deal of emotion. There was what I believe is termed a cut-back, showing scenes from their courtship and early married life and some glimpses of Lovers Through the Ages, and the picture concluded with a close-up of the pair in an embrace, with the child looking on with natural gratification and an organ playing "Hearts and Flowers" in the distance.'

'Proceed, Jeeves,' I said. 'You interest me strangely. I begin to grasp the idea. You mean—?'

'I mean, sir, that, with this young gentleman on the premises, it might be possible to arrange a *dénouement* of a somewhat similar nature in regard to Mr Bullivant and Miss Vickers.'

'Aren't you overlooking the fact that this kid is no relation of Mr Bullivant or Miss Vickers?'

'Even with that handicap, sir, I fancy that good results might ensue. I think that, if it were possible to bring Mr Bullivant and Miss Vickers together for a short space of time in the presence of the child, sir, and if the child were to say something of a touching nature—'

'I follow you absolutely, Jeeves,' I cried with enthusiasm. 'It's big. This is the way I see it. We lay the scene in this room. Child, centre. Girl, L.C. Freddie up stage, playing the piano. No, that won't do. He can only play a little of "The Rosary" with one finger, so we'll have to cut out the soft music. But the rest's all right. Look here,' I said. 'This inkpot is Miss Vickers. This mug with "A Present from Marvis Bay" on it is the child. This penwiper is Mr Bullivant. Start with dialogue leading up to child's line. Child speaks line, let us say, "Boofer lady, does 'oo love Dadda?" Business of outstretched hands. Hold picture for a moment. Freddie crosses L. takes girl's hand. Business of swallowing lump in throat. Then big speech: "Ah, Elizabeth, has not this misunderstanding of ours gone on too long? See! A little child rebukes us!" And so on. I'm just giving you the general outline. Freddie must work up his own part. And we must get a good line for the child. "Boofer lady, does 'oo love Dadda?" isn't definite enough. We want something more—'

'If I might make the suggestion, sir—?'

'Yes?'

'I would advocate the words "Kiss Freddie!" It is short, readily memorised, and has what I believe is technically termed the punch.'

'Genius, Jeeves!'

'Thank you very much, sir.'

'"Kiss Freddie!" it is, then. But, I say, Jeeves, how the deuce are we to get them together in here? Miss Vickers cuts Mr Bullivant. She wouldn't come within a mile of him.'

'It is awkward, sir.'

'It doesn't matter. We shall have to make it an exterior set instead of an interior. We can easily corner her on the beach somewhere, when we're ready. Meanwhile, we must get the kid word-perfect.'

'Yes, sir.'

'Right! First rehearsal for lines and business at eleven sharp tomorrow morning.'

Poor old Freddie was in such a gloomy frame of mind that I decided not to tell him the idea till we had finished coaching the child. He wasn't in the mood to have a thing like that hanging over him. So we concentrated on Tootles. And pretty early in the proceedings we saw that the only way to get Tootles worked up to the spirit of the thing was to introduce sweets of some sort as a sub-motive, so to speak.

'The chief difficulty, sir,' said Jeeves, at the end of the first rehearsal, 'is, as I envisage it, to establish in the young gentleman's mind a connection between the words we desire him to say and the refreshment.'

'Exactly,' I said. 'Once the blighter has grasped the basic fact that those two words, clearly spoken, result automatically in chocolate nougat, we have got a success.'

I've often thought how interesting it must be to be one of those animal-trainer blokes – to stimulate the dawning intelligence and all that. Well, this was every bit as exciting. Some days success seemed to be staring us in the eyeball, and the kid got out the line as if he had been an old professional. And then he would go all to pieces again. And time was flying.

'We must hurry up, Jeeves,' I said. 'The kid's uncle may arrive any day now and take him away.'

'Exactly, sir.'

'And we have no understudy.'

'Very true, sir.'

'We must work! I must say this child is a bit discouraging at times. I should have thought a deaf-mute would have learned his part by now.'

I will say this for the kid, though: he was a trier. Failure didn't damp him. Whenever there was any kind of sweet in sight he had a dash at his line, and kept saying something till he had got what he was after. His chief fault was his uncertainty. Personally, I would have been prepared to risk opening in the act and was ready to start the public performance at the first opportunity, but Jeeves said no.

'I would not advocate undue haste, sir,' he said. 'As long as the young gentleman's memory refuses to act with any certainty, we are running grave risks of failure. Today, if you recollect, sir, he said "Kick Freddie!" That is not a speech to win a young lady's heart, sir.'

'No. And she might do it, too. You're right. We must postpone production.'

But, by Jove, we didn't! The curtain went up the very next afternoon.

It was nobody's fault – certainly not mine. It was just fate. Jeeves was out, and I was alone in the house with Freddie and the child. Freddie had just settled down at the piano, and I was leading the kid out of the place for a bit of exercise, when, just as we'd got on to the veranda, along came the girl Elizabeth on her way to the beach. And at the sight of her the kid set up a matey yell, and she stopped at the foot of the steps.

'Hallo, baby,' she said. 'Good morning,' she said to me. 'May I come up?'

She didn't wait for an answer. She just hopped on to the veranda. She seemed to be that sort of girl. She started fussing over the child. And six feet away, mind you, Freddie smiting the piano in the sitting room. It was a dashed disturbing situation, take it from Bertram. At any minute Freddie might take it into his head to come out on the veranda, and I hadn't even begun to rehearse him in his part.

I tried to break up the scene.

'We were just going down to the beach,' I said.

'Yes?' said the girl. She listened for a moment. 'So you're having your piano tuned?' she said. 'My aunt has been trying to find a tuner for ours. Do you mind if I go in and tell this man to come on to us when he has finished here?'

I mopped the brow.

'Er – I shouldn't go in just now,' I said. 'Not just now, while he's working, if you don't mind. These fellows can't bear to be disturbed when they're at work. It's the artistic temperament. I'll tell him later.'

'Very well. Ask him to call at Pine Bungalow. Vickers is the name . . . Oh, he seems to have stopped. I suppose he will be out in a minute now. I'll wait.'

'Don't you think – shouldn't you be getting on to the beach?' I said.

She had started talking to the kid and didn't hear. She was feeling in her bag for something.

'The beach,' I babbled.

'See what I've got for you, baby,' said the girl. 'I thought I might meet you somewhere, so I bought some of your favourite sweets.'

And, by Jove, she held up in front of the kid's bulging eyes a chunk of toffee about the size of the Albert Memorial!

That finished it. We had just been having a long rehearsal, and the kid was all worked up in his part. He got it right first time.

'Kiss Fweddie!' he shouted.

And the French windows opened and Freddie came out on to the veranda, for all the world as if he had been taking a cue.

'Kiss Fweddie!' shrieked the child.

Freddie looked at the girl, and the girl looked at him. I looked at the ground, and the kid looked at the toffee.

'Kiss Fweddie!' he yelled. 'Kiss Fweddie!'

'What does this mean?' said the girl, turning on me.

'You'd better give it him,' I said. 'He'll go on till you do, you know.'

She gave the kid the toffee and he subsided. Freddie, poor ass, still stood there gaping, without a word.

'What does it mean?' said the girl again. Her face was pink, and her eyes were sparkling in the sort of way, don't you know, that makes a fellow feel as if he hadn't any bones in him, if you know what I mean. Yes, Bertram felt filleted. Did you ever tread on your partner's dress at a dance – I'm speaking now of the days when women wore dresses long enough to be trodden on – and hear it rip and see her smile at you like an angel and say, '*Please* don't apologise. It's nothing,' and then suddenly meet her clear blue eyes and feel as if you had stepped on the teeth of a rake and had the handle jump up and hit you in the face? Well, that's how Freddie's Elizabeth looked.

'*Well?*' she said, and her teeth gave a little click.

I gulped. Then I said it was nothing. Then I said it was

nothing much. Then I said, 'Oh, well, it was this way.' And I told her all about it. And all the while Idiot Freddie stood there gaping, without a word. Not one solitary yip had he let out of himself from the start.

And the girl didn't speak, either. She just stood listening.

And then she began to laugh. I never heard a girl laugh so much. She leaned against the side of the veranda and shrieked. And all the while Freddie, the World's Champion Dumb Brick, standing there, saying nothing.

Well, I finished my story and sidled to the steps. I had said all I had to say, and it seemed to me that about here the stage-direction 'exit cautiously' was written in my part. I gave poor old Freddie up in despair. If only he had said a word it might have been all right. But there he stood, speechless.

Just out of sight of the house I met Jeeves, returning from his stroll.

'Jeeves,' I said, 'all is over. The thing's finished. Poor dear old Freddie has made a complete ass of himself and killed the whole show.'

'Indeed, sir? What has actually happened?'

I told him.

'He fluffed in his lines,' I concluded. 'Just stood there saying nothing, when if ever there was a time for eloquence, this was it. He . . . Great Scott! Look!'

We had come back within view of the cottage, and there in front of it stood six children, a nurse, two loafers, another nurse, and the fellow from the grocer's. They were all staring. Down the road came galloping five more children, a dog, three men and a boy, all about to stare. And on our porch, as unconscious of the spectators as if they had been alone in the Sahara, stood Freddie and his Elizabeth, clasped in each other's arms.

'Great Scott!' I said.

'It would appear, sir,' said Jeeves, 'that everything has concluded most satisfactorily, after all.'

'Yes. Dear old Freddie may have been fluffy in his lines,' I said, 'but his business certainly seems to have gone with a bang.'

'Very true, sir,' said Jeeves.

Comrade Bingo

The thing really started in the Park – at the Marble Arch end – where weird birds of every description collect on Sunday afternoons and stand on soapboxes and make speeches. It isn't often you'll find me there, but it so happened that on the Sabbath after my return to the good old metrop I had a call to pay in Manchester Square, and, taking a stroll round in that direction so as not to arrive too early, I found myself right in the middle of it.

Now that the Empire isn't the place it was, I always think the Park on a Sunday is the centre of London, if you know what I mean. I mean to say, that's the spot that makes the returned exile really sure he's back again. After what you might call my enforced sojourn in New York I'm bound to say that I stood there fairly lapping it all up. It did me good to listen to the lads giving tongue and realise that all had ended happily and Bertram was home again.

On the edge of the mob farthest away from me a gang of top-hatted chappies were starting an open-air missionary service; nearer at hand an atheist was letting himself go with a good deal of vim, though handicapped a bit by having no roof to his mouth; while in front of me there stood a little group of serious thinkers with a banner labelled 'Heralds of the Red Dawn'; and as I came up, one of the heralds, a bearded egg in a slouch hat and a tweed suit, was slipping it into the Idle Rich with such breadth and vigour that I paused for a moment to get an earful. While I was standing there somebody spoke to me.

'Mr Wooster, surely?'

Stout chappie. Couldn't place him for a second. Then I got him. Bingo Little's uncle, the one I had lunch with at the time when young Bingo was in love with that waitress at the Piccadilly bun-shop. No wonder I hadn't recognised him at first. When I had seen him last he had been a rather sloppy old gentleman – coming down to lunch, I remember, in carpet slippers and a velvet smoking jacket; whereas now dapper simply wasn't the word. He absolutely gleamed in the sunlight in a silk hat, morning coat, lavender spats and sponge-bag trousers, as now worn. Dressy to a degree.

'Oh, hallo!' I said. 'Going strong?'

'I am in excellent health, I thank you. And you?'

'In the pink. Just been over to America.'

'Ah! Collecting local colour for one of your delightful romances?'

'Eh?' I had to think a bit before I got on to what he meant. 'Oh, no,' I said. 'Just felt I needed a change. Seen anything of Bingo lately?' I asked quickly, being desirous of heading the old thing off what you might call the literary side of my life.

'Bingo?'

'Your nephew.'

'Oh, Richard? No, not very recently. Since my marriage a little coolness seems to have sprung up.'

'Sorry to hear that. So you've married since I saw you, what? Mrs Little all right?'

'My wife is happily robust. But – er – *not* Mrs Little. Since we last met a gracious Sovereign has been pleased to bestow on me a signal mark of his favour in the shape of – ah – a peerage. On the publication of the last Honours List I became Lord Bittlesham.'

'By Jove! Really? I say, heartiest congratulations. That's the stuff to give the troops, what? Lord Bittlesham?' I said. 'Why, you're the owner of Ocean Breeze.'

'Yes. Marriage has enlarged my horizon in many directions. My wife is interested in horse racing, and I now maintain a small stable. I understand that Ocean Breeze is fancied, as I am told the expression is, for a race which will take place at the end of the month at Goodwood, the Duke of Richmond's seat in Sussex.'

'The Goodwood Cup. Rather! I've got my chemise on it for one.'

'Indeed? Well, I trust the animal will justify your confidence. I know little of these matters myself, but my wife tells me that it is regarded in knowledgeable circles as what I believe is termed a snip.'

At this moment I suddenly noticed that the audience was gazing in our direction with a good deal of interest, and I saw that the bearded chappie was pointing at us.

'Yes, look at them! Drink them in!' he was yelling, his voice rising above the perpetual-motion fellow's and beating the missionary service all to nothing. 'There you see two typical members of the class which has downtrodden the poor for centuries. Idlers! Non-producers! Look at the tall thin one with the face like a motor-mascot. Has he ever done an honest day's work in his life? No! A prowler, a trifler, and a bloodsucker! And I bet he still owes his tailor for those trousers!'

He seemed to me to be verging on the personal, and I

didn't think a lot of it. Old Bittlesham, on the other hand, was pleased and amused.

'A great gift of expression these fellows have,' he chuckled. 'Very trenchant.'

'And the fat one!' proceeded the chappie. 'Don't miss him. Do you know who that is? That's Lord Bittlesham! One of the worst. What has he ever done except eat four square meals a day? His god is his belly, and he sacrifices burnt-offerings to it. If you opened that man now you would find enough lunch to support ten working-class families for a week.'

'You know, that's rather well put,' I said, but the old boy didn't seem to see it. He had turned a brightish magenta and was bubbling like a kettle on the boil.

'Come away, Mr Wooster,' he said. 'I am the last man to oppose the right of free speech, but I refuse to listen to this vulgar abuse any longer.'

We legged it with quiet dignity, the chappie pursuing us with his foul innuendoes to the last. Dashed embarrassing.

Next day I looked in at the club, and found young Bingo in the smoking room.

'Hallo, Bingo,' I said, toddling over to his corner full of *bonhomie*, for I was glad to see the chump. 'How's the boy?'

'Jogging along.'

'I saw your uncle yesterday.'

Young Bingo unleashed a grin that split his face in half.

'I know you did, you trifler. Well, sit down, old thing, and suck a bit of blood. How's the prowling these days?'

'Good Lord! You weren't there!'

'Yes, I was.'

'I didn't see you.'

'Yes, you did. But perhaps you didn't recognise me in the shrubbery.'

'The shrubbery?'

'The beard, my boy. Worth every penny I paid for it. Defies detection. Of course, it's a nuisance having people shouting "Beaver!" at you all the time, but one's got to put up with that.'

I goggled at him.

'I don't understand.'

'It's a long story. Have a martini or a small gore-and-soda, and I'll tell you all about it. Before we start, give me your honest opinion. Isn't she the most wonderful girl you ever saw in your puff?'

He had produced a photograph from somewhere, like a conjurer taking a rabbit out of a hat, and was waving it in front of me. It appeared to be a female of sorts, all eyes and teeth.

'Oh, Great Scott!' I said. 'Don't tell me you're in love again.'

He seemed aggrieved.

'What do you mean – again?'

'Well, to my certain knowledge you've been in love with at least half a dozen girls since the spring, and it's only July now. There was that waitress and Honoria Glossop and—'

'Oh, tush! Not to say pish! Those girls? Mere passing fancies. This is the real thing.'

'Where did you meet her?'

'On top of a bus. Her name is Charlotte Corday Rowbotham.'

'My God!'

'It's not her fault, poor child. Her father had her christened that because he's all for the Revolution, and it seems that the original Charlotte Corday used to go about stabbing oppressors in their baths, which entitles her to consideration and respect. You must meet old Rowbotham, Bertie. A delightful chap. Wants to massacre the *bourgeoisie*, sack Park Lane and disembowel the hereditary aristocracy. Well, nothing could be fairer than that, what? But about Charlotte. We were on top of the bus, and it started to rain. I offered her my umbrella, and we chatted of this and that. I fell in love and got her address, and a couple of days later I bought the beard and toddled round and met the family.'

'But why the beard?'

'Well, she had told me all about her father on the bus, and I saw that to get any footing at all in the home I should have to join these Red Dawn blighters; and naturally, if I was to make speeches in the Park, where at any moment I might run into a dozen people I knew, something in the nature of a disguise was indicated. So I bought the beard, and, by Jove, old boy, I've become dashed attached to the thing. When I take it off to come in here, for instance, I feel absolutely nude. It's done me a lot of good with old Rowbotham. He thinks I'm a Bolshevist of sorts who has to go about disguised because of the police. You really must meet old Rowbotham, Bertie. I tell you what, are you doing anything tomorrow afternoon?'

'Nothing special. Why?'

'Good! Then you can have us all to tea at your flat. I had promised to take the crowd to Lyons' Popular Café after a meeting we're holding down in Lambeth, but I can save money this way; and, believe me, laddie, nowadays, as far as

I'm concerned, a penny saved is a penny earned. My uncle told you he'd got married?'

'Yes. And he said there was a coolness between you.'

'Coolness? I'm down to zero. Ever since he married he's been launching out in every direction and economising on *me*. I suppose that peerage cost the old devil the deuce of a sum. Even baronetcies have gone up frightfully nowadays, I'm told. And he's started a racing-stable. By the way, put your last collar stud on Ocean Breeze for the Goodwood Cup. It's a cert.'

'I'm going to.'

'It can't lose. I mean to win enough on it to marry Charlotte with. You're going to Goodwood, of course?'

'Rather!'

'So are we. We're holding a meeting on Cup day just outside the paddock.'

'But, I say, aren't you taking frightful risks? Your uncle's sure to be at Goodwood. Suppose he spots you? He'll be fed to the gills if he finds out that you're the fellow who ragged him in the Park.'

'How the deuce is he to find out? Use your intelligence, you prowling inhaler of red corpuscles. If he didn't spot me yesterday, why should he spot me at Goodwood? Well, thanks for your cordial invitation for tomorrow, old thing. We shall be delighted to accept. Do us well, laddie, and blessings shall reward you. By the way, I may have misled you by using the word "tea". None of your wafer slices of bread-and-butter. We're good trenchermen, we of the Revolution. What we shall require will be something on the order of scrambled eggs, muffins, jam, ham, cake and sardines. Expect us at five sharp.'

'But, I say, I'm not quite sure—'

'Yes, you are. Silly ass, don't you see that this is going to do you a bit of good when the Revolution breaks loose? When you see old Rowbotham sprinting up Piccadilly with a dripping knife in each hand, you'll be jolly thankful to be able to remind him that he once ate your tea and shrimps. There will be four of us: Charlotte, self, the old man, and Comrade Butt. I suppose he will insist on coming along.'

'Who the devil's Comrade Butt?'

'Did you notice a fellow standing on my left in our little troupe yesterday? Small, shrivelled chap. Looks like a haddock with lung trouble. That's Butt. My rival, dash him. He's sort of semi-engaged to Charlotte at the moment. Till I came along he was the blue-eyed boy. He's got a voice like a foghorn, and old Rowbotham thinks a lot of him. But, hang it, if I can't thoroughly encompass this Butt and cut him out and put him where he belongs among the discards – well, I'm not the man I was, that's all. He may have a big voice, but he hasn't my gift of expression. Thank heaven I was once cox of my college boat. Well, I must be pushing now. I say, you don't know how I could raise fifty quid somehow, do you?'

'Why don't you work?'

'Work?' said young Bingo, surprised. 'What, me? No, I shall have to think of some way. I must put at least fifty on Ocean Breeze. Well, see you tomorrow. God bless you, old sport, and don't forget the muffins.'

I don't know why, ever since I first knew him at school, I should have felt a rummy feeling of responsibility for young Bingo. I mean to say, he's not my son (thank goodness) or my brother or anything like that. He's got absolutely no claim on me at all, and yet a large-sized chunk of my existence seems to be spent in fussing over him like a bally old hen and hauling him out of the soup. I suppose it must be some rare beauty in my nature or something. At any rate, this latest affair of his worried me. He seemed to be doing his best to marry into a family of pronounced loonies, and how the deuce he thought he was going to support even a mentally afflicted wife on nothing a year beat me. Old Bittlesham was bound to knock off his allowance if he did anything of the sort and, with a fellow like young Bingo, if you knocked off his allowance, you might just as well hit him on the head with an axe and make a clean job of it.

'Jeeves,' I said, when I got home, 'I'm worried.'

'Sir?'

'About Mr Little. I won't tell you about it now, because he's bringing some friends of his to tea tomorrow, and then you will be able to judge for yourself. I want you to observe closely, Jeeves, and form your decision.'

'Very good, sir.'

'And about the tea. Get in some muffins.'

'Yes, sir.'

'And some jam, ham, cake, scrambled eggs, and five or six wagonloads of sardines.'

'Sardines, sir?' said Jeeves, with a shudder.

'Sardines.'

There was an awkward pause.

'Don't blame me, Jeeves,' I said. 'It isn't my fault.'

'No, sir.'

'Well, that's that.'

'Yes, sir.'

I could see the man was brooding tensely.

I've found, as a general rule in life, that the things you think are going to be the scaliest nearly always turn out not so bad after all; but it wasn't that way with Bingo's tea party. From the moment he invited himself I felt that the thing was going to be blue round the edges, and it was. And I think the most gruesome part of the whole affair was the fact that, for the first time since I'd known him, I saw Jeeves come very near to being rattled. I suppose there's a chink in everyone's armour, and young Bingo found Jeeves's right at the drop of the flag when he breezed in with six inches or so of brown beard hanging on to his chin. I had forgotten to warn Jeeves about the beard, and it came on him absolutely out of a blue sky. I saw the man's jaw drop, and he clutched at the table for support. I don't blame him, mind you. Few people have ever looked fouler than young Bingo in the fungus. Jeeves paled a little; then the weakness passed and he was himself again. But I could see that he had been shaken.

Young Bingo was too busy introducing the mob to take much notice. They were a very C3 collection. Comrade Butt looked like one of the things that come out of dead trees after the rain; moth-eaten was the word I should have used to describe old Rowbotham; and as for Charlotte, she seemed to take me straight into another and a dreadful world. It wasn't that she was exactly bad-looking. In fact, if she had knocked off starchy foods and done Swedish exercises for a bit, she might have been quite tolerable. But there was too much of her. Billowy curves. Well-nourished, perhaps, expresses it best. And, while she may have had a heart of gold, the thing you noticed about her first was that she had a tooth of gold. I know that young Bingo, when in form, could fall in love with practically anything of the other sex; but this time I couldn't see any excuse for him at all.

'My friend, Mr Wooster,' said Bingo, completing the ceremonial.

Old Rowbotham looked at me and then he looked round the room, and I could see he wasn't particularly braced. There's nothing of absolutely Oriental luxury about the old flat, but I have managed to make myself fairly comfortable, and I suppose the surroundings jarred him a bit.

'Mr Wooster?' said old Rowbotham. 'May I say Comrade Wooster?'

'I beg your pardon?'

'Are you of the movement?'

'Well – er—'

'Do you yearn for the Revolution?'

'Well, I don't know that I exactly yearn. I mean to say, as far as I can make out, the whole hub of the scheme seems to be to massacre coves like me; and I don't mind owning I'm not frightfully keen on the idea.'

'But I'm talking him round,' said Bingo. 'I'm wrestling with him. A few more treatments ought to do the trick.'

Old Rowbotham looked at me a bit doubtfully.

'Comrade Little has great eloquence,' he admitted.

'I think he talks something wonderful,' said the girl, and young Bingo shot a glance of such succulent devotion at her that I reeled in my tracks. It seemed to depress Comrade Butt a good deal too. He scowled at the carpet and said something about dancing on volcanoes.

'Tea is served, sir,' said Jeeves.

'Tea, pa!' said Charlotte, starting at the word like the old war-horse who hears the bugle; and we got down to it.

Funny how one changes as the years roll on. At school, I remember, I would cheerfully have sold my soul for scrambled eggs and sardines at five in the afternoon; but somehow, since reaching man's estate, I had rather dropped out of the habit; and I'm bound to admit I was appalled to a goodish extent at the way the sons and daughter of the Revolution shoved their heads down and went for the foodstuffs. Even Comrade Butt cast off his gloom for a space and immersed his whole being in scrambled eggs, only coming to the surface at intervals to grab another cup of tea. Presently the hot water gave out, and I turned to Jeeves.

'More hot water.'

'Very good, sir.'

'Hey! what's this? What's this?' Old Rowbotham had lowered his cup and was eyeing us sternly. He tapped Jeeves on the shoulder. 'No servility, my lad; no servility!'

'I beg your pardon, sir?'

'Don't call me "sir". Call me Comrade. Do you know what you are, my lad? You're an obsolete relic of an exploded feudal system.'

'Very good, sir.'

'If there's one thing that makes my blood boil in my veins—'

'Have another sardine,' chipped in young Bingo – the

first sensible thing he'd done since I had known him. Old Rowbotham took three and dropped the subject, and Jeeves drifted away. I could see by the look of his back what he felt.

At last, just as I was beginning to feel that it was going on for ever, the thing finished. I woke up to find the party getting ready to leave.

Sardines and about three quarts of tea had mellowed old Rowbotham. There was quite a genial look in his eye as he shook my hand.

'I must thank you for your hospitality, Comrade Wooster,' he said.

'Oh, not at all! Only too glad—'

'Hospitality?' snorted the man Butt, going off in my ear like a depth-charge. He was scowling in a morose sort of manner at young Bingo and the girl, who were giggling together by the window. 'I wonder the food didn't turn to ashes in our mouths! Eggs! Muffins! Sardines! All wrung from the bleeding lips of the starving poor!'

'Oh, I say! What a beastly idea!'

'I will send you some literature on the subject of the Cause,' said old Rowbotham. 'And soon, I hope, we shall see you at one of our little meetings.'

Jeeves came in to clear away, and found me sitting among the ruins. It was all very well for Comrade Butt to knock the food, but he had pretty well finished the ham; and if you had shoved the remainder of the jam into the bleeding lips of the starving poor it would hardly have made them sticky.

'Well, Jeeves,' I said, 'how about it?'

'I would prefer to express no opinion, sir.'

'Jeeves, Mr Little is in love with that female.'

'So I gathered, sir. She was slapping him in the passage.'

I clutched my brow.

'Slapping him?'

'Yes, sir. Roguishly.'

'Great Scott! I didn't know it had got as far as that. How did Comrade Butt seem to be taking it? Or perhaps he didn't see?'

'Yes, sir, he observed the entire proceedings. He struck me as extremely jealous.'

'I don't blame him. Jeeves, what are we to do?'

'I could not say, sir.'

'It's a bit thick.'

'Very much so, sir.'

And that was all the consolation I got from Jeeves.

Bingo has a Bad Goodwood

I had promised to meet young Bingo next day, to tell him what I thought of his infernal Charlotte, and I was mooching slowly up St James's Street, trying to think how the dickens I could explain to him, without hurting his feelings, that I considered her one of the world's foulest, when who should come toddling out of the Devonshire Club but old Bittlesham and Bingo himself. I hurried on and overtook them.

'What ho!' I said.

The result of this simple greeting was a bit of a shock. Old Bittlesham quivered from head to foot like a poleaxed blancmange. His eyes were popping and his face had gone sort of greenish.

'Mr Wooster!' He seemed to recover somewhat, as if I wasn't the worst thing that could have happened to him. 'You gave me a severe start.'

'Oh, sorry!'

'My uncle,' said young Bingo in a hushed, bedside sort of voice, 'isn't feeling quite himself this morning. He's had a threatening letter.'

'I go in fear of my life,' said old Bittlesham.

'Threatening letter?'

'Written,' said old Bittlesham, 'in an uneducated hand and couched in terms of uncompromising menaces. Mr Wooster, do you recall a sinister, bearded man who assailed me in no measured terms in Hyde Park last Sunday?'

I jumped, and shot a look at young Bingo. The only expression on his face was one of grave, kindly concern.

'Why – ah – yes,' I said. 'Bearded man. Chap with a beard.'

'Could you identify him, if necessary?'

'Well, I – er – how do you mean?'

'The fact is, Bertie,' said Bingo, 'we think this man with the beard is at the bottom of all this business. I happened to be walking late last night through Pounceby Gardens, where Uncle Mortimer lives, and as I was passing the house a fellow came hurrying down the steps in a furtive sort of way. Probably he had just been shoving the letter in at the front door. I noticed that he had a beard. I didn't think any more of it, however, until this morning, when Uncle Mortimer showed me the letter he had received and told me about the chap in the Park. I'm going to make inquiries.'

'The police should be informed,' said Lord Bittlesham.

'No,' said young Bingo firmly, 'not at this stage of the proceedings. It would hamper me. Don't you worry, uncle; I think I can track this fellow down. You leave it all to me. I'll pop you into a taxi now, and go and talk it over with Bertie.'

'You're a good boy, Richard,' said old Bittlesham, and we put him in a passing cab and pushed off. I turned and looked young Bingo squarely in the eyeball.

'Did you send that letter?' I said.

'Rather! You ought to have seen it, Bertie! One of the best gent's ordinary threatening letters I ever wrote.'

'But where's the sense of it?'

'Bertie, my lad,' said Bingo, taking me earnestly by the coat-sleeve, 'I had an excellent reason. Posterity may say of me what it will, but one thing it can never say – that I have not a good solid business head. Look here!' He waved a bit of paper in front of my eyes.

'Great Scott!' It was a cheque – an absolute, dashed cheque for fifty of the best, signed Bittlesham, and made out to the order of R. Little.

'What's that for?'

'Expenses,' said Bingo, pouching it. 'You don't suppose an investigation like this can be carried on for nothing, do you! I now proceed to the bank and startle them into a fit with it. Later I edge round to my bookie and put the entire sum on Ocean Breeze. What you want in situations of this kind, Bertie, is tact. If I had gone to my uncle and asked him for fifty quid, would I have got it? No! But by exercising tact— Oh! by the way, what do you think of Charlotte?'

'Well – er—'

Young Bingo massaged my sleeve affectionately.

'I know, old man, I know. Don't try to find words. She bowled you over, eh? Left you speechless, what? *I* know! That's the effect she has on everybody. Well, I leave you here, laddie. Oh, before we part – Butt! What of Butt? Nature's worst blunder, don't you think?'

'I must say I've seen cheerier souls.'

'I think I've got him licked, Bertie. Charlotte is coming to the Zoo with me this afternoon. Alone. And later on to the pictures. That looks like the beginning of the end, what? Well, toodle-oo, friend of my youth. If you've nothing better to do this morning, you might take a stroll along Bond Street and be picking out a wedding present.'

I lost sight of Bingo after that. I left messages a couple of times at the club, asking him to ring me up, but they didn't have any effect. I took it that he was too busy to respond. The Sons of the Red Dawn also passed out of my life, though Jeeves told me he had met Comrade Butt one evening and had a brief chat with him. He reported Butt as gloomier than ever. In the competition for the bulging Charlotte, Butt had apparently gone right back in the betting.

'Mr Little would appear to have eclipsed him entirely, sir,' said Jeeves.

'Bad news, Jeeves; bad news!'

'Yes, sir.'

'I suppose what it amounts to, Jeeves, is that, when young Bingo really takes his coat off and starts in, there is no power of God or man that can prevent him making a chump of himself.'

'It would seem so, sir,' said Jeeves.

Then Goodwood came along, and I dug out the best suit and popped down.

I never know, when I'm telling a story, whether to cut the thing down to plain facts or whether to drool on and shove in a lot of atmosphere, and all that. I mean, many a cove would no doubt edge into the final spasm of this narrative with a long description of Goodwood, featuring the blue sky, the rolling prospect, the joyous crowds of pickpockets, and the parties of the second part who were having their pockets picked, and – in a word, what not. But better give it a miss, I think. Even if I wanted to go into details about the bally meeting I don't think I'd have the heart to. The thing's too recent. The anguish hasn't had time to pass. You see, what happened was that Ocean Breeze (curse him!) finished absolutely nowhere for the Cup. Believe me, nowhere.

These are the times that try men's souls. It's never pleasant to be caught in the machinery when a favourite comes unstitched, and in the case of this particular dashed animal, one had come to look on the running of the race as a pure formality, a sort of quaint, old-world ceremony to be gone through before one sauntered up to the bookie and collected. I had wandered out of the paddock to try and forget, when I bumped into old Bittlesham: and he looked so rattled and purple, and his eyes were standing out of his head at such an angle, that I simply pushed my hand out and shook his in silence.

'Me, too,' I said. 'Me, too. How much did you drop?'

'Drop?'

'On Ocean Breeze.'

'I did not bet on Ocean Breeze.'

'What! You owned the favourite for the Cup, and didn't back it!'

'I never bet on horse racing. It is against my principles. I am told that the animal failed to win the contest.'

'Failed to win! Why, he was so far behind that he nearly came in first in the next race.'

'Tut!' said old Bittlesham.

'Tut is right,' I agreed. Then the rumminess of the thing struck me. 'But if you haven't dropped a parcel over the race,' I said, 'why are you looking so rattled?'

'That fellow is here!'

'What fellow?'

'That bearded man.'

It will show you to what an extent the iron had entered into my soul when I say that this was the first time I had given a thought to young Bingo. I suddenly remembered now that he had told me he would be at Goodwood.

'He is making an inflammatory speech at this very moment, specifically directed at me. Come! Where that crowd is.' He lugged me along and, by using his weight scientifically, got us into the front rank. 'Look! Listen!'

Young Bingo was certainly tearing off some ripe stuff. Inspired by the agony of having put his little all on a stumer that hadn't finished in the first six, he was fairly letting himself go on the subject of the blackness of the hearts of plutocratic owners who allowed a trusting public to imagine a horse was the real goods when it couldn't trot the length of its stable without getting its legs crossed and sitting down to rest. He then went on to draw what I'm bound to say was a most moving picture of a working man's home, due to this dishonesty. He showed us the working man, all optimism and simple trust, believing every word he read in the papers about Ocean Breeze's form; depriving his wife and children of food in order to back the brute; going without beer so as to be able to cram an extra bob on; robbing the baby's money-box with a hatpin on the eve of the race; and finally getting let down with a thud. Dashed impressive it was. I could see old Rowbotham nodding his head gently, while poor old Butt glowered at the speaker with ill-concealed jealousy. The audience ate it.

'But what does Lord Bittlesham care,' shouted Bingo, 'if the poor working man loses his hard-earned savings? I tell you, friends and comrades, you may talk, and you may argue, and you may cheer, and you may pass resolutions, but what you need is Action! Action! The world won't be a fit place for honest men to live in till the blood of Lord Bittlesham and his kind flows down the gutters of Park Lane!'

Roars of approval from the populace, most of whom, I suppose, had had their little bit on blighted Ocean Breeze, and were feeling it deeply. Old Bittlesham bounded over to a large, sad policeman who was watching the proceedings, and appeared to be urging him to rally round. The policeman pulled at his moustache, and smiled gently, but that was as far as he seemed inclined to go; and old Bittlesham came back to me, puffing not a little.

'It's monstrous! The man definitely threatens my personal safety, and that policeman declines to interfere. Said it was just talk! Talk! It's monstrous!'

'Absolutely,' I said, but I can't say it seemed to cheer him up much.

Comrade Butt had taken the centre of the stage now. He had a voice like the Last Trump, and you could hear every word he said, but somehow he didn't seem to be clicking. I suppose the fact was he was too impersonal, if that's the word I want. After Bingo's speech the audience was in the mood for something a good deal snappier than just general remarks about the Cause. They had started to heckle the poor blighter pretty freely, when he stopped in the middle of a sentence, and I saw that he was staring at old Bittlesham.

The crowd thought he had dried up.

'Suck a lozenge,' shouted someone.

Comrade Butt pulled himself together with a jerk, and even from where I stood I could see the nasty gleam in his eye.

'Ah,' he yelled, 'you may mock, comrades; you may jeer

and sneer; and you may scoff; but let me tell you that the movement is spreading every day and every hour. Yes, even amongst the so-called upper classes it's spreading. Perhaps you'll believe me when I tell you that here, today, on this very spot, we have in our little band one of our most earnest workers, the nephew of that very Lord Bittlesham whose name you were hooting but a moment ago.'

And before old Bingo had a notion of what was up, he had reached out a hand and grabbed the beard. It came off all in one piece, and, well as Bingo's speech had gone, it was simply nothing compared with the hit made by this bit of business. I heard old Bittlesham give one short, sharp snort of amazement at my side, and then any remarks he may have made were drowned in thunders of applause.

I'm bound to say that in this crisis young Bingo acted with a good deal of decision and character. To grab Comrade Butt by the neck and try to twist his head off was with him the work of a moment. But before he could get any results the sad policeman, brightening up like magic, had charged in, and the next minute he was shoving his way back through the crowd, with Bingo in his right hand and Comrade Butt in his left.

'Let me pass, sir, please,' he said, civilly, as he came up against old Bittlesham, who was blocking the gangway.

'Eh?' said old Bittlesham, still dazed.

At the sound of his voice young Bingo looked up quickly from under the shadow of the policeman's right hand, and as he did so all the stuffing seemed to go out of him with a rush. For an instant he drooped like a bally lily, and then shuffled brokenly on. His air was the air of a man who has got it in the neck properly.

Sometimes when Jeeves has brought in my morning tea and shoved it on the table beside my bed, he drifts silently from the room and leaves me to go to it: at other times he sort of shimmies respectfully in the middle of the carpet, and then I know that he wants a word or two. On the day after I had got back from Goodwood I was lying on my back, staring at the ceiling, when I noticed that he was still in my midst.

'Oh, hallo,' I said. 'Yes?'

'Mr Little called earlier in the morning, sir.'

'Oh, by Jove, what? Did he tell you about what happened?'

'Yes, sir. It was in connection with that that he wished to see you. He proposes to retire to the country and remain there for some little while.'

'Dashed sensible.'

'That was my opinion, also, sir. There was, however, a slight financial difficulty to be overcome. I took the liberty of advancing him ten pounds on your behalf to meet current expenses. I trust that meets with your approval, sir?'

'Oh, of course. Take a tenner off the dressing table.'

'Very good, sir.'

'Jeeves,' I said.

'Sir?'

'What beats me is how the dickens the thing happened. I mean, how did the chappie Butt ever get to know who he was?'

Jeeves coughed.

'There, sir, I fear I may have been somewhat to blame.'

'You? How?'

'I fear I may carelessly have disclosed Mr Little's identity to Mr Butt on the occasion when I had that conversation with him.'

I sat up.

'What?'

'Indeed, now that I recall the incident, sir, I distinctly remember saying that Mr Little's work for the Cause really seemed to me to deserve something in the nature of public recognition. I greatly regret having been the means of bringing about a temporary estrangement between Mr Little and his lordship. And I am afraid there is another aspect to the matter. I am also responsible for the breaking off of relations between Mr Little and the young lady who came to tea here.'

I sat up again. It's a rummy thing, but the silver lining had absolutely escaped my notice till then.

'Do you mean to say it's off?'

'Completely, sir. I gathered from Mr Little's remarks that his hopes in the direction may now be looked on as definitely quenched. If there were no other obstacle, the young lady's father, I am informed by Mr Little, now regards him as a spy and a deceiver.'

'Well, I'm dashed!'

'I appear inadvertently to have caused much trouble, sir.'

'Jeeves!' I said.

'Sir?'

'How much money is there on the dressing table?'

'In addition to the ten-pound note which you instructed me to take, sir, there are two five-pound notes, three one-pounds, a ten-shillings, two half-crowns, a florin, four shillings, a sixpence, and a halfpenny, sir.'

'Collar it all,' I said. 'You've earned it.'

August

The Great Sermon Handicap

After Goodwood's over, I generally find that I get a bit restless. I'm not much of a lad for the birds and the trees and the great open spaces as a rule, but there's no doubt that London's not at its best in August, and rather tends to give me the pip and make me think of popping down into the country till things have bucked up a trifle. London, about a couple of weeks after that spectacular finish of young Bingo's which I've just been telling you about, was empty and smelled of burning asphalt. All my pals were away, most of the theatres were shut, and they were taking up Piccadilly in large spadefuls.

It was most infernally hot. As I sat in the old flat one night trying to muster up energy enough to go to bed, I felt I couldn't stand it much longer: and when Jeeves came in with the tissue-restorers on a tray I put the thing to him squarely.

'Jeeves,' I said, wiping the brow and gasping like a stranded goldfish, 'it's beastly hot.'

'The weather *is* oppressive, sir.'

'Not all the soda, Jeeves.'

'No, sir.'

'I think we've had about enough of the metrop for the time being, and require a change. Shift ho, I think, Jeeves, what?'

'Just as you say, sir. There is a letter on the tray, sir.'

'By Jove, Jeeves, that was practically poetry. Rhymed, did you notice?' I opened the letter. 'I say, this is rather extraordinary.'

'Sir?'

'You know Twing Hall?'

'Yes, sir.'

'Well, Mr Little is there.'

'Indeed, sir?'

'Absolutely in the flesh. He's had to take another of those tutoring jobs.'

After that fearful mix-up at Goodwood, when young Bingo Little, a broken man, had touched me for a tenner and whizzed silently off into the unknown, I had been all over the place, asking mutual friends if they had heard anything of him, but nobody had. And all the time he had been at Twing Hall. Rummy. And I'll tell you why it was rummy. Twing Hall belongs to old Lord Wickhammersley, a great pal of my guv'nor's when he was alive, and I have a standing invitation to pop down there when I like. I generally put in a week or two some time in the summer, and I was thinking of going there before I read the letter.

'And, what's more, Jeeves, my cousin Claude, and my cousin Eustace – you remember them?'

'Very vividly, sir.'

'Well, they're down there, too, reading for some exam or other with the vicar. I used to read with him myself at one time. He's known far and wide as a pretty hot coach for those of fairly feeble intellect. Well, when I tell you he got *me* through Smalls, you'll gather that he's a bit of a hummer. I call this most extraordinary.'

I read the letter again. It was from Eustace. Claude and Eustace are twins, and more or less generally admitted to be the curse of the human race.

The Vicarage,
Twing, Glos.

DEAR BERTIE – Do you want to make a bit of money? I hear you had a bad Goodwood, so you probably do. Well, come down here quick and get in on the biggest sporting event of the season. I'll explain when I see you, but you can take it from me it's all right.

Claude and I are with a reading party at old Heppenstall's. There are nine of us, not counting your pal Bingo Little, who is tutoring the kid up at the Hall.

Don't miss this golden opportunity, which may never occur again. Come and join us.

Yours,
EUSTACE

I handed this to Jeeves. He studied it thoughtfully.

'What do you make of it? A rummy communication, what?'

'Very high-spirited young gentlemen, sir, Mr Claude and Mr Eustace. Up to some game, I should be disposed to imagine.'

'Yes. But what game, do you think?'

'It is impossible to say, sir. Did you observe that the letter continues over the page?'

'Eh, what?' I grabbed the thing. This was what was on the other side of the last page:

SERMON HANDICAP

RUNNERS AND BETTING

PROBABLE STARTERS

Rev. Joseph Tucker (Badgwick), scratch.

Rev. Leonard Starkie (Stapleton), scratch.

Rev. Alexander Jones (Upper Bingley), receives three minutes.

Rev. W. Dix (Little Clickton-in-the-Wold), receives five minutes.

Rev. Francis Heppenstall (Twing), receives eight minutes.

Rev. Cuthbert Dibble (Boustead Parva), receives nine minutes.

Rev. Orlo Hough (Boustead Magna), receives nine minutes.

Rev. J. J. Roberts (Fale-by-the-Water), receives ten minutes.

Rev. G. Hayward (Lower Bingley), receives twelve minutes.

Rev. James Bates (Gandle-by-the-Hill), receives fifteen minutes.

(The above have arrived.)

Prices. – 5-2, Tucker, Starkie; 3-1, Jones; 9-2, Dix; 6-1, Heppenstall, Dibble, Hough; 100-8 any other.

It baffled me.

'Do you understand it, Jeeves?'

'No, sir.'

'Well, I think we ought to have a look into it, anyway, what?'

'Undoubtedly, sir.'

'Right ho, then. Pack our spare dickey and a toothbrush in a neat brown-paper parcel, send a wire to Lord Wickhammersley to say we're coming, and buy two tickets on the five-ten at Paddington tomorrow.'

The five-ten was late as usual, and everybody was dressing for dinner when I arrived at the Hall. It was only by getting into my evening things in record time and taking the stairs to the dining room in a couple of bounds that I managed to dead heat with the soup. I slid into the vacant chair, and found that I was sitting next to old Wickhammersley's youngest daughter, Cynthia.

'Oh, hallo, old thing,' I said.

Great pals we've always been. In fact, there was a time when I had an idea I was in love with Cynthia. However, it blew over. A dashed pretty and lively and attractive girl, mind you, but full of ideals and all that. I may be wronging her, but I have an idea that she's the sort of girl who would want a fellow to carve out a career and what not. I know I've heard her speak favourably of Napoleon. So what with one thing and another the jolly old frenzy sort of petered out, and now we're just pals. I think she's a topper, and she thinks me next door to a loony, so everything's nice and matey.

'Well, Bertie, so you've arrived?'

'Oh, yes, I've arrived. Yes, here I am. I say, I seem to have plunged into the middle of quite a young dinner party. Who are all these coves?'

'Oh, just people from round about. You know most of them. You remember Colonel Willis, and the Spencers—'

'Of course, yes. And there's old Heppenstall. Who's the other clergyman next to Mrs Spencer?'

'Mr Hayward, from Lower Bingley.'

'What an amazing lot of clergymen there are round here. Why, there's another, next to Mrs Willis.'

'That's Mr Bates, Mr Heppenstall's nephew. He's an assistant master at Eton. He's down here during the summer holidays, acting as *locum tenens* for Mr Spettigue, the rector of Gandle-by-the-Hill.'

'I thought I knew his face. He was in his fourth year at Oxford when I was a fresher. Rather a blood. Got his rowing blue and all that.' I took another look round the table, and spotted young Bingo. 'Ah, there he is,' I said. 'There's the old egg.'

'There's who?'

'Young Bingo Little. Great pal of mine. He's tutoring your brother, you know.'

'Good gracious! Is he a friend of yours?'

'Rather! Known him all my life.'

'Then tell me, Bertie, is he at all weak in the head?'

'Weak in the head?'

'I don't mean simply because he's a friend of yours. But he's so strange in his manner.'

'How do you mean?'

'Well, he keeps looking at me so oddly.'

'Oddly? How? Give me an imitation.'

'I can't in front of all these people.'

'Yes, you can. I'll hold my napkin up.'

'All right, then. Quick. There!'

Considering that she had only about a second and a half to do it in, I must say it was a jolly fine exhibition. She opened her mouth and eyes pretty wide and let her jaw drop sideways, and managed to look so like a dyspeptic calf that I recognised the symptoms immediately.

'Oh, that's all right,' I said. 'No need to be alarmed. He's simply in love with you.'

'In love with me. Don't be absurd.'

'My dear old thing, you don't know young Bingo. He can fall in love with *anybody*.'

'Thank you!'

'Oh, I didn't mean it that way, you know. I don't wonder at his taking to you. Why, I was in love with you myself once.'

'Once? Ah! And all that remains now are the cold ashes? This isn't one of your tactful evenings, Bertie.'

'Well, my dear sweet thing, dash it all, considering that you gave me the bird and nearly laughed yourself into a permanent state of hiccoughs when I asked you—'

'Oh, I'm not reproaching you. No doubt there were faults on both sides. He's very good-looking, isn't he?'

'Good-looking? Bingo? Bingo good-looking? No, I say, come now, really!'

'I mean, compared with some people,' said Cynthia.

Some time after this, Lady Wickhammersley gave the signal for the females of the species to leg it, and they duly stampeded. I didn't get a chance of talking to young Bingo when they'd gone, and later, in the drawing room, he didn't show up. I found him eventually in his room, lying on the bed with his feet on the rail, smoking a toofah. There was a notebook on the counterpane beside him.

'Hallo, old scream,' I said.

'Hallo, Bertie,' he replied, in what seemed to me rather a moody, distrait sort of manner.

'Rummy finding you down here. I take it your uncle cut off your allowance after that Goodwood binge and you had to take this tutoring job to keep the wolf from the door?'

'Correct,' said young Bingo tersely.

'Well, you might have let your pals know where you were.'

He frowned darkly.

'I didn't want them to know where I was. I wanted to

creep away and hide myself. I've been through a bad time, Bertie, these last weeks. The sun ceased to shine—'

'That's curious. We've had gorgeous weather in London.'

'The birds ceased to sing—'

'What birds?'

'What the devil does it matter what birds?' said young Bingo, with some asperity. 'Any birds. The birds round about here. You don't expect me to specify them by their pet names, do you? I tell you, Bertie, it hit me hard at first, very hard.'

'What hit you?' I simply couldn't follow the blighter.

'Charlotte's calculated callousness.'

'Oh, ah!' I've seen poor old Bingo through so many unsuccessful love affairs that I'd almost forgotten there was a girl mixed up with that Goodwood business. Of course! Charlotte Corday Rowbotham. And she had given him the raspberry, I remembered, and gone off with Comrade Butt.

'I went through torments. Recently, however, I've – er – bucked up a bit. Tell me, Bertie, what are you doing down here? I didn't know you knew these people.'

'Me? Why, I've known them since I was a kid.'

Young Bingo put his feet down with a thud.

'Do you mean to say you've known Lady Cynthia all that time?'

'Rather! She can't have been seven when I met her first.'

'Good Lord!' said young Bingo. He looked at me for the first time as though I amounted to something, and swallowed a mouthful of smoke the wrong way. 'I love that girl, Bertie,' he went on, when he'd finished coughing.

'Yes. Nice girl, of course.'

He eyed me with pretty deep loathing.

'Don't speak of her in that horrible casual way. She's an angel. An angel! Was she talking about me at all at dinner, Bertie?'

'Oh, yes.'

'What did she say?'

'I remember one thing. She said she thought you good-looking.'

Young Bingo closed his eyes in a sort of ecstasy. Then he picked up the notebook.

'Pop off now, old man, there's a good chap,' he said, in a hushed, far-away voice. 'I've got a bit of writing to do.'

'Writing?'

'Poetry, if you must know. I wish the dickens,' said young Bingo, not without some bitterness, 'she had been christened something except Cynthia. There isn't a dam' word in the language it rhymes with. Ye gods, how I could have spread myself if she had only been called Jane!'

Bright and early next morning, as I lay in bed blinking at the sunlight on the dressing table and wondering when Jeeves was going to show up with a cup of tea, a heavy weight descended on my toes, and the voice of young Bingo polluted the air. The blighter had apparently risen with the lark.

'Leave me,' I said, 'I would be alone. I can't see anybody till I've had my tea.'

'When Cynthia smiles,' said young Bingo, 'the skies are blue; the world takes on a roseate hue; birds in the garden trill and sing, and Joy is king of everything, when Cynthia smiles.' He coughed, changing gears. 'When Cynthia frowns—'

'What the devil are you talking about?'

'I'm reading you my poem. The one I wrote to Cynthia last night. I'll go on, shall I?'

'No!'

'No?'

'No. I haven't had my tea.'

At this moment Jeeves came in with the good old beverage, and I sprang on it with a glad cry. After a couple of sips things looked a bit brighter. Even young Bingo didn't offend the eye to quite such an extent. By the time I'd finished the first cup I was a new man, so much so that I not only permitted but encouraged the poor fish to read the rest of the bally thing, and even went so far as to criticise the scansion of the fourth line of the fifth verse. We were still arguing the point when the door burst open and in blew Claude and Eustace. One of the things which discourages me about rural life is the frightful earliness with which events begin to break loose. I've stayed at places in the country where they've jerked me out of the dreamless at about six-thirty to go for a jolly swim in the lake. At Twing, thank heaven, they know me, and let me breakfast in bed.

The twins seemed pleased to see me.

'Good old Bertie!' said Claude.

'Stout fellow!' said Eustace. 'The Rev. told us you had arrived. I thought that letter of mine would fetch you.'

'You can always bank on Bertie,' said Claude. 'A sportsman to the fingertips. Well, has Bingo told you about it?'

'Not a word. He's been—'

'We've been talking,' said Bingo hastily, 'of other matters.'

Claude pinched the last slice of thin bread-and-butter, and Eustace poured himself out a cup of tea.

'It's like this, Bertie,' said Eustace, settling down cosily. 'As I told you in my letter, there are nine of us marooned in this desert spot, reading with old Heppenstall. Well, of course, nothing is jollier than sweating up the Classics when it's a hundred in the shade, but there does come a time when you begin to feel the need of a little relaxation; and, by Jove, there are absolutely no facilities for relaxation in this place whatever. And then Steggles got this idea. Steggles is one of our reading party, and, between ourselves, rather a worm as a general thing. Still, you have to give him credit for getting this idea.'

'What idea?'

'Well, you know how many parsons there are round about here. There are about a dozen hamlets within a radius of six miles, and each hamlet has a church and each church has a parson and each parson preaches a sermon every Sunday. Tomorrow week – Sunday the twenty-third – we're running off the great Sermon Handicap. Steggles is making the book. Each parson is to be clocked by a reliable steward of the course, and the one that preaches the longest sermon wins. Did you study the race-card I sent you?'

'I couldn't understand what it was all about.'

'Why, you chump, it gives the handicaps and the current odds on each starter. I've got another one here, in case you've lost yours. Take a careful look at it. It gives you the thing in a nutshell. Jeeves, old son, do you want a sporting flutter?'

'Sir?' said Jeeves, who had just meandered in with my breakfast.

Claude explained the scheme. Amazing the way Jeeves

grasped it right off. But he merely smiled in a paternal sort of way.

'Thank you, sir, I think not.'

'Well, you're with us, Bertie, aren't you?' said Claude, sneaking a roll and a slice of bacon. 'Have you studied that card? Well, tell me, does anything strike you about it?'

Of course it did. It had struck me the moment I looked at it.

'Why, it's a sitter for old Heppenstall,' I said. 'He's got the event sewed up in a parcel. There isn't a parson in the land who could give him eight minutes. Your pal Steggles must be an ass, giving him a handicap like that. Why, in the days when I was with him, old Heppenstall never used to preach under half an hour, and there was one sermon of his on Brotherly Love which lasted forty-five minutes if it lasted a second. Has he lost his vim lately, or what is it?'

'Not a bit of it,' said Eustace. 'Tell him what happened, Claude.'

'Why,' said Claude, 'the first Sunday we were here, we all went to Twing church, and old Heppenstall preached a sermon that was well under twenty minutes. This is what happened. Steggles didn't notice it, and the Rev. didn't notice it himself, but Eustace and I both spotted that he had dropped a chunk of at least half a dozen pages out of his sermon-case as he was walking up to the pulpit. He sort of flickered when he got to the gap in the manuscript, but carried on all right, and Steggles went away with the impression that twenty minutes or a bit under was his usual form. The next Sunday we heard Tucker and Starkie, and they both went well over the thirty-five minutes, so Steggles arranged the handicapping as you see on the card.

You must come into this, Bertie. You see, the trouble is that I haven't a bean, and Eustace hasn't a bean, and Bingo Little hasn't a bean, so you'll have to finance the syndicate. Don't weaken! It's just putting money in all our pockets. Well, we'll have to be getting back now. Think the thing over, and phone me later in the day. And, if you let us down, Bertie, may a cousin's curse—Come on, Claude, old thing.'

The more I studied the scheme, the better it looked.

'How about it, Jeeves?' I said.

Jeeves smiled gently, and drifted out.

'Jeeves has no sporting blood,' said Bingo.

'Well, I have. I'm coming into this. Claude's quite right. It's like finding money by the wayside.'

'Good man!' said Bingo. 'Now I can see daylight. Say I have a tenner on Heppenstall, and cop; that'll give me a bit in hand to back Pink Pill with in the two o'clock at Gatwick the week after next: cop on that, put the pile on Musk-Rat for the one-thirty at Lewes, and there I am with a nice little sum to take to Alexandra Park on September the tenth, when I've got a tip straight from the stable.'

It sounded like a bit out of *Smiles's Self-Help*.

'And then,' said young Bingo, 'I'll be in a position to go to my uncle and beard him in his lair somewhat. He's quite a bit of a snob, you know, and when he hears that I'm going to marry the daughter of an earl—'

'I say, old man,' I couldn't help saying, 'aren't you looking ahead rather far?'

'Oh, that's all right. It's true nothing's actually settled yet, but she practically told me the other day she was fond of me.'

'What!'

'Well, she said that the sort of man she liked was the self-reliant, manly man with strength, good looks, character, ambition, and initiative.'

'Leave me, laddie,' I said. 'Leave me to my fried egg.'

Directly I'd got up I went to the phone, snatched Eustace away from his morning's work, and instructed him to put a tenner on the Twing flier at current odds for each of the syndicate; and after lunch Eustace rang me up to say that he had done business at a snappy seven to one, the odds having lengthened owing to a rumour in knowledgeable circles that the Rev. was subject to hay fever, and was taking big chances strolling in the paddock behind the Vicarage in the early mornings. And it was dashed lucky, I thought next day, that we had managed to get the money on in time, for on the Sunday morning old Heppenstall fairly took the bit between his teeth, and gave us thirty-six solid minutes on Certain Popular Superstitions. I was sitting next to Steggles in the pew, and I saw him blench visibly. He was a little rat-faced fellow, with shifty eyes and a suspicious nature. The first thing he did when we emerged into the open air was to announce, formally, that anyone who fancied the Rev. could now be accommodated at fifteen to eight on, and he added, in a rather nasty manner, that if he had his way, this sort of in-and-out running would be brought to the attention of the Jockey Club, but that he supposed that there was nothing to be done about it. This ruinous price checked the punters at once, and there was little money in sight. And so matters stood till just after lunch on Tuesday afternoon, when, as I was strolling up and down in front of the house with a cigarette, Claude and Eustace came bursting up the drive on bicycles, dripping with momentous news.

'Bertie,' said Claude, deeply agitated, 'unless we take immediate action and do a bit of quick thinking, we're in the cart.'

'What's the matter?'

'G. Hayward's the matter,' said Eustace morosely. 'The Lower Bingley starter.'

'We never even considered him,' said Claude. 'Somehow or other, he got overlooked. It's always the way. Steggles overlooked him. We all overlooked him. But Eustace and I happened by the merest fluke to be riding through Lower Bingley this morning, and there was a wedding on at the church, and it suddenly struck us that it wouldn't be a bad move to get a line on G. Hayward's form, in case he might be a dark horse.'

'And it was jolly lucky we did,' said Eustace. 'He delivered an address of twenty-six minutes by Claude's stopwatch. At a village wedding, mark you! What'll he do when he really extends himself!'

'There's only one thing to be done, Bertie,' said Claude. 'You must spring some more funds, so that we can hedge on Hayward and save ourselves.'

'But—'

'Well, it's the only way out.'

'But I say, you know, I hate the idea of all that money we put on Heppenstall being chucked away.'

'What else can you suggest? You don't suppose the Rev. can give this absolute marvel a handicap and win, do you?'

'I've got it!' I said.

'What?'

'I see a way by which we can make it safe for our nominee. I'll pop over this afternoon, and ask him as a personal favour to preach that sermon of his on Brotherly Love on Sunday.'

Claude and Eustace looked at each other, like those chappies in the poem, with a wild surmise.

'It's a scheme,' said Claude.

'A jolly brainy scheme,' said Eustace. 'I didn't think you had it in you, Bertie.'

'But even so,' said Claude, 'fizzer as that sermon no doubt is, will it be good enough in the face of a four-minute handicap?'

'Rather!' I said. 'When I told you it lasted forty-five minutes, I was probably understating it. I should call it – from my recollection of the thing – nearer fifty.'

'Then carry on,' said Claude.

I toddled over in the evening and fixed the thing up. Old Heppenstall was most decent about the whole affair. He seemed pleased and touched that I should have remembered the sermon all these years, and said he had once or twice had an idea of preaching it again, only it had seemed to him, on reflection, that it was perhaps a trifle long for a rustic congregation.

'And in these restless times, my dear Wooster,' he said, 'I fear that brevity in the pulpit is becoming more and more desiderated by even the bucolic churchgoer, who one might have supposed would be less afflicted with the spirit of hurry and impatience than his metropolitan brother. I have had many arguments on the subject with my nephew, young Bates, who is taking my old friend Spettigue's cure over at Gandle-by-the-Hill. His view is that a sermon nowadays should be a bright, brisk, straight-from-the-shoulder address, never lasting more than ten or twelve minutes.'

'Long?' I said. 'Why, my goodness! you don't call that Brotherly Love sermon of yours *long*, do you?'

'It takes fully fifty minutes to deliver.'

'Surely not?'

'Your incredulity, my dear Wooster, is extremely flattering – far more flattering, of course, than I deserve. Nevertheless, the facts are as I have stated. You are sure that I would not be well advised to make certain excisions and eliminations? You do not think it would be a good thing to cut, to prune? I might, for example, delete the rather exhaustive excursus into the family life of the early Assyrians?'

'Don't touch a word of it, or you'll spoil the whole thing,' I said earnestly.

'I am delighted to hear you say so, and I shall preach the sermon without fail next Sunday morning.'

What I have always said, and what I always shall say, is, that this ante-post betting is a mistake, an error, and a mug's game. You never can tell what's going to happen. If fellows would only stick to the good old S.P. there would be fewer young men go wrong. I'd hardly finished my breakfast on the Saturday morning, when Jeeves came to my bedside to say that Eustace wanted me on the telephone.

'Good Lord, Jeeves, what's the matter, do you think?'

I'm bound to say I was beginning to get a bit jumpy by this time.

'Mr Eustace did not confide in me, sir.'

'Has he got the wind up?'

'Somewhat vertically, sir, to judge by his voice.'

'Do you know what I think, Jeeves? Something's gone wrong with the favourite.'

'Which is the favourite, sir?'

'Mr Heppenstall. He's gone to odds on. He was intending to preach a sermon on Brotherly Love which would have brought him home by lengths. I wonder if anything's happened to him.'

'You could ascertain, sir, by speaking to Mr Eustace on the telephone. He is holding the wire.'

'By Jove, yes!'

I shoved on a dressing gown, and flew downstairs like a mighty, rushing wind. The moment I heard Eustace's voice I knew we were for it. It had a croak of agony in it.

'Bertie?'

'Here I am.'

'Deuce of a time you've been. Bertie, we're sunk. The favourite's blown up.'

'No!'

'Yes. Coughing in his stable all last night.'

'What!'

'Absolutely! Hay fever.'

'Oh, my sainted aunt!'

'The doctor is with him now, and it's only a question of minutes before he's officially scratched. That means the curate will show up at the post instead, and he's no good at all. He is being offered at a hundred to six, but no takers. What shall we do?'

I had to grapple with the thing for a moment in silence.

'Eustace.'

'Hallo?'

'What can you get on G. Hayward?'

'Only four to one now. I think there's been a leak, and Steggles has heard something. The odds shortened late last night in a significant manner.'

'Well, four to one will clear us. Put another fiver all round on G. Hayward for the syndicate. That'll bring us out on the right side of the ledger.'

'If he wins.'

'What do you mean? I thought you considered him a cert, bar Heppenstall.'

'I'm beginning to wonder,' said Eustace gloomily, 'if there's such a thing as a cert in this world. I'm told the Rev. Joseph Tucker did an extraordinarily fine trial gallop at a mothers' meeting over at Badgwick yesterday. However, it seems our only chance. So long.'

Not being one of the official stewards, I had my choice of churches next morning, and naturally I didn't hesitate. The only drawback to going to Lower Bingley was that it was ten miles away, which meant an early start, but I borrowed a bicycle from one of the grooms and tooled off. I had only Eustace's word for it that G. Hayward was such a stayer, and it might have been that he had showed too flattering form at that wedding where the twins had heard him preach; but any misgivings I may have had disappeared the moment he got into the pulpit. Eustace had been right. The man was a trier. He was a tall, rangy-looking greybeard, and he went off from the start with a nice, easy action, pausing and clearing his throat at the end of each sentence, and it wasn't five minutes before I realised that here was the winner. His habit of stopping dead and looking round the church at intervals was worth minutes to us, and in the home stretch we gained no little advantage owing to his dropping his pince-nez and having to grope for them. At the twenty-minute mark he had merely settled down. Twenty-five minutes saw him going strong. And when he finally finished with a good burst, the clock showed thirty-five minutes fourteen seconds. With the handicap which he had been given, this seemed to me to make the event easy for him, and it was with much *bonhomie* and goodwill to all men that I hopped on to the old bike and started back to the Hall for lunch.

Bingo was talking on the phone when I arrived.

'Fine! Splendid! Topping!' he was saying. 'Eh? Oh, we needn't worry about him. Right ho, I'll tell Bertie.' He hung up the receiver and caught sight of me. 'Oh, hallo, Bertie; I was just talking to Eustace. It's all right, old man. The report from Lower Bingley has just got in. G. Hayward romps home.'

'I knew he would. I've just come from there.'

'Oh, were you there? I went to Badgwick. Tucker ran a splendid race, but the handicap was too much for him. Starkie had a sore throat and was nowhere. Roberts, of Fale-by-the-Water, ran third. Good old G. Hayward!' said Bingo affectionately, and we strolled out on to the terrace.

'Are all the returns in, then?' I asked.

'All except Gandle-by-the-Hill. But we needn't worry about Bates. He never had a chance. By the way, poor old Jeeves loses his tenner. Silly ass!'

'Jeeves? How do you mean?'

'He came to me this morning, just after you had left, and asked me to put a tenner on Bates for him. I told him he was a chump, and begged him not to throw his money away, but he would do it.'

'I beg your pardon, sir. This note arrived for you just after you had left the house this morning.'

Jeeves had materialised from nowhere, and was standing at my elbow.

'Eh? What? Note?'

'The Reverend Mr Heppenstall's butler brought it over from the Vicarage, sir. It came too late to be delivered to you at the moment.'

Young Bingo was talking to Jeeves like a father on the subject of betting against the form book. The yell I gave made him bite his tongue in the middle of a sentence.

'What the dickens is the matter?' he asked, not a little peeved.

'We're dished! Listen to this!'

I read him the note:

The Vicarage,
Twing, Glos.

My Dear Wooster – As you may have heard, circumstances over which I have no control will prevent my preaching the sermon on Brotherly Love for which you made such a flattering request. I am unwilling, however, that you shall be disappointed, so, if you will attend divine service at Gandle-by-the-Hill this morning, you will hear my sermon preached by young Bates, my nephew. I have lent him the manuscript at his urgent desire, for, between ourselves, there are wheels within wheels. My nephew is one of the candidates for the headmastership of a well-known public school, and the choice has narrowed down between him and one rival.

Late yesterday evening James received private information that the head of the Board of Governors of the school proposed to sit under him this Sunday in order to judge of the merits of his preaching, a most important item in swaying the Board's choice. I acceded to his plea that I lend him my sermon on Brotherly Love, of which, like you, he apparently retains a vivid recollection. It would have been too late for him to compose a sermon of suitable length in place of the brief address which – mistakenly, in my opinion – he had designed to deliver to his rustic flock, and I wished to help the boy.

Trusting that his preaching of the sermon will supply you with as pleasant memories as you say you have of mine, I remain,

Cordially yours,
F. Heppenstall

PS – The hay fever has rendered my eyes unpleasantly weak for the time being, so I am dictating this letter to my butler, Brookfield, who will convey it to you.

I don't know when I've experienced a more massive silence than the one that followed my reading of this cheery epistle. Young Bingo gulped once or twice, and practically every known emotion came and went on his face. Jeeves coughed one soft, low, gentle cough like a sheep with a blade of grass stuck in its throat, and then stood gazing serenely at the landscape. Finally young Bingo spoke.

'Great Scott!' he whispered hoarsely. 'An SP job!'

'I believe that is the technical term, sir,' said Jeeves.

'So you had inside information, dash it!' said young Bingo.

'Why, yes, sir,' said Jeeves. 'Brookfield happened to

mention the contents of the note to me when he brought it. We are old friends.'

Bingo registered grief, anguish, rage, despair and resentment.

'Well, all I can say,' he cried, 'is that it's a bit thick! Preaching another man's sermon! Do you call that honest? Do you call that playing the game?'

'Well, my dear old thing,' I said, 'be fair. It's quite within the rules. Clergymen do it all the time. They aren't expected always to make up the sermons they preach.'

Jeeves coughed again, and fixed me with an expressionless eye.

'And in the present case, sir, if I may be permitted to take the liberty of making the observation, I think we should make allowances. We should remember that the securing of this headmastership meant everything to the young couple.'

'Young couple? What young couple?'

'The Reverend James Bates, sir, and Lady Cynthia. I am informed by her ladyship's maid that they have been engaged to be married for some weeks – provisionally, so to speak; and his lordship made his consent conditional on Mr Bates securing a really important and remunerative position.'

Young Bingo turned a light green.

'Engaged to be married!'

'Yes, sir.'

There was a silence.

'I think I'll go for a walk,' said Bingo.

'But, my dear old thing,' I said, 'it's just lunchtime. The gong will be going any minute now.'

'I don't want any lunch!' said Bingo.

Noblesse Oblige

On the usually unruffled brow of the Bean who had just entered the smoking room of the Drones Club there was a furrow of perplexity. He crossed pensively to the settee in the corner and addressed the group of Eggs and Crumpets assembled there.

'I say,' he said, 'in re Freddie Widgeon, do any of you chaps happen to know if he's gone off his rocker?'

An Egg asked what made him think so.

'Well, he's out in the bar, drinking Lizard's Breaths . . .'

'Nothing unbalanced about that.'

'No, but his manner is strange. It so happens that at the seminary where he and I were educated they are getting up a fund for some new racquets courts, and when I tackled Freddie just now and said that he ought to chip in and rally round the dear old school, he replied that he was fed to the tonsils with dear old schools and never wished to hear anyone talk about dear old schools again.'

'Rummy,' agreed the Egg.

'He then gave a hideous laugh and added that, if anybody was interested in his plans, he was going to join the Foreign Legion, that Cohort of the Damned in which broken men may toil and die and, dying, forget.'

'Beau Widgeon?' said the Egg, impressed. 'What ho!'

A Crumpet shook his head.

'You won't catch Freddie joining any Foreign Legion,

once he gets on to the fact that it means missing his morning cup of tea. All the same, I can understand his feeling a bit upset at the moment, poor old blighter. Tragedy has come into his life. He's just lost the only girl in the world.'

'Well, he ought to be used to that by this time.'

'Yes. But he also got touched for his only tenner in the world, and on top of that his uncle, old Blicester, has cut his allowance in half.'

'Ah,' said the Egg understandingly.

'It was at Cannes that it all happened,' proceeded the Crumpet. 'Old Blicester had been ordered there by his doctor, and he offered to take Freddie along, paying all expenses. A glittering prospect, of course, for there are few juicier spots than the South of France during the summer season: nevertheless, I warned the poor fish not to go. I told him no good could come of it, pointing out the unexampled opportunities he would have of making some sort of a bloomer and alienating the old boy, if cooped up with him at a foreign resort for a matter of six weeks. But he merely blushed prettily and said that, while nobody was more alive to that possibility than himself, he was jolly well going to go, because this girl was at Cannes.'

'Who was this girl?'

'I forget her name. Drusilla something. Never met her myself. He described her to me, and I received the impression of a sort of blend of Tallulah Bankhead and a policewoman. Fascinating exterior, I mean to say, but full of ideas at variance with the spirit of modern progress. Apparently she sprang from a long line of bishops and archdeacons and what not, and was strongly opposed to all forms of gambling, smoking, and cocktail-drinking. And Freddie had made an excellent first impression on her owing to the fact that he never gambled, never smoked, and looked on cocktails as the curse of the age.'

'Freddie?' said the Egg, startled.

'That was what he had told her, and I consider it a justifiable stratagem. I mean to say, if you don't kid the delicately nurtured along a bit in the initial stages, where are you?'

'True,' said the Egg.

Well, that is how matters stood when Freddie arrived at Cannes, and as he sauntered along the Croisette on the fourth or fifth day of his visit I don't suppose there was a happier bloke in all that gay throng. The sun was shining, the sea was blue, the girl had promised to have tea with him that afternoon at the Casino, and he knew he was looking absolutely his best. Always a natty dresser, today he had eclipsed himself. The glistening trousers, the spotless shirt, the form-fitting blue coat . . . all these combined to present an intoxicating picture. And this picture he had topped off with a superb tie which he had contrived to pinch overnight from his uncle's effects. Gold and lavender in its general colour scheme, with a red stripe thrown in for good measure. Lots of fellows, he tells me, couldn't have carried it off, but it made him look positively godlike.

Well, when I tell you that he hadn't been out on the Croisette ten minutes before a French bloke came up and offered him five hundred francs to judge a Peasant Mothers Baby Competition down by the harbour, where they were having some sort of local fete or jamboree in honour of a saint whose name has escaped me, you will admit that he must have looked pretty impressive. These knowledgeable Gauls don't waste their money on tramps.

Now, you might have thought that as old Blicester, the world's greatest exponent of the one-way pocket, consistently refused to slip him so much as a franc for current expenses, Freddie would have jumped at this chance of making a bit. But it so happened that he had recently wired to a staunch pal in London for a tenner and had received intimation that the sum would be arriving by that afternoon's post. He had no need, accordingly, for the gold the chap was dangling before his eyes. However, he was pleased by the compliment, and said he would most certainly look in, if he could, and lend the binge the prestige of his presence, and they parted on cordial terms.

It was almost immediately after this that the bird in the shabby reach-me-downs accosted him.

His watch having told him that the afternoon post would be in any minute now, Freddie, in his perambulations, had not moved very far from the Carlton, which was the hotel where he and his uncle and also the girl were stopping, and he was manoeuvring up and down about opposite it when a voice at his elbow, speaking in that sort of surprised and joyful manner in which one addresses an old friend encountered in a foreign spot, said:

'Why, hullo!'

And, turning, he perceived the above-mentioned bird in the reach-me-downs as described. A tallish, thinnish chap.

'Well, well, well!' said the bird.

Freddie goggled at him. As far as memory served, he didn't know the blighter from Adam.

'Hullo,' he said, playing for time.

'Fancy running into you,' said the chap.

'Ah,' said Freddie.

'It's a long time since we met.'

'Absolutely,' said Freddie, the persp beginning to start out a bit on the brow. Because if there's one thing that makes a man feel a chump it is this business of meeting ancient cronies and not being able to put a name to them.

'I don't suppose you see any of the old crowd now?' said the chap.

'Not many,' said Freddie.

'They scatter.'

'They do scatter.'

'I came across Smith a few weeks ago.'

'Oh, yes?'

'T. T. Smith, I mean.'

'Oh, T. T. Smith?'

'Yes. Not J. B. I hear J. B.'s gone to the Malay States. T. T's in some sort of agency business. Rather prosperous.'

'That's good.'

'You seem to be doing pretty well, yourself.'

'Oh, fairly.'

'Well, I'm not surprised,' said the chap. 'One always knew you would, even at school.'

The word, Freddie tells me, was like a lifebelt. He grabbed at it. So this was a fellow he had known at school. That narrowed it down a lot. Surely now, he felt, the old brain would begin to function. Then he took another look at the chap, and the momentary exhilaration ebbed. He had not known him from Adam, and he still did not know him from Adam. The situation had thus become more awkward than ever, because the odds were that in the end this fellow was going to turn out to be someone he had shared a study with and ought to be falling on the neck of and swopping reminiscences of the time when old Boko Jervis brought the white rabbit into chapel and what not.

'Yes,' said the chap. 'Even then one could tell that you were bound to go up and up. Gosh, how I used to admire you at the dear old school. You were my hero.'

'What!' yipped Freddie. He hadn't the foggiest that he had been anyone's hero at school. His career there hadn't been so dashed distinguished as all that. He had scraped into the cricket team in his last year, true: but even so he couldn't imagine any of his contemporaries looking up to him much.

'You were,' said the chap. 'I thought you a marvel.'

'No, really?' said Freddie, suffused with coy blushes. 'Well, well, well, fancy that. Have a cigarette?'

'Thanks,' said the chap. 'But what I really want is a meal. I'm right on my uppers. We aren't all like you, you see. While you've been going up and up, some of us have been going down and down. If I don't get a meal today, I don't know what I shall do.'

Freddie tells me the thing came on him as a complete surprise. You might have supposed that a wary bird like him, who has been a member of this club since he came down from Oxford, would have known better, but he insists that he had absolutely no suspicion that a touch was in the air till it suddenly hit him like this. And his first impulse, he says, was to mumble something at the back of his throat and slide off.

And he was just going to when a sudden surge of generous emotion swept over him. Could he let a fellow down who had not only been at school with him but who, when at school, had looked upon him as a hero? Imposs, felt Freddie. There had been six hundred and forty-seven chaps at the old school. Was he to hand the callous mitten to the only one of those six hundred and forty-seven who had admired him? Absolutely out of the q., was Freddie's verdict. A *mille* was the dickens of a sum of money, of course – present rate of exchange a bit more than a tenner – but it would have to be found somehow. *Noblesse oblige,* he meant to say.

And just when the fervour was at its height he recollected this cheque which was arriving by the afternoon post. In the stress of emotion it had quite slipped his mind.

'By Jove!' he said. 'Yes, I can fix you up. Suppose we meet at the Casino a couple of hours from now.'

'God bless you,' said the chap.

'Not at all,' said Freddie.

It was with mixed feelings that he went into the hotel to see if the post had come. On the one hand, there was the solemn anguish of parting with a tenner which he had earmarked for quite a different end. On the other, there was the quiet chestiness induced by the realisation that here he had been jogging along through the world, not thinking such a frightful lot of himself, and all the while in the background was this bloke treasuring his memory and saying to himself: 'Ah, if we could all be like Freddie Widgeon!' Cheap at a tenner, he told himself, the sensation of spiritual yeastiness which this reflection gave him.

All the same, he wished the chap could have done with five, because there was a bookie in London to whom he had owed a fiver for some months now and recent correspondence had shown that this hell-hound was on the verge of becoming a bit unpleasant. Until this episode had occurred, he had fully intended to send the man thirty bob or so, to sweeten him. Now, of course, this was out of the question. The entire sum must go unbroken to this old school-fellow whose name he wished he could remember.

Spivis? . . . Brent? . . . Jerningham? . . . Fosway? . . .

No.

Brewster? . . . Goggs? . . . Bootle? . . . Finsbury? . . .

No.

He gave it up and went to the desk. The letter was there, and in it the cheque. The very decent johnny behind the counter cashed it for him without a murmur, and he was just gathering up the loot when somebody behind him said 'Ah!'

Now, in the word 'Ah!' you might say that there is nothing really to fill a fellow with a nameless dread. Nevertheless, that is what this 'Ah!' filled Freddie with. For he had recognised the voice. It was none other than that of the bookie to whom he owed the fiver. That is the trouble about Cannes in August – it becomes very mixed. You get your Freddie Widgeons there – splendid chaps who were worshipped by their schoolmates – and you also get men like this bookie. All sorts, if you follow me, from the highest to the lowest.

From the moment when he turned and gazed into the fellow's steely eyes, Freddie tells me he hadn't a hope. But he did his best.

'Hullo, Mr McIntosh!' he said. 'You here? Well, well, well! Ha, ha!'

'Yes,' said the bookie.

'I never thought I should run into you in these parts.'

'You have,' the bookie assured him.

'Come down here for a nice holiday, what? Taking a perfect rest, eh? Going to bask in the lovely sunshine and put all thoughts of business completely out of your head, yes?'

'Well, not quite all,' said the bookie, producing the little black book. 'Now, let me see, Mr Widgeon . . . Ah, yes, five pounds on Marmalade to cop in the second at Ally Pally. Should have won by the form book, but ran third. Well, that's life, isn't it? I think it comes to a little more than four hundred and fifty francs, really, but we'll call it four-fifty. One doesn't want any haggling among friends.'

'I'm awfully sorry,' said Freddie. 'Some other time, what? I can't manage it just at the moment. I haven't any money.'

'No?'

'I mean to say, I want this for a poor man.'

'So do I,' said the bookie.

And the upshot and outcome, of course, was that poor old Freddie had to brass up. You can't appeal to a bookie's better feelings, because he hasn't any. He pushed over the four hundred and fifty.

'Oh, very well,' he said. 'Here you are. And let me tell you, Mr McIntosh, that the curse of the Widgeons goes with it.'

'Right,' said the bookie.

So there Freddie was with five hundred and fifty francs in his kick, and needing a thousand.

I must say I wouldn't have blamed him if, in these circs, he had decided to give a miss to the old school-friend. Allowing fifty francs for lushing up the girl Drusilla at the tea table, he would in that case have had a cool five hundred with which to plunge into the variegated pleasures of Cannes in the summertime. A very nice sum, indeed.

But, though tempted, he was strong. This old admirer of his – Muttlebury? . . . Jukes? . . . Ferguson? . . . Braithwaite? . . . – had said that he needed a *mille,* and a *mille* he must have.

But how to raise the other five hundred? That was the prob.

For some moments he toyed with mad schemes like trying to borrow it from his uncle. Then it suddenly flashed upon him that the sum he required was the exact amount which the intelligent Gaul had offered him if he would come down to the jamboree by the harbour and judge the Peasant Mothers Baby Competition.

Now, Freddie's views on babies are well defined. He is prepared to cope with them singly, if all avenues of escape are blocked and there is a nurse or mother standing by to lend aid in case of sudden hiccoughs, retchings, or nauseas. Under such conditions he has even been known to offer his watch to one related by ties of blood in order that the little stranger might listen to the tick-tick. But it would be paltering with the truth to say that he likes babies. They give him, he says, a sort of grey feeling. He resents their cold stare and the supercilious and upstage way in which they dribble out of the corner of their mouths on seeing him. Eyeing them, he is conscious of doubts as to whether Man can really be Nature's last word.

This being so, you will readily understand that, even for so stupendous a fee as five hundred francs, he shrank from being closeted with a whole platoon of the little brutes.

And I think it is greatly to his credit that after only the shortest of internal struggles he set his teeth, clenched his fists, and made for the harbour with a steady step. How different it would all have been, he felt wistfully, if he were being called upon to judge a contest of Bathing Belles.

There was the possibility, of course, that in the interval since he had met the intelligent Gaul the post of judge would have been filled. But no. The fellow welcomed him with open arms and led him joyfully into a sort of marquee place crowded with as tough-looking a bunch of mothers and as hard-boiled a gaggle of issue as anybody could wish to see. He made a short speech in French which was much too rapid for Freddie to follow, and the mothers all applauded, and the babies all yelled, and then he was conducted along the line, with all the mothers glaring at him in an intimidating way, as much as to warn him that if he dared give the prize to anybody else's offspring he had jolly well better look out for himself. Dashed unpleasant, the whole thing, Freddie tells me, and I see his viewpoint.

He kept his head, however. This was the first time he had ever been let in for anything of this nature, but a sort of instinct told him to adopt the policy followed by all experienced judges at these affairs – viz. to ignore the babies absolutely and concentrate entirely on the mothers. So many points for ferocity of demeanour, that is to say, and so many for possibility of knife concealed in stocking, and so on and so forth. You ask any curate how he works the gaff at the annual Baby Competition in his village, and he will tell you that these, broadly, are the lines on which he goes.

There were, it seemed, to be three prizes and about the

first one there could be no question at all. It went automatically to a heavyweight mother with beetling eyebrows who looked as if she had just come from doing a spot of knitting at the foot of the guillotine. Just to see those eyebrows, Freddie tells me, was to hear the heads dropping into the basket, and he had no hesitation, as I say, in declaring her progeny the big winner.

The second and third prizes were a bit more difficult, but after some consideration he awarded them to two other female pluguglies with suspicious bulges in their stockings. This done, he sidled up to the intelligent Gaul to receive his wage, doing his best not to listen to the angry mutterings from the losers which were already beginning to rumble through the air.

The brand of English which this bird affected was not of the best, and it took Freddie some moments to get his drift. When he did, he reeled and came very near clutching for support at the other's beard. Because what the Gaul was endeavouring to communicate was the fact that, so far from being paid five hundred francs for his services, Freddie was expected to cough up that sum.

It was an old Cannes custom, the man explained, for some rich visiting milord to take on the providing of the prizes on this occasion, his reward being the compliment implied in the invitation.

He said that when he had perceived Freddie promenading himself on the Croisette he had been so struck by his appearance of the most elegant and his altogether of a superbness so unparalleled that he had picked him without another look at the field.

Well, dashed gratifying, of course, from one point of

view and a handsome tribute to the way Freddie had got himself up that day: but it was not long before he was looking in a tentative sort of manner at the nearest exit. And I think that, had that exit been just a shade closer, he would have put his fortune to the test, to win or lose it all.

But to edge out and leg it would have taken that ten seconds or so which make all the difference. Those mothers would have been on his very heels, and the prospect of sprinting along the streets of Cannes under such conditions was too much for him. Quite possibly he might have shown a flash of speed sufficient to shake off their challenge, but it would have been a very close thing, with nothing in it for the first five hundred yards or so, and he could not have failed to make himself conspicuous.

So, with a heavy sigh, he forked out the five h., and tottered into the open. So sombre was his mood that he scarcely heard the mutterings of the disappointed losers, who were now calling him an *espèce de* something and hinting rather broadly in the local *patois* that he had been fixed.

And the thing that weighed so heavily upon him was the thought that, unless some miracle occurred, he would now be forced to let down his old chum Bulstrode, Waters, Parsloe, Bingley, Murgatroyd, or whatever the blighter's name might be.

He had told the fellow to meet him outside the Casino – which in summer at Cannes is, of course, the Palm Beach at the far end of the Croisette – so he directed his steps thither. And jolly halting steps they were, he tells me. The urge to give the school-chum his *mille* had now become with Frederick Widgeon a regular obsession. He felt that his honour was involved. And he shuddered at the thought of the meeting that lay before him. Up the chap would come frisking, with his hand outstretched and the light of expectation in his eyes, and what would ensue? The miss-in-balk.

He groaned in spirit. He could see the other's pained and disillusioned look. He could hear him saying to himself: 'This is not the old Widgeon form. The boy I admired so much in the dear old days of school would not have foozled a small loan like this. A pretty serious change for the worse there must have been in Frederick W. since the time when we used to sport together in the shade of the old cloisters.' The thought was agony.

All the way along the Croisette he pondered deeply. To the gay throng around him he paid no attention. There were girls within a biscuit-throw in bathing suits which began at the base of the spine and ended two inches lower down, but he did not give them so much as a glance. His whole being was absorbed in this reverie of his.

By the time he reached the Casino, he had made up his mind. Visionary, chimerical though the idea would have seemed to anybody who knew the latter and his views on parting with cash, he had resolved to make the attempt to borrow a thousand francs from his uncle. With this end, therefore, he proceeded to the Baccarat rooms. The other, he knew, was always to be found at this hour seated at one of the three-louis chemmy tables. For, definite though the Earl of Blicester's creed was on the subject of his nephew gambling, he himself enjoyed a modest flutter.

He found the old boy, as expected, hunched up over the green cloth. At the moment of Freddie's arrival he was just scooping in three pink counters with a holy light of exaltation on his face. For there was nothing spacious and sensational about Lord Blicester's methods of play. He was not one of those punters you read about in the papers who rook the Greek Syndicate of three million francs in an evening. If he came out one-and-sixpence ahead of the game, he considered his day well spent.

It looked to Freddie, examining the counters in front of his relative, as if the moment were propitious for a touch. There must have been fully five bob's worth of them, which meant that the other had struck one of those big winning streaks which come to all gamblers sooner or later. His mood, accordingly, ought to be sunny.

'I say, Uncle,' he said, sidling up.

'Get to hell out of here,' replied Lord Blicester, not half so sunny as might have been expected. 'Banco!' he cried, and a second later was gathering in another sixty francs.

'I say, Uncle . . .'

'Well, what is it?'

'I say, Uncle, will you lend me . . .'

'No.'

'I only want . . .'

'Well, you won't get it.'

'It's not for myself . . .'

'Go to blazes,' said old Blicester.

Freddie receded. Though he had never really expected any solid results, his heart was pretty well bowed down with weight of care. He had shot his bolt. His last source of supply had proved a washout.

He looked at his watch. About now, the old schoolmate would be approaching the tryst. He would be walking – so firm would be his faith in his hero – with elastic steps.

Possibly he would even be humming some gay air. Had he a stick? Freddie could not remember. But if he had he would be twirling it.

And then would come the meeting . . . the confession of failure . . . the harsh awakening and the brutal shattering of dreams . . .

It was at this moment that he was roused from his meditations by the one word in the French language capable of bringing him back to the world.

'*Un mille.*'

It was the voice of the croupier, chanting his litany.

'*Cinquante louis à la banque. Un banco de mille.*'

I can't do the dialect, you understand, but what he meant was that somebody holding the bank had run it up to a thousand francs. And Freddie, waking with a start, perceived that a pile of assorted counters, presumably amounting to that sum, now lay in the centre of the board.

Well, a thousand francs isn't much, of course, to the nibs at the big tables, but among the three-louis-minimum lizards if you run a bank up to a *mille* you make a pretty big sensation. There was quite a crowd round the table now, and over their heads Freddie could see that pile of counters, and it seemed to smile up at him.

For an instant he hesitated, while his past life seemed to flit before him as if he had been a drowning man. Then he heard a voice croak '*Banco*' and there seemed something oddly familiar about it, and he suddenly realised that it was his own. He had taken the plunge.

It was a pretty agonising moment for old Freddie, as you may well imagine. I mean to say, he had bancoed this fellow, whoever he was, and if he happened to lose the *coup* all he would have to offer him would be fifty francs and his apologies. There would, he could not conceal it from himself, be the devil of a row. What exactly, he wondered, did they do to you at these French casinos if you lost and couldn't pay up? Something sticky, beyond a question. Hardly the guillotine, perhaps, and possibly not even Devil's Island. But something nasty, undoubtedly. With a dim recollection of a movie he had once seen, he pictured himself in the middle of a hollow square formed by punters and croupiers with the managing director of the place snipping off his coat buttons.

Or was it trouser buttons? No, in a mixed company like this it would hardly be trouser buttons. Still, even coat buttons would be bad enough.

And, if the moment was agonising for Freddie, it was scarcely less so for his uncle, Lord Blicester. It was his bank which had been running up to such impressive proportions, and he was now faced with the problem of whether to take a chance on doubling his loot or to pass the hand.

Lord Blicester was a man who, when in the feverish atmosphere of the gaming rooms, believed in small profits and quick returns. He was accustomed to start his bank at the minimum, run it twice with his heart in his mouth, and then pass. But on the present occasion he had been carried away to such an extent that he had worked the kitty up to a solid *mille*. It was a fearful sum to risk losing. On the other hand, suppose he didn't lose? Someone in the crowd outside his line of vision had said, 'Banco!' and with a bit of luck he might be two *mille* up instead of one, just like that.

What to do? It was a man's crossroads.

In the end, he decided to take the big chance. And it was as the croupier pushed the cards along the table and the crowd opened up a bit to let the challenger get at them that he recognised in the individual leaning forward his nephew Frederick.

'Brzzghl!' gasped Lord Blicester. 'Gor! Woosh!'

What he meant was that the deal was off because the young hound who had just come into the picture was his late sister's son Frederick Fotheringay Widgeon, who had never had a penny except what he allowed him and certainly hadn't a hundredth part of the sum necessary for cashing in if he lost. But he hadn't made himself clear enough. The next moment, with infinite emotion, Freddie was chucking down a nine and the croupier was pushing all old Blicester's hard-earned at him.

It was as he was gathering it up that he caught the old boy's eye. The effect of it was to cause him to spill a hundred-franc counter, two louis counters, and a five-franc counter. And he had just straightened himself after picking these up, when a voice spoke.

'Good afternoon, Mr Widgeon,' said the girl Drusilla.

'Oh, ah,' said Freddie.

You couldn't say it was a frightfully bright remark, but he considers it was dashed good going to utter even as much as that. In the matter of eyes, he tells me, there was not much to choose between this girl's and his uncle's. Their gazes differed in quality, it is true, because, whereas old Blicester's had been piping hot and had expressed hate, fury and the desire to skin, the girl Drusilla's was right off the ice and conveyed a sort of sick disillusionment and a loathing contempt. But as to which he would rather have met on a dark night down a lonely alley, Freddie couldn't have told you.

'You appear to have been lucky,' said this Drusilla.

'Oh, ah,' said Freddie.

He looked quickly away, and ran up against old Blicester's eye again. Then he looked back and caught Drusilla's. The whole situation, he tells me, was extraordinarily like that of an African explorer who, endeavouring to ignore one of the local serpents, finds himself exchanging glances with a man-eating tiger.

The girl was now wrinkling her nose as if a particularly foul brand of poison gas had begun to permeate the Casino and she was standing nearest it.

'I must confess I am a little surprised,' she said, 'because I was under the impression that you had told me that you never gambled.'

'Oh, ah,' said Freddie.

'If I remember rightly, you described gambling as a cancer in the body politic.'

'Oh, ah,' said Freddie.

She took a final sniff, as if she had been hoping against hope that he was not a main sewer and was now reluctantly compelled to realise that he was.

'I am afraid I shall not be able to come to tea this afternoon. Goodbye, Mr Widgeon.'

'Oh, ah,' said Freddie.

He watched her go, knowing that she was going out of his life and that any chance of the scent of orange blossoms and the amble up the aisle with the organ playing 'O Perfect Love' was now blue round the edges; and it was as if there was a dull weight pressing on him.

And then he found that there was a dull weight pressing on him, viz. that of all the counters he was loaded down with. And it was at this point that it dawned upon him that, though he had in prospect an interview with old Blicester which would undoubtedly lower all previous records, and though a life's romance had gone phut, he was at least in a position to satisfy the *noblesse oblige* of the Widgeons.

So he tottered to the cashier's desk and changed the stuff into a pink note, and then he tottered out of the Casino, and was tottering down the steps when he perceived the school-friend in the immediate offing, looking bright and expectant.

'Here I am,' said the school-friend.

'Oh, ah,' said Freddie.

And with a supreme gesture of resignation he pressed the *mille* into the man's hand.

There was never any doubt about the chap taking it. He took it like a trout sucking down a mayfly and shoved it away in a pocket at the back of his costume. But what was odd was that he seemed stupefied. His eyes grew round, his jaw fell, and he stared at Freddie in awestruck amazement.

'I say,' he said, 'don't think I'm raising any objections or anything of that sort, because I'm not. I am heart and soul in this scheme of giving me a *mille*. But it's an awful lot, isn't it? I don't mind telling you that what I had been sketching out as more or less the sum that was going to change hands was something in the nature of fifty francs.'

Freddie was a bit surprised too. He couldn't make this out.

'But you said you had to have a *mille*.'

'And a meal is just what I'm going to have,' replied the

chap, enthusiastically. 'I haven't had a bite to eat since breakfast.'

Freddie was stunned. He isn't what you would call a quick thinker, but he was beginning to see that there had been a confusion of ideas.

'Do you mean to tell me,' he cried, 'that when you said a *mille* what you meant was a meal?'

'I don't suppose anyone ever meant a meal more,' said the chap. He stood awhile in thought. '*Hors d'oeuvres*, I think, to start with,' he went on, passing his tongue meditatively over his lips. 'Then perhaps a touch of clear soup, followed by some fish of the country and a good steak *minute* with fried potatoes and a salad. Cheese, of course, and the usual etceteras, and then coffee, liqueur, and a cigar to wind up with. Yes, you may certainly take it as official that I intend to have a meal. Ah, yes, and I was forgetting. A bot of some nice, dry wine to wash things down. Yes, yes, yes, to be sure. You see this stomach?' he said, patting it. 'Here stands a stomach that is scheduled in about a quarter of an hour to get the surprise of its young life.'

Freddie saw it all now, and the irony of the situation seemed to hit him like a bit of lead piping on the base of the skull. Just because of this footling business of having words in one language which meant something quite different in another language – a thing which could so easily have been prevented by the responsible heads of the French and English nations getting together across a round table and coming to some sensible arrangement – here he was deeper in the soup than he had ever been in the whole course of his career.

He tells me he chafed, and I don't blame him. Anybody

would have chafed in the circs. For about half a minute he had half a mind to leap at the chap and wrench the *mille* out of him and substitute for it the fifty francs which he had been anticipating.

Then the old *noblesse oblige* spirit awoke once more. He might be in the soup, he might be a financial wreck, he might be faced with a *tête-à-tête* with his uncle, Lord Blicester, in the course of which the testy old man would in all probability endeavour to bite a piece out of the fleshy part of his leg, but at least he had done the fine, square thing. He had not let down a fellow who had admired him at school.

The chap had begun to speak again. At first, all he said was a brief word or two revising that passage in his previous address which had dealt with steak *minute.* A steak *minute,* he told Freddie, had among its obvious merits one fault – to wit, that it was not as filling as it might be. A more prudent move, he considered, and he called on Freddie to endorse this view, would be a couple of chump chops. Then he turned from that subject.

'Well, it was certainly a bit of luck running into you, Postlethwaite,' he said.

Freddie was a trifle stymied.

'Postlethwaite?' he said. 'How do you mean, Postlethwaite?'

The chap seemed surprised.

'How do you mean, how do I mean Postlethwaite?'

'I mean, why Postlethwaite? How has this Postlethwaite stuff crept in?'

'But, Postlethwaite, your name's Postlethwaite.'

'My name's Widgeon.'

'Widgeon?'

'Widgeon.'

'*Not* Postlethwaite?'

'Certainly not.'

The chap uttered an indulgent laugh.

'Ha, ha. Still the same old jovial, merry, kidding Postlethwaite, I see.'

'I'm not the same old jovial, merry, kidding Postlethwaite,' said Freddie, with heat. 'I never was the jovial, merry, kidding Postlethwaite.'

The chap stared.

'You aren't the Postlethwaite I used to admire so much at dear old Bingleton?'

'I've never been near dear old Bingleton in my life.'

'But you're wearing an Old Bingletonian tie.'

Freddie reeled.

'Is this beastly thing an Old Bingletonian tie? It's one I sneaked from my uncle.'

The chap laughed heartily.

'Well, of all the absurd mix-ups! You look like Postlethwaite and you're wearing an OB tie. Naturally, I thought you *were* Postlethwaite. And all the time we were thinking of a couple of other fellows! Well, well, well! However, it's all worked out for the best, what? Goodbye,' he added hastily, and was round the corner like a streak.

Freddie looked after him dully. He was totting up in his mind the final returns. On the debit side, he had lost Drusilla whatever-her-name-was. He had alienated his uncle, old Blicester. He was down a tenner. And, scaliest thought of all, he hadn't been anybody's hero at school. On the credit side, he had fifty francs.

At the Palm Beach Casino at Cannes you can get five martini cocktails for fifty francs. Freddie went and had them.

Then, wiping his lips with the napkin provided by the management, he strode from the bar to face the hopeless dawn.

The Love that Purifies

There is a ghastly moment in the year, generally about the beginning of August, when Jeeves insists on taking a holiday, the slacker, and legs it off to some seaside resort for a couple of weeks, leaving me stranded. This moment had now arrived, and we were discussing what was to be done with the young master.

'I had gathered the impression, sir,' said Jeeves, 'that you were proposing to accept Mr Sipperley's invitation to join him at his Hampshire residence.'

I laughed. One of those bitter, rasping ones.

'Correct, Jeeves. I was. But mercifully I was enabled to discover young Sippy's foul plot in time. Do you know what?'

'No, sir.'

'My spies informed me that Sippy's fiancée, Miss Moon, was to be there. Also his fiancée's mother, Mrs Moon, and his fiancée's small brother, Master Moon. You see the hideous treachery lurking behind the invitation? You see the man's loathsome design? Obviously my job was to be the task of keeping Mrs Moon and little Sebastian Moon interested and amused while Sippy and his blighted girl went off for the day, roaming the pleasant woodlands and talking of this and that. I doubt if anyone has ever had a narrower escape. You remember little Sebastian?'

'Yes, sir.'

'His goggle eyes? His golden curls?'

'Yes, sir.'

'I don't know why it is, but I've never been able to bear with fortitude anything in the shape of a kid with golden curls. Confronted with one, I feel the urge to step on him or drop things on him from a height.'

'Many strong natures are affected in the same way, sir.'

'So no *chez* Sippy for me. Was that the front-door bell ringing?'

'Yes, sir.'

'Somebody stands without.'

'Yes, sir.'

'Better go and see who it is.'

'Yes, sir.'

He oozed off, to return a moment later bearing a telegram. I opened it, and a soft smile played about the lips.

'Amazing how often things happen as if on a cue, Jeeves. This is from my Aunt Dahlia, inviting me down to her place in Worcestershire.'

'Most satisfactory, sir.'

'Yes. How I came to overlook her when searching for a haven, I can't think. The ideal home from home. Picturesque surroundings. Company's own water, and the best cook in England. You have not forgotten Anatole?'

'No, sir.'

'And above all, Jeeves, at Aunt Dahlia's there should be an almost total shortage of blasted kids. True, there is her son Bonzo, who, I take it, will be home for the holidays, but I don't mind Bonzo. Buzz off and send a wire, accepting.'

'Yes, sir.'

'And then shove a few necessaries together, including golf-clubs and tennis racquet.'

'Very good, sir. I am glad that matters have been so happily adjusted.'

I think I have mentioned before that my Aunt Dahlia stands alone in the grim regiment of my aunts as a real good sort and a chirpy sportsman. She is the one, if you remember, who married old Tom Travers and, with the assistance of Jeeves, lured Mrs Bingo Little's French cook, Anatole, away from Mrs B. L. and into her own employment. To visit her is always a pleasure. She generally has some cheery birds staying with her, and there is none of that rot about getting up for breakfast which one is sadly apt to find at country houses.

It was, accordingly, with unalloyed lightness of heart that I edged the two-seater into the garage at Brinkley Court, Worc., and strolled round to the house by way of the shrubbery and the tennis-lawn, to report arrival. I had just got across the lawn when a head poked itself out of the smoking room window and beamed at me in an amiable sort of way.

'Ah, Mr Wooster,' it said. 'Ha, ha!'

'Ho, ho!' I replied, not to be outdone in the courtesies.

It had taken me a couple of seconds to place this head. I now perceived that it belonged to a rather moth-eaten septuagenarian of the name of Anstruther, an old friend of Aunt Dahlia's late father. I had met him at her house in London once or twice. An agreeable cove, but somewhat given to nervous breakdowns.

'Just arrived?' he asked, beaming as before.

'This minute,' I said, also beaming.

'I fancy you will find our good hostess in the drawing room.'

'Right,' I said, and after a bit more beaming to and fro I pushed on.

Aunt Dahlia was in the drawing room, and welcomed me with gratifying enthusiasm. She beamed, too. It was one of those big days for beamers.

'Hullo, ugly,' she said. 'So here you are. Thank heaven you were able to come.'

It was the right tone, and one I should be glad to hear in others of the family circle, notably my Aunt Agatha.

'Always a pleasure to enjoy your hosp, Aunt Dahlia,' I said cordially. 'I anticipate a delightful and restful visit. I see you've got Mr Anstruther staying here. Anybody else?'

'Do you know Lord Snettisham?'

'I've met him, racing.'

'He's here, and Lady Snettisham.'

'And Bonzo, of course?'

'Yes. And Thomas.'

'Uncle Thomas?'

'No, he's in Scotland. Your Cousin Thomas.'

'You don't mean Aunt Agatha's loathly son?'

'Of course I do. How many Cousin Thomases do you think you've got, fathead? Agatha has gone to Homburg and planted the child on me.'

I was visibly agitated.

'But, Aunt Dahlia! Do you realise what you've taken on? Have you an inkling of the sort of scourge you've introduced into your home? In the society of young Thos, strong men quail. He is England's premier fiend in human shape. There is no devilry beyond his scope.'

'That's what I have always gathered from the form book,' agreed the relative. 'But just now, curse him, he's behaving like something out of a Sunday School story. You see, poor old Mr Anstruther is very frail these days, and when he found he was in a house containing two small boys he acted promptly. He offered a prize of five pounds to whichever behaved best during his stay. The consequence is that, ever since, Thomas has had large white wings sprouting out of his shoulders.' A shadow seemed to pass across her face. She appeared embittered. 'Mercenary little brute!' she said. 'I never saw such a sickeningly well-behaved kid in my life. It's enough to make one despair of human nature.'

I couldn't follow her.

'But isn't that all to the good?'

'No, it's not.'

'I can't see why. Surely a smug, oily Thos about the house is better than a Thos, raging hither and thither and being a menace to society? Stands to reason.'

'It doesn't stand to anything of the kind. You see, Bertie, this Good Conduct prize has made matters a bit complex. There are wheels within wheels. The thing stirred Jane Snettisham's sporting blood to such an extent that she insisted on having a bet on the result.'

A great light shone upon me. I got what she was driving at.

'Ah!' I said. 'Now I follow. Now I see. Now I comprehend. She's betting on Thos, is she?'

'Yes. And naturally, knowing him, I thought the thing was in the bag.'

'Of course.'

'I couldn't see myself losing. Heaven knows I have no illusions about my darling Bonzo. Bonzo is, and has been from the cradle, a pest. But to back him to win a Good Conduct contest with Thomas seemed to me simply money for jam.'

'Absolutely.'

'When it comes to devilry, Bonzo is just a good, ordinary selling-plater. Whereas Thomas is a classic yearling.'

'Exactly. I don't see that you have any cause to worry, Aunt Dahlia. Thos can't last. He's bound to crack.'

'Yes. But before that the mischief may be done.'

'Mischief?'

'Yes. There is dirty work afoot, Bertie,' said Aunt Dahlia gravely. 'When I booked this bet, I reckoned without the hideous blackness of the Snettishams' souls. Only yesterday it came to my knowledge that Jack Snettisham had been urging Bonzo to climb on the roof and boo down Mr Anstruther's chimney.'

'No!'

'Yes. Mr Anstruther is very frail, poor old fellow, and it would have frightened him into a fit. On coming out of which, his first action would have been to disqualify Bonzo and declare Thomas the winner by default.'

'But Bonzo did not boo?'

'No,' said Aunt Dahlia, and a mother's pride rang in her voice. 'He firmly refused to boo. Mercifully, he is in love at the moment, and it has quite altered his nature. He scorned the tempter.'

'In love? Who with?'

'Lilian Gish. We had an old film of hers at the Bijou

Dream in the village a week ago, and Bonzo saw her for the first time. He came out with a pale, set face, and ever since has been trying to lead a finer, better life. So the peril was averted.'

'That's good.'

'Yes. But now it's my turn. You don't suppose I am going to take a thing like that lying down, do you? Treat me right, and I am fairness itself: but try any of this nobbling of starters, and I can play that game, too. If this Good Conduct contest is to be run on rough lines, I can do my bit as well as anyone. Far too much hangs on the issue for me to handicap myself by remembering the lessons I learned at my mother's knee.'

'Lot of money involved?'

'Much more than mere money. I've betted Anatole against Jane Snettisham's kitchen maid.'

'Great Scott! Uncle Thomas will have something to say if he comes back and finds Anatole gone.'

'And won't he say it!'

'Pretty long odds you gave her, didn't you? I mean, Anatole is famed far and wide as a hash-slinger without peer.'

'Well, Jane Snettisham's kitchen maid is not to be sneezed at. She is very hot stuff, they tell me, and good kitchen maids nowadays are about as rare as original Holbeins. Besides, I had to give her a shade the best of the odds. She stood out for it. Well, anyway, to get back to what I was saying, if the opposition are going to place temptations in Bonzo's path, they shall jolly well be placed in Thomas's path, too, and plenty of them. So ring for Jeeves and let him get his brain working.'

'But I haven't brought Jeeves.'

'You haven't brought Jeeves?'

'No. He always takes his holiday at this time of year. He's down at Bognor for the shrimping.'

Aunt Dahlia registered deep concern.

'Then send for him at once! What earthly use do you suppose you are without Jeeves, you poor ditherer?'

I drew myself up a trifle – in fact, to my full height. Nobody has a greater respect for Jeeves than I have, but the Wooster pride was stung.

'Jeeves isn't the only one with brains,' I said coldly. 'Leave this thing to me, Aunt Dahlia. By dinnertime tonight I shall hope to have a fully matured scheme to submit for your approval. If I can't thoroughly encompass this Thos, I'll eat my hat.'

'About all you'll get to eat if Anatole leaves,' said Aunt Dahlia in a pessimistic manner which I did not like to see.

I was brooding pretty tensely as I left the presence. I have always had a suspicion that Aunt Dahlia, while invariably matey and bonhomous and seeming to take pleasure in my society, has a lower opinion of my intelligence than I quite like. Too often it is her practice to address me as 'fathead', and if I put forward any little thought or idea or fancy in her hearing it is apt to be greeted with the affectionate but jarring guffaw. In our recent interview she had hinted quite plainly that she considered me negligible in a crisis which, like the present one, called for initiative and resource. It was my intention to show her how greatly she had underestimated me.

To let you see the sort of fellow I really am, I got a ripe, excellent idea before I had gone halfway down the corridor. I examined it for the space of one and a half cigarettes, and could see no flaw in it, provided – I say, provided old Mr Anstruther's notion of what constituted bad conduct squared with mine.

The great thing on these occasions, as Jeeves will tell you, is to get a toe-hold on the psychology of the individual. Study the individual, and you will bring home the bacon. Now, I had been studying young Thos for years, and I knew his psychology from caviare to nuts. He is one of those kids who never let the sun go down on their wrath, if you know what I mean. I mean to say, do something to annoy or offend or upset this juvenile thug, and he will proceed at the earliest possible opp to wreak a hideous vengeance upon you. Only the previous summer, for instance, it having been drawn to his attention that the latter had reported him for smoking, he had marooned a Cabinet Minister on an island in the lake, at Aunt Agatha's place in Hertfordshire – in the rain, mark you, and with no company but that of one of the nastiest-minded swans I have ever encountered. Well, I mean!

So now it seemed to me that a few well-chosen taunts, or jibes, directed at his more sensitive points, must infallibly induce in this Thos a frame of mind which would lead to his working some sensational violence upon me. And, if you wonder that I was willing to sacrifice myself to this frightful extent in order to do Aunt Dahlia a bit of good, I can only say that we Woosters are like that.

The one point that seemed to me to want a spot of clearing up was this: viz., would old Mr Anstruther consider an outrage perpetrated on the person of Bertram Wooster a crime sufficiently black to cause him to rule

Thos out of the race? Or would he just give a senile chuckle and mumble something about boys being boys? Because, if the latter, the thing was off. I decided to have a word with the old boy and make sure.

He was still in the smoking room, looking very frail over the morning *Times*. I got to the point at once.

'Oh, Mr Anstruther,' I said. 'What ho!'

'I don't like the way the American market is shaping,' he said. 'I don't like this strong Bear movement.'

'No?' I said. 'Well, be that as it may, about this Good Conduct prize of yours?'

'Ah, you have heard of that, eh?'

'I don't quite understand how you are doing the judging.'

'No? It is very simple. I have a system of daily marks. At the beginning of each day I accord the two lads twenty marks apiece. These are subject to withdrawal either in small or large quantities according to the magnitude of the offence. To take a simple example, shouting outside my bedroom in the early morning would involve a loss of three marks – whistling two. The penalty for a more serious lapse would be correspondingly greater. Before retiring to rest at night I record the day's marks in my little book. Simple, but, I think, ingenious, Mr Wooster?'

'Absolutely.'

'So far the result has been extremely gratifying. Neither of the little fellows has lost a single mark, and my nervous system is acquiring a tone which, when I learned that two lads of immature years would be staying in the house during my visit, I confess I had not dared to anticipate.'

'I see,' I said. 'Great work. And how do you react to what I might call general moral turpitude?'

'I beg your pardon?'

'Well, I mean when the thing doesn't affect you personally. Suppose one of them did something to me, for instance? Set a booby-trap or something? Or, shall we say, put a toad or so in my bed?'

He seemed shocked at the very idea.

'I would certainly in such circumstances deprive the culprit of a full ten marks.'

'Only ten?'

'Fifteen, then.'

'Twenty is a nice, round number.'

'Well, possibly even twenty. I have a peculiar horror of practical joking.'

'Me, too.'

'You will not fail to advise me, Mr Wooster, should such an outrage occur?'

'You shall have the news before anyone,' I assured him.

And so out into the garden, ranging to and fro in quest of young Thos. I knew where I was now. Bertram's feet were on solid ground.

I hadn't been hunting long before I found him in the summer-house, reading an improving book.

'Hullo,' he said, smiling a saintlike smile.

This scourge of humanity was a chunky kid whom a too indulgent public had allowed to infest the country for a matter of fourteen years. His nose was snub, his eyes green, his general aspect that of one studying to be a gangster. I had never liked his looks much, and with a saintlike smile added to them they became ghastly to a degree.

I ran over in my mind a few assorted taunts.

'Well, young Thos,' I said. 'So there you are. You're getting as fat as a pig.'

It seemed as good an opening as any other. Experience had taught me that if there was a subject on which he was unlikely to accept persiflage in a spirit of amused geniality it was this matter of his bulging tum. On the last occasion when I made a remark of this nature, he had replied to me, child though he was, in terms which I would have been proud to have had in my own vocabulary. But now, though a sort of wistful gleam did flit for a moment into his eyes, he merely smiled in a more saintlike manner than ever.

'Yes, I think I have been putting on a little weight,' he said gently. 'I must try and exercise a lot while I'm here. Won't you sit down, Bertie?' he asked, rising. 'You must be tired after your journey. I'll get you a cushion. Have you cigarettes? And matches? I could bring you some from the smoking room. Would you like me to fetch you something to drink?'

It is not too much to say that I felt baffled. In spite of what Aunt Dahlia had told me, I don't think that until this moment I had really believed there could have been anything in the nature of a genuinely sensational change in this young plugugly's attitude towards his fellows. But now, hearing him talk as if he were a combination of Boy Scout and delivery wagon, I felt definitely baffled. However, I stuck at it in the old bulldog way.

'Are you still at that rotten kids' school of yours?' I asked.

He might have been proof against jibes at his *embonpoint*, but it seemed to me incredible that he could have sold himself for gold so completely as to lie down under taunts directed at his school. I was wrong. The money-lust evidently held him in its grip. He merely shook his head.

'I left this term. I'm going to Pevenhurst next term.'

'They wear mortar-boards there, don't they?'

'Yes.'

'With pink tassels?'

'Yes.'

'What a priceless ass you'll look!' I said, but without much hope. And I laughed heartily.

'I expect I shall,' he said, and laughed still more heartily.

'Mortar-boards!'

'Ha, ha!'

'Pink tassels!'

'Ha, ha!'

I gave the thing up.

'Well, teuf-teuf,' I said moodily, and withdrew.

A couple of days later I realised that the virus had gone even deeper than I had thought. The kid was irredeemably sordid.

It was old Mr Anstruther who sprang the bad news.

'Oh, Mr Wooster,' he said, meeting me on the stairs as I came down after a refreshing breakfast. 'You were good enough to express an interest in this little prize for Good Conduct which I am offering.'

'Oh, ah?'

'I explained to you my system of marking, I believe. Well, this morning I was impelled to vary it somewhat. The circumstances seemed to me to demand it. I happened to encounter our hostess's nephew, the boy Thomas, returning to the house, his aspect somewhat weary, it appeared to me, and travel-stained. I inquired of him where he had been at that early hour – it was not yet breakfast-time – and he replied that he had heard you mention overnight a regret that you had omitted to order the *Sporting Times* to be sent to you before leaving London, and he had actually walked all the way to the railway station, a distance of more than three miles, to procure it for you.'

The old boy swam before my eyes. He looked like two old Mr Anstruthers, both flickering at the edges.

'What!'

'I can understand your emotion, Mr Wooster. I can appreciate it. It is indeed rarely that one encounters such unselfish kindliness in a lad of his age. So genuinely touched was I by the goodness of heart which the episode showed that I have deviated from my original system and awarded the little fellow a bonus of fifteen marks.'

'Fifteen!'

'On second thoughts, I shall make it twenty. That, as you yourself suggested, is a nice, round number.'

He doddered away, and I bounded off to find Aunt Dahlia.

'Aunt Dahlia,' I said, 'matters have taken a sinister turn.'

'You bet your Sunday spats they have,' agreed Aunt Dahlia emphatically. 'Do you know what happened just now? That crook Snettisham, who ought to be warned off the turf and hounded out of his clubs, offered Bonzo ten shillings if he would burst a paper bag behind Mr Anstruther's chair at breakfast. Thank heaven the love of a good woman triumphed again. My sweet Bonzo merely looked at him and walked away in a marked manner. But it just shows you what we are up against.'

'We are up against worse than that, Aunt Dahlia,' I said. And I told her what had happened.

She was stunned. Aghast, you might call it.

'*Thomas* did that?'

'Thos in person.'

'Walked six miles to get you a paper?'

'Six miles and a bit.'

'The young hound! Good heavens, Bertie, do you realise that he may go on doing these Acts of Kindness daily – perhaps twice a day? Is there no way of stopping him?'

'None that I can think of. No, Aunt Dahlia, I must confess it. I am baffled. There is only one thing to do. We must send for Jeeves.'

'And about time,' said the relative churlishly. 'He ought to have been here from the start. Wire him this morning.'

There is good stuff in Jeeves. His heart is in the right place. The acid test does not find him wanting. Many men in his position, summoned back by telegram in the middle of their annual vacation, might have cut up rough a bit. But not Jeeves. On the following afternoon in he blew, looking bronzed and fit, and I gave him the scenario without delay.

'So there you have it, Jeeves,' I said, having sketched out the facts. 'The problem is one that will exercise your intelligence to the utmost. Rest now, and tonight, after a light repast, withdraw to some solitary place and get down to it. Is there any particularly stimulating food or beverage you would like for dinner? Anything that you feel would give the old brain just that extra fillip? If so, name it.'

'Thank you very much, sir, but I have already hit upon a plan which should, I fancy, prove effective.'

I gazed at the man with some awe.

'Already?'

'Yes, sir.'

'Not *already*?'

'Yes, sir.'

'Something to do with the psychology of the individual?'

'Precisely, sir.'

I shook my head, a bit discouraged. Doubts had begun to creep in.

'Well, spring it, Jeeves,' I said. 'But I have not much hope. Having only just arrived, you cannot possibly be aware of the frightful change that has taken place in young Thos. You are probably building on your knowledge of him, when last seen. Useless, Jeeves. Stirred by the prospect of getting his hooks on five of the best, this blighted boy has become so dashed virtuous that his armour seems to contain no chink. I mocked at his waistline and sneered at his school and he merely smiled in a pale, dying-duck sort of way. Well, that'll show you. However, let us hear what you have to suggest.'

'It occurred to me, sir, that the most judicious plan in the circumstances would be for you to request Mrs Travers to invite Master Sebastian Moon here for a short visit.'

I shook the onion again. The scheme sounded to me like apple sauce, and Grade A apple sauce, at that.

'What earthly good would that do?' I asked, not without a touch of asperity. 'Why Sebastian Moon?'

'He has golden curls, sir.'

'What of it?'

'The strongest natures are sometimes not proof against long golden curls.'

Well, it was a thought, of course. But I can't say I was leaping about to any great extent. It might be that the sight of Sebastian Moon would break down Thos's iron self-control to the extent of causing him to inflict mayhem on the person, but I wasn't any too hopeful.

'It may be so, Jeeves.'

'I do not think I am too sanguine, sir. You must remember that Master Moon, apart from his curls, has a personality which is not uniformly pleasing. He is apt to express himself with a breezy candour which I fancy Master Thomas might feel inclined to resent in one some years his junior.'

I had had a feeling all along that there was a flaw somewhere, and now it seemed to me that I had spotted it.

'But, Jeeves. Granted that little Sebastian is the pot of poison you indicate, why won't he act just as forcibly on young Bonzo as on Thos? Pretty silly we should look if our nominee started putting it across him. Never forget that already Bonzo is twenty marks down and falling back in the betting.'

'I do not anticipate any such contingency, sir. Master Travers is in love, and love is a very powerful restraining influence at the age of thirteen.'

'H'm.' I mused. 'Well, we can but try, Jeeves.'

'Yes, sir.'

'I'll get Aunt Dahlia to write to Sippy tonight.'

I'm bound to say that the spectacle of little Sebastian when he arrived two days later did much to remove pessimism from my outlook. If ever there was a kid whose whole appearance seemed to call aloud to any right-minded boy to lure him into a quiet spot and inflict violence upon him, that kid was undeniably Sebastian Moon. He reminded me strongly of Little Lord Fauntleroy. I marked young Thos's demeanour closely at the moment of their meeting and, unless I was much mistaken, there came into his eyes the sort of look which would come into those of an Indian chief – Chinchagook, let us say, or Sitting Bull – just before he started reaching for his scalping-knife. He had the air of one who is about ready to begin.

True, his manner as he shook hands was guarded. Only a keen observer could have detected that he was stirred to his depths. But I had seen, and I summoned Jeeves forthwith.

'Jeeves,' I said, 'if I appeared to think poorly of that scheme of yours, I now withdraw my remarks. I believe you have found the way. I was noticing Thos at the moment of impact. His eyes had a strange gleam.'

'Indeed, sir?'

'He shifted uneasily on his feet and his ears wiggled. He had, in short, the appearance of a boy who was holding himself in with an effort almost too great for his frail body.'

'Yes, sir?'

'Yes, Jeeves. I received a distinct impression of something being on the point of exploding. Tomorrow I shall ask Aunt Dahlia to take the two warts for a country ramble, to lose them in some sequestered spot, and to leave the rest to Nature.'

'It is a good idea, sir.'

'It is more than a good idea, Jeeves,' I said. 'It is a pip.'

You know, the older I get the more firmly do I become convinced that there is no such thing as a pip in existence.

Again and again have I seen the apparently sure thing go phut, and now it is rarely indeed that I can be lured from my aloof scepticism. Fellows come sidling up to me at the Drones and elsewhere, urging me to invest on some horse that can't lose even if it gets struck by lightning at the starting-post, but Bertram Wooster shakes his head. He has seen too much of life to be certain of anything.

If anyone had told me that my Cousin Thos, left alone for an extended period of time with a kid of the superlative foulness of Sebastian Moon, would not only refrain from cutting off his curls with a pocket knife and chasing him across country into a muddy pond but would actually return home carrying the gruesome kid on his back because he had got a blister on his foot, I would have laughed scornfully. I knew Thos. I knew his work. I had seen him in action. And I was convinced that not even the prospect of collecting five pounds would be enough to give him pause.

And yet what happened? In the quiet evenfall, when the little birds were singing their sweetest and all Nature seemed to whisper of hope and happiness, the blow fell. I was chatting with old Mr Anstruther on the terrace when suddenly round a bend in the drive the two kids hove in view. Sebastian, seated on Thos's back, his hat off and his golden curls floating on the breeze, was singing as much as he could remember of a comic song, and Thos, bowed down by the burden but carrying on gamely, was trudging along, smiling that bally saintlike smile of his. He parked the kid on the front steps and came across to us.

'Sebastian got a nail in his shoe,' he said in a low, virtuous voice. 'It hurt him to walk, so I gave him a piggyback.'

I heard old Mr Anstruther draw in his breath sharply.

'All the way home?'

'Yes, sir.'

'In this hot sunshine?'

'Yes, sir.'

'But was he not very heavy?'

'He was a little, sir,' said Thos, uncorking the saintlike once more. 'But it would have hurt him awfully to walk.'

I pushed off. I had had enough. If ever a septuagenarian looked on the point of handing out another bonus, that septuagenarian was old Mr Anstruther. He had the unmistakable bonus glitter in his eye. I withdrew, and found Jeeves in my bedroom messing about with ties and things.

He pursed the lips a bit on hearing the news.

'Serious, sir.'

'Very serious, Jeeves.'

'I had feared this, sir.'

'Had you? I hadn't. I was convinced Thos would have massacred young Sebastian. I banked on it. It just shows what the greed for money will do. This is a commercial age, Jeeves. When I was a boy, I would cheerfully have forfeited five quid in order to deal faithfully with a kid like Sebastian. I would have considered it money well spent.'

'You are mistaken, sir, in your estimate of the motives actuating Master Thomas. It was not a mere desire to win five pounds that caused him to curb his natural impulses.'

'Eh?'

'I have ascertained the true reason for his change of heart, sir.'

I felt fogged.

'Religion, Jeeves?'

'No, sir. Love.'

'Love?'

'Yes, sir. The young gentleman confided in me during a brief conversation in the hall shortly after luncheon. We had been speaking for a while on neutral subjects, when he suddenly turned a deeper shade of pink and after some slight hesitation inquired of me if I did not think Miss Greta Garbo the most beautiful woman at present in existence.'

I clutched the brow.

'Jeeves! Don't tell me Thos is in love with Greta Garbo?'

'Yes, sir. Unfortunately such is the case. He gave me to understand that it had been coming on for some time, and her last picture settled the issue. His voice shook with an emotion which it was impossible to misread. I gathered from his observations, sir, that he proposes to spend the remainder of his life trying to make himself worthy of her.'

It was a knockout. This was the end.

'This is the end, Jeeves,' I said. 'Bonzo must be a good forty marks behind by now. Only some sensational and spectacular outrage upon the public weal on the part of young Thos could have enabled him to wipe out the lead. And of that there is now, apparently, no chance.'

'The eventuality does appear remote, sir.'

I brooded.

'Uncle Thomas will have a fit when he comes back and finds Anatole gone.'

'Yes, sir.'

'Aunt Dahlia will drain the bitter cup to the dregs.'

'Yes, sir.'

'And, speaking from a purely selfish point of view, the

finest cooking I have ever bitten will pass out of my life for ever, unless the Snettishams invite me in some night to take pot luck. And that eventuality is also remote.'

'Yes, sir.'

'Then the only thing I can do is square the shoulders and face the inevitable.'

'Yes, sir.'

'Like some aristocrat of the French Revolution popping into the tumbril, what? The brave smile. The stiff upper lip.'

'Yes, sir.'

'Right ho, then. Is the shirt studded?'

'Yes, sir.'

'The tie chosen?'

'Yes, sir.'

'The collar and evening underwear all in order?'

'Yes, sir.'

'Then I'll have a bath and be with you in two ticks.'

It is all very well to talk about the brave smile and the stiff upper lip, but my experience – and I daresay others have found the same – is that they are a dashed sight easier to talk about than actually to fix on the face. For the next few days, I'm bound to admit, I found myself, in spite of every effort, registering gloom pretty consistently. For, as if to make things tougher than they might have been, Anatole at this juncture suddenly developed a cooking streak which put all his previous efforts in the shade.

Night after night we sat at the dinner table, the food melting in our mouths, and Aunt Dahlia would look at me and I would look at Aunt Dahlia, and the male Snettisham would ask the female Snettisham in a ghastly, gloating sort of way if she had ever tasted such cooking and the female Snettisham would smirk at the male Snettisham and say she never had in all her puff, and I would look at Aunt Dahlia and Aunt Dahlia would look at me and our eyes would be full of unshed tears, if you know what I mean.

And all the time old Mr Anstruther's visit drawing to a close.

The sands running out, so to speak.

And then, on the very last afternoon of his stay, the thing happened.

It was one of those warm, drowsy, peaceful afternoons. I was up in my bedroom, getting off a spot of correspondence which I had neglected of late, and from where I sat I looked down on the shady lawn, fringed with its gay flower beds. There was a bird or two hopping about, a butterfly or so fluttering to and fro, and an assortment of bees buzzing hither and thither. In a garden chair sat old Mr Anstruther, getting his eight hours. It was a sight which, had I had less on my mind, would no doubt have soothed the old soul a bit. The only blot on the landscape was Lady Snettisham, walking among the flower beds and probably sketching out future menus, curse her.

And so for a time everything carried on. The birds hopped, the butterflies fluttered, the bees buzzed, and old Mr Anstruther snored – all in accordance with the programme. And I worked through a letter to my tailor to the point where I proposed to say something pretty strong about the way the right sleeve of my last coat bagged.

There was a tap on the door, and Jeeves entered,

bringing the second post. I laid the letters listlessly on the table beside me.

'Well, Jeeves,' I said sombrely.

'Sir?'

'Mr Anstruther leaves tomorrow.'

'Yes, sir.'

I gazed down at the sleeping septuagenarian.

'In my young days, Jeeves,' I said, 'however much I might have been in love, I could never have resisted the spectacle of an old gentleman asleep like that in a deck chair. I would have done *something* to him, no matter what the cost.'

'Indeed, sir?'

'Yes. Probably with a pea-shooter. But the modern boy is degenerate. He has lost his vim. I suppose Thos is indoors on this lovely afternoon, showing Sebastian his stamp-album or something. Ha!' I said, and I said it rather nastily.

'I fancy Master Thomas and Master Sebastian are playing in the stable-yard, sir. I encountered Master Sebastian not long back and he informed me he was on his way thither.'

'The motion-pictures, Jeeves,' I said, 'are the curse of the age. But for them, if Thos had found himself alone in a stable-yard with a kid like Sebastian—'

I broke off. From some point to the south-west, out of my line of vision, there had proceeded a piercing squeal.

It cut through the air like a knife, and old Mr Anstruther leaped up as if it had run into the fleshy part of his leg. And the next moment little Sebastian appeared, going well and followed at a short interval by Thos, who was going even better. In spite of the fact that he was hampered in his movements by a large stable-bucket which he bore in his right hand, Thos was running a great race. He had almost come up with Sebastian, when the latter, with great presence of mind, dodged behind Mr Anstruther, and there for a moment the matter rested.

But only for a moment. Thos, for some reason plainly stirred to the depths of his being, moved adroitly to one side and, poising the bucket for an instant, discharged its contents. And Mr Anstruther, who had just moved to the same side, received, as far as I could gather from a distance, the entire consignment. In one second, without any previous training or upbringing, he had become the wettest man in Worcestershire.

'Jeeves!' I cried.

'Yes, indeed, sir,' said Jeeves, and seemed to me to put the whole thing in a nutshell.

Down below, things were hotting up nicely. Old Mr Anstruther may have been frail, but he undoubtedly had his moments. I have rarely seen a man of his years conduct himself with such a lissom abandon. There was a stick lying beside the chair, and with this in hand he went into action like a two-year-old. A moment later, he and Thos had passed out of the picture round the side of the house, Thos cutting out a rare pace but, judging from the sounds of anguish, not quite good enough to distance the field.

The tumult and the shouting died; and, after gazing for a while with considerable satisfaction at the Snettisham, who was standing there with a sandbagged look watching her nominee pass right out of the betting, I turned to Jeeves. I felt quietly triumphant. It is not often that I score off him, but now I had scored in no uncertain manner.

'You see, Jeeves,' I said, 'I was right and you were wrong. Blood will tell. Once a Thos, always a Thos. Can the leopard change his spots or the Ethiopian his whatnot? What was that thing they used to teach us at school about expelling Nature?'

'You may expel Nature with a pitchfork, sir, but she will always return? In the original Latin—'

'Never mind about the original Latin. The point is that I told you Thos could not resist those curls, and he couldn't. You would have it that he could.'

'I do not fancy it was the curls that caused the upheaval, sir.'

'Must have been.'

'No, sir. I think Master Sebastian had been speaking disparagingly of Miss Garbo.'

'Eh? Why would he do that?'

'I suggested that he should do so, sir, not long ago when I encountered him on his way to the stable-yard. It was a move which he was very willing to take, as he informed me that in his opinion Miss Garbo was definitely inferior both in beauty and talent to Miss Clara Bow, for whom he has long nourished a deep regard. From what we have just witnessed, sir, I imagine that Master Sebastian must have introduced the topic into the conversation at an early point.'

I sank into a chair. The Wooster system can stand just so much.

'Jeeves!'

'Sir?'

'You tell me that Sebastian Moon, a stripling of such tender years that he can go about the place with long curls without causing mob violence, is in love with Clara Bow?'

'And has been for some little time, he gave me to understand, sir.'

'Jeeves, this Younger Generation is hot stuff.'

'Yes, sir.'

'Were you like that in your day?'

'No, sir.'

'Nor I, Jeeves. At the age of fourteen I once wrote to Marie Lloyd for her autograph, but apart from that my private life could bear the strictest investigation. However, that is not the point. The point is, Jeeves, that once more I must pay you a marked tribute.'

'Thank you very much, sir.'

'Once more you have stepped forward like the great man you are and spread sweetness and light in no uncertain measure.'

'I am glad to have given satisfaction, sir. Would you be requiring my services any further?'

'You mean you wish to return to Bognor and its shrimps? Do so, Jeeves, and stay there another fortnight, if you wish. And may success attend your net.'

'Thank you very much, sir.'

I eyed the man fixedly. His head stuck out at the back, and his eyes sparkled with the light of pure intelligence.

'I am sorry for the shrimp that tries to pit its feeble cunning against you, Jeeves,' I said.

And I meant it.

DIVE INTO THE HILARIOUS WORLD OF WODEHOUSE

'The purest kind of comedy'

Independent

WHAT HO!

For more gloriously witty goings on,
join the P. G. Wodehouse community.

Visit the official website
www.wodehouse.co.uk

Follow on Twitter
@wodehouseoffice

Become a fan on Facebook
facebook.com/wodehousepage

Revel with fellow aficionados as a
member of the P. G. Wodehouse society
www.pgwodehousesociety.org.uk